What happened in the dark w...
scandalous, absolutely improp...
But oh, how she longs for it
to happen again!

Siusan heard the door open.
Her breath seized in her lungs.

Moonlight just touched the angular face of a large man, hardly two strides away.

Her heart pounded. How respectable would it appear for her to be found in a room meant for family, not guests? Thankfully, the library was cloaked in night. If she didn't move . . . barely breathed, the man mightn't even know she was in the room with him.

But then his eyes shifted to her and she saw a smile roll across his lips. "There you are," he whispered, striding fast toward her.

Siusan's heart thudded harder in her chest. Panicking, she opened her mouth to tell him that she was not who he thought her to be, when suddenly his lips were moving over hers. She shivered as she felt his tongue ease into her mouth and begin stroking the insides of her cheeks, twirling around her tongue.

In this man's arms something miraculous was happening. And she did not want him to stop.

Her eyes snapped open. She could do it. She could let herself have this.

Just one night of sin. That was all.

By Kathryn Caskie

THE DUKE'S NIGHT OF SIN
THE MOST WICKED OF SINS
TO SIN WITH A STRANGER
HOW TO PROPOSE TO A PRINCE
HOW TO ENGAGE AN EARL
HOW TO SEDUCE A DUKE

KATHRYN CASKIE

THE DUKE'S NIGHT OF SIN

AVON
An Imprint of HarperCollinsPublishers

This is a work of fiction. Names, characters, places, and incidents are products of the author's imagination or are used fictitiously and are not to be construed as real. Any resemblance to actual events, locales, organizations, or persons, living or dead, is entirely coincidental.

AVON BOOKS
An Imprint of HarperCollins*Publishers*
10 East 53rd Street
New York, New York 10022–5299

Copyright © 2010 by Kathryn Caskie
Untitled excerpt copyright © 2012 by Kathryn Caskie
ISBN 978–0–06–149103–0
www.avonromance.com

First Avon Books paperback printing: December 2010

Avon Trademark Reg. U.S. Pat. Off. and in Other Countries, Marca Registrada, Hecho en U.S.A.
HarperCollins® is a registered trademark of HarperCollins Publishers.

Printed in the U.S.A.

10 9 8 7 6 5 4 3 2 1

For Kim Castillo,
who took care of everything
so I could tell Siusan's story.

Author's Note

Dear Readers,

As you read this book you may think it odd that London's late summer and autumn temperatures would vary so greatly from the usual. The reason for this is that the weather of 1816 was unique, not only in London, but across the Northern Hemisphere.

On April 10, 1815, Mount Tambora in the Dutch East Indies erupted, ultimately killing tens of thousands of people. The explosion was so intense that miles of thick ash spewed into the stratosphere. By 1816, that massive ash cloud had reached the Northern Hemisphere.

The volcano's dust in the atmosphere greatly reduced the amount of sunlight passing through to the earth, causing unseasonably cold temperatures and an extreme change in weather patterns, so much so that 1816 became known as the Year Without Summer, or worse, the Year of Poverty.

In England, Europe, and America, there was snow in early June. In July, August, and September, daytime temperatures were cold and nighttime temperatures frigid. The lack of sunlight stunted plant growth and what crops managed to survive the spring withered during the droughts of July and August, or died from the biting cold and frosts of September. There were mass food shortages, raiding of public food stores, political unrest, chaos, and protests in the streets.

By September, the Thames was frozen and the people of London were in dire times indeed.

This is the climate in which the Sinclairs find themselves in *The Duke's Night of Sin*.

His Grace, William **········· m. ········** Her Grace, Patience
The Duke of Sinclair   The Duchess of Sinclair
(1754–)   (1768–1795)

Sterling Sinclair   Lady Siusan   Lord Grant
Marquess of Blackburn   (1790–)   (1791–)
(1788–)

···· m. ····   **···· m. ····**

Isobel Carington   Sebastian Beaufort
                              The Duke of Exeter
(To Sin With a Stranger)   *(The Duke's Night of Sin)*

Sinclair Family Tree

Lord Lachlan
(1793–)

Lady Ivy
(1794–)

···· m. ····

Lord Killian
(1795–)

(twins)

Lady Priscilla
(1795–)

**Dominic Sheridan
Marquess of Counterton**

(The Most Wicked of Sins)

The Duke's Night of Sin

Chapter 1

It has been said that idleness is the parent of mischief, which is very true; but mischief itself is merely an attempt to escape from the dreary vacuum of idleness.

George Borrow

Late August 1816
Blackwood Hall, outside London

The ancient hall was bustling with excited guests waiting for the presentation of the new Duke of Exeter. It was to be the bachelor's grand debut in London Society since ascending to the title—which, of course brought everyone with a daughter even close to marriageable age to seek an invitation to the glittering event.

After all, a young, fit, unmarried man was all

too quickly becoming a rare commodity in these turbulent war-torn times, but a duke . . . and a handsome one at that (or so it was rumored—for no member of the *ton* had actually reported *seeing* the man), well, he was a rare prize indeed.

Even so, the novelty of the evening had already worn gossamer thin for Lady Siusan Sinclair. She was very likely the only miss in the hall who did not wish to be there. "I daresay, we've stayed long enough, Priscilla. No man is worth waiting about for four long hours—especially in this crowd."

Her younger sister's eyes went wide at Siusan's sacrilegious words. "An unmarried duke is entirely worth the wait!"

Siusan rolled her eyes as she dabbed her moist neck with her handkerchief.

"And do not dare perspire," Priscilla warned, critically studying the cerulean silk dress Siusan wore. "I only lent you the gown upon your solemn oath that you would not ruin it. That includes perspiring." She snatched up Siusan's wrist. "Come now, make use of your fan. Mine is keeping me sufficiently cool. A true lady does not perspire. Remember that."

"Aye, Priscilla, I know, however if we do not leave at once—"

"I am certain you can manage to refrain from glowing for a few more minutes." Priscilla narrowed her eyes at Siusan, then rose to her toes to survey the ballroom. "The duke will appear at any moment, I have no doubt. I shouldn't need to remind you of our predicament. His Grace is unmarried and from the country, some dreary old place in Devonshire. I am sure he has never even heard of the Sinclairs, and that fact works in our favor. Our chances of snaring his ring are as good as any other noble miss's."

Siusan stood on the tips of her toes as well and glanced about before returning her heels to the floor, pulling Priscilla down along with her. She moved her mouth close to her younger sister's ear, for as the daughter of a duke herself, Siusan was nothing if not well trained. Like her brothers and sisters, she simply did not always choose to adhere to the rules of propriety in the *strictest* sense. "Keeping us all waiting for his glorious presence, bah. I daresay, the duke is clearly very rude. Perhaps you are right, Priscilla. He may fit in with the Seven Deadly Sins nicely."

"Hush. Do not refer to our family so vilely. That others do does not make it acceptable." Priscilla glanced around them to be sure Siusan's assertion was not overheard. Convinced that it was not, she growled into Siusan's ear. "And besides, *my* future husband is not rude."

"*Your* husband, dear? Did you not just claim that *our* chance for winning his ring were just as favorable as anyone else's?"

"Aye, but I meant that *my* chances are equal. Not yours. Do you not recall that I voiced my claim on the duke the moment we stepped down from the carriage?"

"Good Lord, are you still six years old?" Her sister's reliance on an old game might have been diverting at another time, but not tonight. "The wretched duke still hasn't had the courtesy to grace those waiting for him with his esteemed noble presence. Besides which, Priscilla, you cannot claim the duke unless you see him *first*. That is the primary rule of the game."

Priscilla suddenly looked very determined. "Then I shall ensure that I do see him first." She started off through the crowd, leaving Siusan to scurrying to catch up. Within a minute, Priscilla had climbed a step and positioned herself on the far edge of the musicians' dais.

"Priscilla, you are being a great goose. Come down. Please, let us find our brothers and away."

Priscilla's gaze swept the ballroom as she replied. "I have an elevated view of the ballroom from here, and I will signal you posthaste the moment the duke appears." She turned her eyes back upon Siusan. "That way you will know he has arrived . . . and that *I* saw him first."

Her sister was being ridiculous. Siusan swiped her cutwork fan before her face, hoping to coax the humid air into cooling her face. On another night, the prospect of meeting a strikingly handsome unmarried duke might have been sufficient incentive for Siusan to cram herself into a rented coach with her brothers and sister and ride eight dusty miles outside of Town.

But not tonight . . . of all painful nights.

All she wanted tonight was to be alone with her memories. But solitude wasn't a luxury she could afford. She and her wayward siblings, widely known within Society as the Seven Deadly Sins, had only accepted tonight's invitation for one simple reason—they were willing to do anything to earn back their father's approval. Not because they were truly ashamed of their wild and wicked ways, for indeed they were not.

Their motivation did not run quite so clear and deep. It was because the money their father, the Duke of Sinclair, provided them was only just enough to meet their most basic of needs, and even those funds were quickly dwindling. Their father's man of affairs had made it startlingly clear that no further pouches of coin were to make their way into the Sinclair brothers' and sisters' hands until they changed their wild ways and earned the respect the Sinclair name deserved. They all knew that time was fast running out.

And, well, there was an unmarried duke to be had. What quicker way for her or her sister to restore respectability than to marry a duke?

She glanced up at Priscilla, who was earnestly sweeping the dance floor with her gaze.

Well, her sister could have him. Tonight, Siusan just didn't care—about dukes, money, even her father's respect. With a sniff, Siusan raised her chin and surreptitiously dabbed a lace handkerchief to an errant tear budding in her eye.

Tonight marked one year. A full heart-breaking year without Simon. And despite her brother Grant's good intentions, no amount of whisky en route to the gala could lessen the aching heaviness in her heart this night. The spirits only made her head spin.

Gads, she wanted nothing more than to leave this place and to be alone. The moist heat emanating from the sweating hordes of ladies in pale silk gowns and gentlemen in dark coats thickened the air, adding to her irritation.

It was hard enough for Siusan to breathe in her overtight corset, but the stays were a necessary evil to fit into Priscilla's cerulean gown. *Simon had always favored her in blue, and this gown in particular.*

The backs of her eyes began to sting anew. Lud, the crush of perspiring bodies was unbearable! What benefit would the beautiful silk gown be to either of the Sinclair sisters if it became sodden with perspiration and ruined?

Nay, she had to remove herself from the crowd, if she could just slip outside into the unseasonably cool air for just a few moments, maybe she would be able to rein in her grief and mask herself with the composure expected of a Sinclair.

She made her way through the ballroom into a grand entry hall. The vaulted ceilings were higher there, but three small windows were no match for the body heat of hundreds below.

Och, where was the door? Like the other Sinclairs, Siusan was extraordinarily tall, and by standing on her toes, she barely managed to see over the shifting sea of guests to a darkened passage just ahead to her left. She made for it, but the crush of humanity was too great. She could not move through the crowd. And then she saw him. A tall officer with gleaming red hair . . . and God above, could she be mistaken, or was he wearing

the uniform of the Royal Scots Greys? It was eerie
how much he resembled Simon.

Her heart thrummed in her chest. *Simon*? Of
course, it could not be . . . and yet—she had to
get closer. She tried to follow him through the
crowd. Aye, his tunic was scarlet with blue garter
facings and a gold-and-blue-striped sash around
the waist. Simon's regimental dress uniform. The
one he'd been wearing when he asked her father
for her hand.

Gritting her teeth, she focused on the shifting
sea of people.

"Sir. I say, sir!" she called out to him. A quartet of
people parted to let Siusan through. "Please, wait
for me. I see you." She pushed forward, squeezing her way down the hall. "Please do excuse me.
He is just *there*. Thank you. Thank you ever so
much." She edged her hip sideways through the
next gathering, but she was losing sight of him.
She raised her hand into the air. "Please wait. Just
another moment."

But after a minute, he had disappeared. She had
crossed the entire grand hall, but he was gone.
Siusan started back, still scanning the crowd for
any glimpse of the officer. Of course it was not
Simon, but rather her mind playing tricks on
her eyes, filling in Simon's features for those she

hadn't seen clearly enough. Her eyes were stinging. Logically, she knew this, but still she kept searching. She had to see his face fully to tamp out this foolish fantasy that somehow Simon was here and had not died from his wounds.

Stop this folly, Siusan! Simon died, she reminded herself. *You saw him die.*

She spun around, unable to give up her search. Mayhap he knew her Simon, could tell more about what happened at Waterloo. After Simon returned from the battle, his mind was oft dull with laudanum. The words he managed to speak were sharp and cruel, likely coaxed between his lips from pain.

Suddenly, she spied a hallway she hadn't noticed before. Perhaps he went down the passage. It was possible.

The temperature of the dimly lit passage was somewhat cooler, but her head was whirling from the whisky and the heat of her rush through grand hall. What she truly required was an open window and some time alone to calm herself. To evict this all-too-vivid memory of Simon from her head.

She hurried to the first door. After a wary glance behind her to be certain she had not been observed leaving the gala, she pressed down on the latch and peered inside. A wand of moonlight reached between the drawn curtains, allowing just enough light for Siusan to discern a snug library. She slipped inside and pressed the door back with her hip, closing it behind her.

She could smell the oiled books on the shelves lining the walls though she could not see them. But for the thin swathe of moonlight coming through a break in the curtains, the room was utterly black.

Siusan started for the window, but within her first three steps her knee slammed into something low and hard—*a table*? She bit into her lower lip to stifle a whimper. Her knee throbbed.

Reaching out, she felt for a place to sit down, her hand finally finding a cushioned sofa. Limping around its arm, she sat down and hoisted her skirt up and pulled the ribbon at her thigh, then drew down her stocking to rub her barked knee. It wasn't bleeding, which was a good thing, since this was her last pair of silk stockings, and she hadn't the money to buy another if they were ruined.

Just then, she heard the door open. Her breath seized in her lungs.

Moonlight just barely touched the angular face of a large man. He was hardly two strides away.

Her heart pounded. How respectable would it

appear for her to be found in a room meant for family, not guests? Thankfully, the library was cloaked in night. If she didn't move . . . barely breathed, the man mightn't even know she was in the library with him.

But then, his eyes shifted to her, and she saw a smile roll across his lips. She followed his gaze and saw that the lone shaft of moonlight was draped across her bare thigh.

"There you are. I couldn't recall if you said the anteparlor or the library," he whispered, striding unsteadily toward her. "Suppose I guessed right, eh?"

Siusan sat stunned, her mind all a jumble about what to do.

"I apologize for leaving you to wait. Went out for a long ride. Had to. I cannot endure the crowds and all of this meaningless fuss." He came and stood before her, his feet firmly positioned either side of hers. His hand shot out and one finger slid alongside her jaw, easing her head back against the sofa cushion.

Siusan's heart thudded harder in her chest. Panicked, she opened her mouth to tell him that she was not who he thought her to be, when suddenly his lips were moving over hers. She shivered as she felt his tongue ease into her mouth and began stroking the insides of her cheeks, twirling around her tongue. The peaty notes of brandy lingered on her tongue, and as she focused on the taste of his mouth, she didn't at first feel his other hand move between her legs and begin to caress her thigh.

When she did, Siusan clamped her legs together. He lifted his mouth a scant breath from hers and exhaled a short laugh. "Come now, it is not as if it is the first time." He nudged her knees open just a bit, then touched her bare thigh again, softly moving his fingers higher between her legs. Touching her just *there*. "And I know you like this quite a lot."

God, she did. A low moan slipped from her lips. *But how*—Siusan's eyes went wide—*how, pray, could he possibly know this?* Her mind spun like a leaf caught in a whirlwind. *No one else knew. Except Simon, of course—but he's*—

Suddenly, he was lifting her, and her back brushed the seat of the long sofa. He stood beside her as he shed his coat and his waistcoat, dropping them to the floor. Within an instant, he'd unwound his neckcloth and pulled his lawn shirt over his head.

She peered up at him. His face was obscured by darkness, but the shaft of moonlight cut across his muscled chest, scored his abdomen, and defined the hardness beneath his breeches.

Lord above. He was so very, very male. To her own embarrassment, moist heat began to collect between her thighs.

What was she doing? Aye, she was no longer a maid, but no one knew this. And it had only been Simon, her betrothed, the man she would have married.

Until Waterloo left him torn in shreds.

Simon hadn't been expected to survive the night, let alone his transport home. But somehow he did, if only to writhe in agony for weeks at her side, muttering the most hurtful things, untruths meant to drive her from his side. To spare her from seeing him finally succumb. One year ago . . . tonight.

He moved from the light, and she felt him part her knees. The cushion beneath her gave, and she felt him move between her legs.

She couldn't see him now, and she knew he couldn't see her face as he leaned over her and began kissing her again. She closed her eyes and remembered Simon. How she missed him. How she missed the feel of him. Tears welled in her eyes. She felt part of herself die alongside him that night, one year ago.

But in this man's arms, something miraculous was happening. She could scarce believe it, but there was no denying . . . she was beginning to feel again. As if . . . as if his tenderness, his kisses pressing down on her lips, her neck . . . my God, it was as though he was raising her from the dead.

And she did not want him to stop.

Aye, it was wicked, but her body and her mind needed this confirmation of life.

Her eyes snapped open. She could let herself have this. Reclaim her life.

Just one night.

No one would know. Even he thought her to be someone else.

Just one night of sin. That was all.

And in that moment, her decision was made. She raised a hand and ran it through his thick hair, holding him to her as she responded to his passionate kiss while she stroked his muscled chest.

"Mmm," he moaned, stealing one last kiss. He leaned back slightly and ran his fingertips over her breasts, making her arch into his touch. He moved lower and eased his hands over her belly, then beneath the rumpled skirts about her hips. He pushed up her silk chemise and petticoat. His mouth was searing as he kissed the insides of her thighs as he eased her legs wider, opening her sex to him.

Siusan closed her eyes. *Oh, God, this is madness.* But she wasn't going to stop him now. His touches and kisses had wound her body so achingly tight. He made her feel so alive again, the way she had when she was with Simon.

Aye, Simon. She would think of Simon.

His mouth centered on the heat between her thighs. He sucked on her core, flicking her, swirling his tongue with all-knowing surety.

Simon. Simon. She struggled to hold an image of him in her mind. Only, Simon had never done *this*—so wicked a thing. Oh, God. *Oh, God.*

A warm shiver shook her. Simon never made her feel this way. Ever.

She trembled as his fingers spread her folds, then eased inside, slipping into her, curling up slightly as he circled her womanhood with his masterful tongue. She moaned and twisted as heat spiraled tighter and tighter inside her.

Her legs began to quiver uncontrollably. An urgency grew within her, one that she knew only a man could quell.

With both hands, she grasped his head and

turned it up toward hers. When she felt him face her, she leaned down and caught his arms, dragging him back up to her.

In the darkness, she heard him laugh softly, and he moved and rose to kneel between her legs. She extended her arm until her hand felt his breeches stretched tight over his erection. With both hands she searched and finally found the buttons to his front fall. Against the strain of fabric, she fumbled to release them.

His hands came down over hers, then moved them aside to release each button himself. At once the front fall opened, and she felt the heavy weight of his cock bounce down against her before rising again.

She grasped its long thickness and skimmed her fingertips up its shaft to its plump head the way Simon had once tutored her, hardening him to stone. In the wedge of moonlight, she saw a droplet pearl at his tip. She spread it over its crown, making it slick . . . for her.

The sound of the crowd in the ballroom swelled, and she felt his body twist. He was looking toward the door.

Nay, we've not gone this far only to stop now. Siusan pumped her hand once more, then boldly set his plum-shaped tip against the entrance to her wetness.

He groaned aloud and arched his body over hers, poised to take her.

Her anticipation was so great, she could scarcely catch her breath, but when the musk scent of him filled her senses, her yearning grew ever more intense.

She thrilled at the sensation of his hot, muscled body between her thighs. She needed to feel him inside her. Needed to feed a hunger like no other she'd felt.

He eased his hardness into her moist folds, brushing past that place he'd made so sensitive with his skilled tongue. She shivered and brought her legs up and nearly around him.

In a low voice, he swore beneath his breath, then all at once, he grasped her wrists and held them on either side of her head as he thrust into her sheath. She gasped as her body stretched to him. Unbidden, her muscles gripped him, and she arched up, driving him deeper inside.

He slammed harder into her, filling her, almost to the point that she could not bear it. His fully aroused penis stroking her so forcefully created a mutiny of sensation, pushing her to the edge of sanity.

A whimper of carnal pleasure slipped from her mouth, drawing his attention. He kissed her again, hard at first, then slower and more gently, all the while pressing into her again and again, making her even wetter.

She gasped against his mouth, then again and again. He thrust into her harder and faster, until her muscles spasmed with an intensity she'd never known, overwhelming every inch of her with pulsing ecstasy.

With his last stroke, he swore and tried to pull back, but her legs held him in place. Too long. His body suddenly arched and jerked into hers until his weight collapsed atop her. A sheen of perspiration broke over his back.

Panting, he rested upon her. "I'm sorry. I tried—Christ, I've always been able to stop. *Always.*" He pushed up finally and came to his feet, busying himself with dressing.

Siusan slid to the corner of the sofa, her fingers scrabbling for the ribbon to her stocking. In the black of the room, she couldn't find it anywhere. So, instead, she rolled the top of her stocking to hold it in place, then, with a yank, she returned her skirts to her ankles. She sat still, keeping to the darkness, until she could make her escape.

He bent to retrieve what Siusan guessed to be

his waistcoat. This was her moment. As quietly as possible, she rose from the sofa, slipped around behind it, and started for the door.

"Wait." His hand curled around her wrist. "I would be remiss if I allowed you to forget this." There was a clink of coins as he pressed a small leather bag into her palm.

She couldn't help herself. Siusan turned, her face catching the moonlight momentarily as she looked down at the bag, torn between her family's dire need of the money and feeling like she would have sold herself if she took it.

He released her wrist, and his hand dropped to his side. "You are not . . . oh God, you are not Clarissa."

"Nay, I am not." *Blast, I should not have said anything!* Abruptly, she dropped the bag on the floor, and when he instinctively bent to retrieve it, she opened the door and ran down the passage, chancing a hunted glance over her shoulder.

"Oof!" She'd slammed into a stocky, auburn-haired man rounding the corner into the passage just as she turned. She glanced back again as she twisted, and as she slid around him, she saw the man look down the passage toward the library.

Her secret lover stepped from the library at that very moment. Siusan lunged for the crowd. Suddenly the masses surged forward, and she was swallowed up into the swell.

She heard the bang of the liveried footman's staff on the floor behind her. "All hail, His Grace, the Duke of Exeter!"

Siusan pushed against the current of guests rushing forward to see the duke, just catching notice of her sister amongst their number.

"Priscilla!" She lunged forward and caught her sister's arm.

Startled, Priscilla turned to her. "There you are, Su! We've been looking everywhere for you. But here you are and just in time too. The Duke of Exeter has just been announced!"

"I am aware, but we have to find our brothers and leave at once." She tugged on Priscilla's arm.

"I daresay, I am not going anywhere." She furrowed her brow, annoyed.

Siusan grabbed her sister's shoulders. "Listen to me. We *must* leave."

A young woman bumped into Priscilla while blindly racing forward to join the crowd. This only raised her sister's ire. "I haven't yet met the duke."

"But Priscilla, *I have*, and if we do not quit this gala, the duke may recognize me and—oh God—

Da will never forgive me for what I have done. Do you understand? He will toss me to the street before the week is out."

Priscilla's eyes rounded. "Gads, Su, what have you done now?"

Heat washed into her cheeks. "I-I will admit all to you later. I swear. Presently, though, I need for you to locate our brothers. We must away. I will meet you in the carriage." She pinned Priscilla with her gaze, hoping to impart the urgency of her words.

Priscilla nodded, then plunged into the crowd.

Siusan hurriedly descended the staircase. Budding tears stung her eyes as the liveried footman opened the doors, releasing her into the night. She could scarcely catch her breath.

She was such a fool. A damnable weak fool.

One night of sin . . . might well have cost her future.

Chapter 2

To do nothing at all is the most difficult thing in the world, the most difficult and the most intellectual.
Oscar Wilde

The next day

The morning sun cut through the break in the heavy library draperies, rousing Sebastian Beaufort from the sofa where he had sought sleep but never found it. Staggering forward, he yanked open the curtains and peered through the rippled windowpanes at the dew-gilded fields that stretched as far as his bleary eyes could see.

It belonged to him now. *Everything.*

Though he wanted none of it.

Not the houses or the properties and certainly not the title . . . Duke of Exeter.

The weight of responsibility made his head ache and his empty stomach churn. His hand fell to a crystal glass on the table, and, pensively, he ran his thumb around its rim.

This was never meant to be his life. His older brother had assumed the damnable legacy of the Exeter title.

This life was to have been Quinn's.

But now, instead, the task of redeeming the soiled family name was settled firmly upon Sebastian's shoulders, and there wasn't a damned thing he could do to change his circumstance.

After all, he had earned this hellish fate.

A wave of sudden dizziness compelled him to return to the sofa. As he collapsed into it, he glimpsed a pale blue ribbon poking out from beneath a cushion. Slipping it free, he lifted it before his eyes and stared.

Damn it. Sebastian blinked hard, trying to convince himself that it wasn't really what he thought it was. Maybe a bookmarker, or something dropped by a maid. He worked his imagination, but ultimately he resigned himself that it was exactly what he first thought—a garter. There was no way he could brush off what had happened as a liquorish dream now, though he wished he could.

Sebastian sighed, gazing at the silken reminder of his indiscretion. He was sure it belonged to her, the Society chit, a guest of his grandmother's whom he'd recklessly bedded in this very room. *Bloody hell.* He was as much a scoundrel as his lying, wenching father.

Leaning back, Sebastian gazed through the window once more. He raised the crystal to his mouth and tipped it, just enough for the brandy to wet his dry lips, then exhaled a derisive laugh and drained the glass. Why the hell shouldn't he drink it all? The sun had only just risen, and he'd already failed his family.

He slammed the crystal back down upon the glossy surface of a small table beside the sofa, recalling his heartfelt vow. After the casket closed, sealing Quinn's remains, and the title of Duke of Exeter was abruptly thrust upon him, Sebastian had sworn a solemn oath to be different. To change his careless, rakish ways. To become the man the family needed. A good man. A moral man, loyal and trustworthy.

He lowered his head in shame. Well, that vow had lasted all of a month. One bloody month.

He was every bit as worthless as his father had always predicted he would be.

"There you are, dear." His grandmother's frail feminine hand settled gently upon his shoulder. "Admiring your northern domain, I see. It really is quite something, but I daresay nothing compared to Exeter, eh?"

Sebastian turned more fully toward his grandmother as he stealthily returned the blue ribbon to its hiding place between the cushions. But when his gaze met her smiling eyes, he couldn't face her. He shifted his focus out the window again. "It is lovely . . . but I must admit, all of this is quite overwhelming."

She squeezed his shoulder. "I know your ascension was sudden and horribly unexpected, Sebastian, but you were meant to be the Duke of Exeter. I feel it in my heart. You are so like your grandfather when he was your age. You resemble him greatly, did you know that?"

Sebastian nodded. There were six portraits of the first Duke of Exeter hanging in Blackwood Hall alone. Who would have ever imagined that, within a span of four years' time, two dukes would die tragically and that he would become the fourth Duke of Exeter? Certainly not he.

"But more importantly, you, Sebastian, are the only male of your generation who had the morality, propriety, and fortitude to restore dignity to our family. To reclaim what your father lost."

He winced at that. It wasn't true. Quinn was meant to be *the one.* The one groomed for the position, educated, polished. Not he.

As if knowing his thoughts, his grandmother moved around the sofa and stood before him. "Believe me, Sebastian. You are the one. You will do it. Yes, I will concede that Quinn had tremendous potential, but too many of your father's weaknesses were mirrored in your brother. He always needed adventure, excitement. Always associating with the wrong sort and getting himself into dark mischief."

Sebastian shook his head. "It's not true." She didn't know Quinn like he did. She didn't know *him* either. Not really. He was far more like his father than she knew. Worse. Hell, last night only verified it. Oh, he had fooled himself for a month that he could be the man the duchy needed him to be, but last night proved him wholly wrong.

Christ, last eve, he'd been so bleeding sotted, he hadn't known the difference between the high-priced whore, Clarissa, and an innocent miss.

Sebastian glared down at the empty glass beside

him, then set his fingers to his throbbing temples and tried to remember her and what happened between them.

She seemed so willing. So . . . passionate. Responsive to his touch. But, God, had she truly been?

Or had his drink-fogged brain only told him so? Pins of guilt pricked at the backs of his eyes. Sebastian closed them for a moment and struggled to recall her. But he couldn't. He'd never really seen her face, even when he lay intimately atop her, here on the sofa, in the darkness. His only memory was a parting glimpse of her dark hair and blue gown as she ran from him down the dark hall before disappearing into the crowd in the grand hall. Nothing more.

"I've brought a stack of invitations. Do you have a few moments to sort through them with me?"

Sebastian exhaled resignedly. Evidently, she was oblivious to his supremely pained state.

She flashed him a curious smile, an excited light gleaming in her aged brown eyes. "We shall have to be most selective. I shall warn you of this now. Your time in London is short and the invitations many. We will need to ensure you use every moment to its best advantage if you are to make powerful connections."

"C-connections?" What was she talking about? He was here to formally take his seat in the House of Lords, then return to Exeter, nothing more.

"Well, of course. Political alliances . . . but also connections with notable families. I do not jest when I tell you that everyone expects your foray to London to result in an engagement, and well . . . it would be so good for Gemma to have a . . . a woman to mother her."

"Gemma?" Sebastian straightened. Now she had his full attention.

"I need not remind you that as her guardian, the responsibility of her care is yours. I expect you to carry on for Quinn. She has no one else, and dare I say it, she looks so like your brother that though we may not speak of it outwardly, the Beaufort blood fills her veins." Her gaze changed. She was studying him now. "I have placed her in a school for young gentlewomen. It is expensive, but it actually focuses on education rather than painting with watercolors and such affected notions as how to sprinkle French into conversation. At first, I thought this school suited her quiet nature, but her increasingly frequent letters suggest she is not at all happy there. The other wicked chits know the circumstances of her birth and taunt her constantly." Her eyes fixed on his. "You may choose to engage a governess and take her to Exeter or her to remain where she is if you prefer though you ought make your decision soon."

A dry cough raced up his throat. Sebastian hadn't considered Gemma's future. Hadn't even thought of Quinn's child. His grandmother had taken the girl in after Quinn's death, and it never occurred to him that this arrangement should change. Lord knows, his grandmother was far more suited to deciding the child's future than the man . . . who was to blame for her father's—his own brother's—death.

"Either way, you are nearing thirty. It is time for you to find yourself a bride. I trust we understand each other on this point, Sebastian. It is your *duty*." She rubbed her hands together as if brushing dirt from them. Then her expression brightened. "Now then, tell me, dear, did any of the young ladies in attendance last evening strike your fancy?"

A dukedom, a charge, and a bride. Bloody hell. He shoved his fingers through his hair. Everything was happening too quickly for his brandy-dulled mind to follow.

"Well?" she prodded.

"I-I might have glimpsed someone of interest."

His grandmother clapped her hands excitedly. Such a change in her demeanor from only a moment ago. "What is her name? Who are her people?"

Damn. Had he completely lost his wits? He shouldn't have admitted anything. "We were never introduced." Sebastian couldn't let on about the truth of the matter . . . that a young lady did rouse his passions like never before. But not in the genteel way his grandmother meant.

"Well then, we shall endeavor with all earnestness to learn her name and ensure that proper introductions are arranged. My man will begin making inquires today. Why delay?" There was an eagerness to his grandmother's voice that set Sebastian's nerves on edge. Given her ways, he had no doubt she would work through last night's guest list, interviewing young ladies, until one of them happened upon a certain tearful miss—who would shock her with a most salacious story . . . involving the new duke.

He shoved his fingers between the cushions and drew the ribbon into his fist. There was no choice. He would have to locate the lady first. He had to learn what really happened and beg her forgiveness, then make whatever amends she demanded, if the worst of his suspicions revealed itself to be the truth.

He had to locate her with all due haste.

As he rose from the sofa, he smiled at his grandmother, feigning interest in her stack of cards and letters. Then something occurred to him. "Might there be any invitations to a ball? I would wager that the number of Society events is greatly reduced now that the Season has ended, so the chances of our paths crossing would be greater."

"Yes, you are entirely correct, dear boy." His grandmother said, looking proudly upon him. "The most-heavily-attended events, such as balls, as you mentioned, will allow us to efficiently sort through the unmarried ladies of the *ton*. We shall concentrate on those invitations first."

The old woman dropped into the chair behind the writing desk and began hurriedly thumbing through the invitations. "There is one extremely notable event that caught my notice. Not a ball— so much better than that." Her eyes lit suddenly. "Ah, here it is." Her eyes raced over the embossed card. "Perfect!"

Sebastian walked over to view her treasure.

She turned her head up and gazed triumphantly at him. "The Lord Mayor's annual dinner. Everyone of political or social consequence will be in attendance, which means, no doubt *she will* be as well." She rose and embraced him. "Are you not excited, dear? Perhaps I am being a little optimistic, but who knows? We may meet your future bride in as little as a sennight!"

Sebastian clenched his fist tightly around the garter ribbon. "Seven days," he echoed.

If he didn't manage to find her before then.

Noon
The Sinclair residence
No. 1 Grosvenor Square, London

Siusan set her hand atop her belly and peered into the mirror. Her father's learning of her indiscretion was not her only worry. Even if she somehow succeeded in eluding the Duke of Exeter until he returned to the country and managed to keep the incident in the library concealed from Society, there was another worry. One more frightening than even her father in one of his rages.

She could be with child. And in time, there would no concealing that. Setting her fingers to her temples, she began to pace. There was no way to know. She would have to worry and wonder for nearly a month if her wanton coupling with the Duke of Exeter had taken root. Nearly a month. How could she bear the wait?

* * *

Confessing a sin, even one so great as the one Siusan had committed with the Duke of Exeter, had never been difficult for the Sinclair siblings, at least not for many years.

After their mother died when they were but children, and their father found solace in the depths of a bottle, the Sinclairs reveled in regaling each other with tales of shocking behavior. Bragging about their sins.

It was not because their souls were shadowed that they sought out bad behavior, for indeed, all seven of the Sinclairs were generous, kind, and loving. But their hearts were wounded, torn open by the members of Edinburgh Society, who saw only unruly children and referred to the Sinclairs quite publicly as the Seven Deadly Sins.

Even their governess taunted them cruelly with this epithet as she forced them to their knees in Rosslyn Chapel to pray for their salvation.

But the Sinclairs were nothing if not proud Scots, and to be reduced to tears by another's words was not acceptable to the seven children, and especially not to Sterling Sinclair, the eldest.

Perhaps, because of this, Fate would choose Sterling to forge the armor that would protect them all from the stinging blows of the hurtful designation.

It had been a day not unlike any other when Sterling's mind strayed from his prayers once more and his gaze wandered upward to a nearby stone archway. He'd glanced at it any number of times, he was sure, but today the light illuminated the carving most exceptionally, drawing out intricate detail. What he saw sent him to his feet, despite the immediate barrage of slaps levied upon his head by their governess.

For there, to his complete astonishment, was a depiction of the Procession of the Seven Deadly Sins. He couldn't believe it, but there it was. The solution had been there before them for their entire lives, there, in a chapel built by their own ancestor, William St. Clair, hundreds of years before!

In that moment, he came to a realization that would change all of their lives forever. To remove the power and the pain, they had to embrace the title the Seven Deadly Sins.

And so they did. Each of them claimed ownership one of the sins and did everything each could to embody that sin when in public. The sins became the weapons with which to slice through

Edinburgh Society and the armor with which to protect themselves from pain and humiliation.

By the time the children were young adults, the sinful behavior was no longer just a way to cope with the hurtful barbs of others—now they embraced the sins completely. Every action was influenced by the learned habit.

And so, when Sinclairs gathered in the resplendent parlor of their otherwise-sparsely-dressed Grosvenor Square town house, and Siusan admitted her intimate indiscretion with none other than the Duke of Exeter, no one even blinked.

Though Priscilla did sulk childishly. "So *you* saw him first! How horrid of you, Siusan. You saw me on the dais. You knew I had set my cap at him."

"Gorblimey, Priscilla!" Lachlan narrowed his eyes at the youngest Sinclair. "Do cease thinking about yourself for once. We have a grave problem here."

Siusan raised her chin. "My actions were risky and dangerous." Her words were strong, and yet her chin began to wobble with weakness. And then, her eyes began to sting, and she knew in another moment her act of strength would disintegrate in a wash of tears.

Her brother Grant rose from the chair nearest the door and took Siusan's shoulders, raising her from her place on the settee. "It was because of Simon. You miss him so greatly. We should have never forced you to attend the gala on the anniversary of his passing." He hugged her to him. "I am sorry, Siusan."

Her shoulders began to shake, and as she had anticipated, the tears came. "What I felt is no excuse." She pushed gently back from Grant and peered up at her brothers and her sister. "I have put you all at risk."

Killian, Priscilla's twin brother, rose and crossed the room to take Siusan's hand. "You said he never saw your face."

"That's right!" Priscilla exclaimed. "He hasn't a clue about your identity." She fashioned a smile for her. "Don't you see? You have nothing to fear, Su."

Siusan shook her head. "Someone may have recognized me when I left the library. A crowd was standing at the other end of the hall—I bumped into a man as I turned into the crowd."

"That may be true, but the passage was unlit. You said it yourself," Grant recounted in a very logical manner. "No one expected the duke to emerge from the passageway, and therefore I would venture to say that no one paid any mind to it until the duke stepped into the grand hall and was announced."

"Even if someone did recognize you, no one but the few of us knows what happened in the library," Lachlan reminded her.

"*He* knows." Siusan sniffled.

"Aye," Lachlan admitted, but waved her words from the air as if they mattered naught. "As an unmarried man—and a newly ascended duke— he is certainly not looking for scandal—or to be leg-shackled to a lass simply because he sought to brag about a tumble in his library. You see, there is very little cause for worry."

Lachlan, who had more than his share of tumbles with the ladies, presented the soundest reasoning. The duke was not about to risk everything on some quest to identify her. A tiny smile tugged at Siusan's lips. "Thank you, Lachlan. Of course, you are right." She gave an embarrassed laugh.

Priscilla scrunched up her nose in confusion. "Why are you laughing?"

"Because my portmanteau is packed. After last night, I saw no recourse but to leave London immediately, to protect all of you from Father's wrath once he learned the shame I have brought the Sinclair family." Siusan looked down, not wanting her brothers and sister to see the redness she felt rising into her cheeks.

Surprise widened Grant's eyes. "And just where do you think you were going . . . without coin?"

Siusan shrugged. "I hoped that I could convince Mrs. Wimpole to allow me to stay with her until the duke leaves."

"Do you not think those in service will hear of a lady hiding out with a cook? I declare, that lot loves gossip more than the *ton*." When Siusan did not reply, Priscilla rushed forward and took her hand. "Well, no need for that, is there now?"

Siusan smiled feebly, wanting to believe they truly had forgiven her for endangering their futures. From the soft smiles on their faces, she knew they had. If only their father could see the goodness in his children—instead of only their faults.

"Come, let me help you unpack your things—" Priscilla pulled her out of the parlor and toward the stairs. "And any of *my things* you might have placed in the case by mistake."

Siusan laughed as they ascended the staircase. Until she remembered Priscilla's blue satin slippers . . . which might have made their way into her portmanteau, accidentally, of course.

That evening
Vauxhall Gardens

Though Siusan trusted the truth of Lachlan's logic, it seemed dreadfully unwise to venture into Society so soon. And yet, here she was less than twenty-four hours later, down the lamplit Grand Walk at Vauxhall Gardens.

"It is as I said, Siusan." Lachlan took no measure to obscure how pleased he was with himself. "Nothing to fret about." He bowed his head and tipped his beaver hat at a comely lady who passed by, ignoring the gentleman at her side. He turned his head to Siusan then, and grinned, as if he'd just proved his assertion again.

A sense of unease prickled Siusan's skin each time they left the ebbing glow of one lamp to step into the golden halo of the next. Lud, she wished the lamps were not so bright, and that this night, the moon merely grinned instead of glowing pure and white like a great pearl.

"I will concede that your keen assessment of the situation seems correct, brother." And it did, for in the past quarter-hour alone they'd encountered more than a dozen members of the *ton*, and not one had viewed them with a sickened gaze. All simply gawked at them, which was completely normal behavior whenever the striking Sinclairs appeared *en masse.*

Still, Siusan could not allow herself to relax and enjoy the cool air and the troops of lively entertainers performing throughout the Gardens. "The night is not yet over, dear brother," she reminded Lachlan. Though she wished it were, and that they were headed for the carriage and home—instead of tromping toward the center of the Gardens.

Just then, Siusan turned and had not Lachlan caught her arm, she would have fallen, bringing unwanted attention to herself. Priscilla, caring sister that she was, had condescended to allow Siusan to wear the very blue slippers she had mistakenly packed in her portmanteau. At first Siusan thought this gesture supremely gracious. But now, as the shoes' low, but too-narrow heels spiked deep into the gravel with every step, dangerously challenging her balance, Siusan began to wonder if allowing her to wear the beautiful shoes was truly meant to be some wicked form of penance for accidentally placing them in her portmanteau.

"Perhaps a glass of arrack punch would steady your frayed nerves, Su." Grant raised his chin to the supper boxes in the distance ahead of them.

Siusan stilled her step. "Nay. Too many lamps. Too many people," she muttered in reply.

"Och, weel of course there are," Grant told her, as they cut a shorter path through the stands of elms. "While the food is predictably horrid, the wine is of superb vintage and not to be missed." He chuckled. "There, do you see? No one—except those with infantile palates and corseted bellies—is eating. Only sampling the wine."

She smiled weakly back at him. God, she was being the veriest goose. Lachlan was correct, she reminded herself. He *was*.

As they entered the dining area, Grant spoke to a barrel-chested man in a dark suit of clothes, and before Siusan could reconsider, their party was ushered into a private booth.

A quart of arrack was instantly set upon their table, along with several thick glasses, while a slightly dusty bottle was presented to Grant, who approved the wine to be opened and a glass poured.

An hour passed, and the brothers were standing a few yards from the dining booth, glasses in hand, reminiscing in slightly slurred, loud voices with Gentleman John Jackson about their brother Sterling's short-lived career in pugilism. Another younger pugilist, judging by his enormous size, had just joined the quartet of half-inebriated men.

"Do you think we can convince one of our

brothers to escort us home?" Siusan asked, not really expecting a reply, when she saw Jackson throw a treacle-slow mock punch at Killian, who pretended to take a blow to his jaw and was now slowly staggering backward. The men burst into riotous laughter.

"Och, *men*. How can they make light of Sterling's bout with the Irishman? Sterling could have been killed by that blow." Priscilla narrowed her eyes at the gathering. "Lud, you do not think that Jackson and that other fellow are trying to persuade Killian to reenter the ring? Not with his fast temper."

Siusan shook her head. *What a ridiculous notion.* "He is merely enjoying the folly." Priscilla did not appear convinced. "I vow that even if your twin sought a life in pugilism, he would never get a match. The whole of England has heard the rumor that he killed a man. Only a fighter with a supreme wish for death would dare enter the ropes with Lord Killian Sinclair."

"I do not agree." Priscilla's eyes fixed on the conversation behind her. "I canna make out what they are saying? Can you, Su?"

With a bored sigh parting her lips, Siusan rose slightly from the bench and leaned forward to peer over Priscilla's shoulder. "If I am not mis-

taken . . . I heard them mention White's. Wait
. . . no, Watier's—" Thinking to hear better, she
leaned farther over the table, setting her hand
down for balance.

Just then, her hand caught the lip of a glass, top-
pling it. Siusan winced as she saw a torrent of red
liquid coursing toward Priscilla's lap. Siusan's
eyes went wide, and she shrieked a warning to
her sister, who was too absorbed in the gentlemen's conversation to have noticed that something was amiss.

It was too late. The wine was pouring off the
table like a crimson waterfall.

Priscilla yelped as the wine drenched her blue
satin gown. She shot to her feet and glared at
Siusan. "I canna believe you did this! You sought
to ruin my gown last night at the gala, and you
could not rest until you succeeded, could you?"

"Nay, Priscilla. Nay, it was an accident." Siusan
held out her lace handkerchief to her sister, but
Priscilla slapped it away. Everyone within fifty
paces was staring at them. "Please, Priscilla,
lower your voice. Everyone is—"

"Nay!" Angry tears erupted in Priscilla's eyes.
"You've always wanted this gown, admit it why
don't you! You've coveted it ever since Simon
said he admired it—"

The blood seemed to rush from Siusan's head, and her knees wobbled beneath her. She dropped back down to the bench, leveled by the blow of her sister's words.

Priscilla gasped at her own outburst and clapped her hand to her mouth. She stood still as a statue for several moments, staring, before finally rushing around the table to Siusan. "Oh God, Siusan, please forgive me . . . I am so sorry. I swear on Mother's grave that I did not mean what I said. Truly, I didn't."

Tears flooded Siusan's eyes. She propelled herself from the box and raced into the shadows of the elms. God, she didn't know where she was going, only that she had to be alone.

Priscilla called after her. "Wait for me. Please!" With a pleading glance back at her brothers, she turned and gave chase.

"It is a lovely evening to stroll Vauxhall Gardens, Sebastian, but I must sit down and rest for a few minutes if you do not mind," his grandmother said.

"Of course." Sebastian led her to a marble bench along the Grand Walk and settled his grandmother down upon it. It was an unusually pleasant evening, but Sebastian, feeling caged within

Blackwood Hall, would have spent it in the fresh air even if torrents of rain were falling from the sky. He had bent his knees to sit beside his grandmother when he saw *her* pass beneath a lamp.

There was no mistake. Even across the distance, he recognized the miss from the library.

The same dark, wavy hair he saw as she escaped down the dim hallway. The very same blue gown. As she passed beneath an unusually bright lamp, he could see the color clearly. Only . . . dear God, was that blood? No, no. Surely he was wrong.

Widening his eyes, he tracked her until she darted into a clutch of elm trees and disappeared from his sight.

His heart pounded inside his chest, and he shot to his feet. "I am dreadfully sorry, Grandmother. But I must leave for a moment—just a moment. I promise you."

"What are you about, Sebastian?" It was evident that she was not appreciative at being left, especially not in the Gardens.

He knelt before his grandmother. "I believe I have just seen *her*."

"The miss you saw last evening?" Her eyes widened excitedly.

"Yes"—he came to his feet—"but I fear she may

be in some manner of distress." He turned and looked toward the elms.

Just then, he and his grandmother witnessed three towering men plunge into the darkness under the trees at breakneck speed.

Bloody hell!

"Go then, Sebastian. I will be fine here in the light. But do take care!"

Instantly, Sebastian tore across the Grand Walk and, without a thought, ducked into the grove of elms.

Chapter 3

The quantity of riches one must earn can be compared to the shoes one wears; if too small, they cause pain; if too big, they are a hindrance to physical and mental comfort. When we have more, it breeds pride, sloth and contempt for others.

Bhagawan Sri Sathya Sai Baba

Sebastian could hear the crunch of gravel and knew that the men—and his passionate lady from the library, too, were not far ahead.

Then, there was a loud crack trailed by a violent shiver of branches and leaves. "Damn me!"

Sebastian froze and listened.

"Hold up, Grant. I slammed me noggin into a great branch, and I'm surely bleeding." A Scotsman, his clear voice low and deep.

Sebastian crept closer. Ghostly bones of white moonlight reached between the trees, and he could now discern two unusually large men.

"Och, ye clumsy buffoon. You're not bleeding at all. You spilled the wine when you fell. He reached down, snatched up the bottle, and only after holding it into the moonlight, did he turn and pull the other man to his feet. "You're damned lucky you didn't spill it all. Do you know what I paid for this?"

"Too much, when our pockets are damn near empty," the other man snapped back.

A breeze picked up behind Sebastian, tumbling dried leaves in erratic circles around him and pricking up the hair on the back of his neck. Huge branches just above him creaked and groaned in the wind.

He stared up, waiting for one to choose its moment and crash down upon him, killing him instantly. Sebastian had no doubt just this sort of freakish accident would claim his life, for it was the way of things. The way every other Duke of Exeter had met his end.

He was wary now, his thoughts of his own demise warring his instinct to attack the Scots.

Three men had entered the trees behind the woman. He glanced around but detected no other.

Ahead, he could see two of them arguing about spilled wine. No longer three, as there had been when he first saw them enter the grove of trees. Where was the third man? Likely still pursuing the young lady.

Ah, but one man he could handle, even one rivaling the size of these two Scottish hulks.

Sebastian backed silently onto the trail, keeping the two men in his sight. He would circle around them quickly, though, and if the stars in the sky above were with him, on the far side of the elm grove, he would come upon his miss . . . and the third man.

Damn it, though. It might already be too late to offer his protection.

"You canna mean that my sister took the carriage and left the Gardens alone!" Priscilla set her hands on her hips, practically daring the transport waiter to tell her otherwise.

"I am afraid she did, miss." He turned his round, bald head and peered up at her through tiny dark eyes. "She and her driver left 'bout two minutes past. If ye listen, might even hear the carriage headed for the bridge." He cupped a hand to his ear, then nodded at Priscilla, urging her to listen.

Priscilla stilled and listened, and aye, she heard something, though she could see very little beyond the glow of the lamp they stood beneath. It was a rattle of gravel they heard; however, the sound came from opposite the direction the transport waiter had indicated. It sounded more like rapid footsteps of another. Her body tensed, and she whirled around until she finally recognized the silhouette of her twin brother running toward them from the direction of the trees.

The waiter nervously backed far away and stood at the side of the road leading to the bridge.

"Killian!" Priscilla rushed forward, extending a pleading hand to her brother. "Thank goodness you have come." She took his hand and pulled him to her. "I have done something terrible, wicked, and I require your help."

"What did you do?" He looked down at her sodden gown, then grabbed her shoulders and held her back so he could see her more clearly. "Lord above, Priscilla, are you hurt?"

"Nay, Killian, I am not, but I wounded Siusan!"

Confusion filled his eyes. "What can you mean? You would never hurt our sister. You are exaggerating, surely."

"And yet, I did hurt her." She paused momentarily, then lowered her voice to confess. "I . . . I said a terrible thing to her . . . about Simon," she added sheepishly.

"Ah, Christ, why did you go and do something like that? She was already fragile as a wee bird after what happened last night." He shook his head with disgust.

"On my honor, I did not mean to do it. I simply reacted and . . . I hurt her." She curled her fingers and gestured to her gown. "She spilled wine all over it, my very favorite dress, ruining it. I canna say why I said what I did . . . I only know that at that moment I wanted to make her feel as horrid as I." Priscilla sniffled. "But I am sorry for hurting her. I am! You know I love her dearly."

Killian narrowed his eyes at her, as if assessing her honesty. "Oh, Priscilla . . ."

"Killian, I swear to you, I *am* sorry. I need to tell her so. Truly!" Priscilla pleaded.

"So why haven't you?" Killian asked. "Where is she?"

"She's taken the carriage. She's alone, Killian, and after last night . . . well, you said it yourself, she's fragile now. I fear she may attempt something rash." She peered up at her brother as her eyes flooded with salty tears.

Killian's eyes widened as he divined her meaning—she would leave home, just as she had thought to do last night. He charged across the gravel. "You there. Come here!" he shouted.

The waiter, seeing a huge, angry-sounding man charging at him like a horned bull, retreated. Killian's hand shot out and caught the waiter's shoulder and forcefully whirled him around. "I shall have a hackney at once." His flame blue eyes flashed, and instantly the waiter began to shake.

"Killian, nay!" Priscilla pried her brother's large hand from the waiter and fumbled in her reticule for a coin. She pressed it into the waiter's trembling hand. "Please, good sir, will you tell us where we might find a driver . . . or a hackney stand?"

"Yes, my lady. Johnny Bowen's rig is tied off near the river. I'll fetch him for you. He'll take you anywhere you like." When the waiter turned and hurried away, Priscilla narrowed her eyes at her twin.

"You dinna need to hand over a coin, Priscilla," Killian growled. "Grant already squandered too much on tonight's outing. Besides, I clearly had the situation well in hand."

"Is that so?" She flicked her brow. "I daresay, another moment in your hand, and the waiter would have soiled himself, and we'd still be standing here, no closer to hiring a hackney." Priscilla suddenly straightened and looked around. "Where are Grant and Lachlan? Our eyes met just before I raced after Siusan."

The waiter sidled up and gave a nod, letting Priscilla know that the hackney was on its way.

Priscilla squinted into the direction of the elms. In the light of the ripe moon, had her brothers been about, she should have been able to see them. "Where are they?"

"We all followed after you. And I could have sworn they trailed me through the wood, though they were both a bit foxed." Killian shrugged. "Och, probably thought that you and I could deal with whatever the problem was and went back to finish off the wine."

"Weel, if that is where their sisters' distress ranks, then they can devise their own means to return to Mayfair." Priscilla nodded firmly. "We shall away without them."

"Or we could wait for a few minutes more."

"Why ever would we do that? Have you forgotten, dear brother? Siusan is terribly shaken."

"By-your-own-words!"

Priscilla waved a dismissive hand. "Nay, we canna wait. We must attend to her at once."

A hackney drew up before them, and the waiter hurried over to hand Priscilla up into the vehicle.

She smiled politely at him. "Och, if only all men were so considerate," she said, as she stepped inside, flashing a wry gaze at her twin as he leaped in, and the waiter shut the door behind him.

In a great burst, Sebastian broke through the trees just in time to see the miss handed up into a hackney. An angry-looking gentleman hurried inside behind her.

The music of Vauxhall Gardens rode the cool night air, but the crack of a whip was distinct over the din. The hackney lurched forward.

Sebastian charged for the hackney, his breathing fast and hard, but he'd managed no more than five yards before the carriage evaporated into the darkness.

He stared into the emptiness. *Bloody hell.* Bending at the waist, he propped his hands on his knees and gulped air into his burning lungs.

"I beg your pardon, sir."

Sebastian looked up. It was the transport waiter who'd assisted the couple into the hackney.

"I could not have held them any longer. While he wanted to wait a while longer for you, the lady could not be persuaded."

"The woman, was she injured?" He straightened and stared down at the waiter.

"Blimey, you're . . . English." The waiter's beady eyes narrowed into tight slits. "I beg your pardon, sir. I mistook you for someone else."

"Damn it, man, was she hurt?" There was only a stride between them now. "I demand you answer me at once."

The waiter started. "No, no! Her gown was wet with what smelled like wine, but she didn't appear injured in any way."

Sebastian's breath came easier now that his fear for her well-being had been extinguished. "I probably appeared a madman just now, eh?"

The waiter didn't dare reply.

"You see, I saw a woman who seemed to be in great distress, and I wondered if she required assistance."

The waiter's expression flattened in apparent relief, and a slight chuckle escaped his lips. "Ah, I understand now. And I apologize, sir, for mistaking you for one of the brothers they spoke of. For it's plain you ain't a bleedin' Scot like them."

"The man *and* the woman—they were both Scots?" Yes, now that he thought about it, he almost remembered having the faintest impression of that when she fled the library. Now this bit of information interested him, and he stepped forward. His sudden movement seemed to startle the waiter.

The man's little eyes went wide as an owl's. "I-I do not know for certain, sir, but they talked a bit like a Scottish scullery gel I once knew . . . except, you know, *Quality*."

The two other men in the elm stand were Scots and certainly the brothers the waiter had overheard mentioned. "Did they happen to tell you their names?"

"No, sir. Why would they? As I informed you, the lady was not hurt." The waiter's growing discomfort and wariness was transparent even in the moonlight. "Again, sir, I apologize for my mistake."

He had pressed his luck with this man long enough. Any additional questions might seem suspicious and draw unwanted attention to him. "My thanks for putting my mind at ease, good man. Good evening." He flipped a coin to the waiter and hurried back in the direction of the Grand Walk, where his grandmother awaited.

So, he hadn't yet met the lady, but tonight was a very productive evening, indeed.

Siusan sat in the dark parlor, waiting. Wax candles were dear, and it would be best to spare what tapers they had. She didn't mind the darkness. It

never frightened her, as it had her sisters Ivy and
Priscilla.

Besides which, she knew she wouldn't be alone
for long. She'd heard Priscilla call out to her
when she ran from the supper boxes at Vauxhall
Gardens. She would come, as would her brothers,
to try to soothe her wounds, as they always did.
During the few days bracketing the anniversary of
Simon's death, it was as if her skin was gossamer
thin, and even the slightest pitying glance could
tear through to her heart, where she held her
memories of Simon, her beloved.

The sound of hoofbeats in the square drew her
gaze out of the parlor's front window to a hackney taking the corner at too fast a pace. The carriage slowed at the pavers before the house, as
she knew it would. Priscilla. It had to be.

The hackney door swung open, and without
waiting for the driver to pull his horses to a complete halt, Killian leaped out. He whirled just in
time to catch Priscilla as she flung herself through
the open cab door, and together they ran up the
stairs to the house.

The front door slammed open, and a scatter of
footfalls filled the entryway.

"Siusan! Siusan? Are you here?" Priscilla's silhouette appeared in the parlor doorway. "My God, Killian, what if she's gone?"

"I haven't," Siusan said. From where she sat on the settee before the window, the moonlight outlined little more than her profile. They wouldn't see that she wasn't crying anymore. That the mask had come up again.

She heard tapers rolling inside the candlebox, then saw Killian cross to the hearth and grasp the tinderbox. She saw sparks as he struck the steel with the flint, then the blue glow of a brimstone-dipped match as he lit the candle Priscilla held out.

"We can spare a candle, Siusan." Priscilla carried a table lamp and set it on the tea table before her. "There, much better now, is it not?"

Killian returned to stand before the parlor doorway. "We were concerned about you. You ought not have left the Gardens alone."

Priscilla sank down on her knees before her. "I apologize for what I said, Su. I did not mean to hurt you." She laid her cheek on Siusan's lap. "I dinna know why I spoke to you with such daggered words, you, my sister, whom I love so dearly. It is as though during the past sennight, I have trod far out of my way to hurt you."

Siusan stroked her sister's hair. "Truly, do you not know?"

Priscilla lifted head. The moonlight touched her skull, transforming her hair into ebony silk, her skin into whitest porcelain. Her eyes were wide and glistening. She said nothing for several long moments, then collapsed into tears. Struggling to her feet, she backed into the center of the room.

Siusan started to rise, but Priscilla halted her with raised palm.

"Y-you know. You know, don't you?" She trembled.

"That you were in love with Simon?" Siusan asked, more as a courtesy because she already knew the truth. "Aye, I knew you were smitten with him. We all did, Priscilla."

If Siusan hadn't had her eyes fixed on her sister, she might have missed Priscilla's glance at her twin for confirmation of this assertion.

"You should despise me. Do you not see? Something inside of me wants to wound you as he hurt me when he chose you, Siusan the older bookish one, instead of me, the—"

"—the pretty one?" Siusan finished. "Priscilla, I do not despise you. Why, you were hardly more than a child when Simon offered for me. What you felt was childish infatuation."

Priscilla bristled. "What I felt was far deeper than you know."

Siusan sighed and slowly rose from the settee. "I daresay, you only believe that because you have never truly been in love. Had you, you would have known the difference." She walked around the settee and leaned her forehead against the cool windowpane. She sighed. "Be grateful you did not love Simon with all of your heart . . . because the pain of being without him is nearly too much to bear."

Killian crossed the room and settled his hand on Siusan's shoulder. "Grant used nearly the same words to describe the heartache and loneliness you and the others felt when our mother died."

Siusan turned her head to look at him. "The two of you were only newly born, so you wouldn't have felt it, but, aye, losing someone you love is the greatest pain that you will ever experience. And sadly, no one escapes that fate."

"Unless you never love anyone," Priscilla said, her voice as chill as a tombstone.

Siusan slowly turned to peer out of the window into the moon-iced square. "Sad, isn't it? The truth of your statement. But you are entirely correct— the only sure way to escape that pain . . . is never to love."

Again.

Chapter 4

A life of leisure and a life of laziness are two different things.

Benjamin Franklin

Mansion House
London

The Lord Mayor's annual dinner was, without question, the grandest event Sebastian had ever attended. It was held in Mansion House, the glittering residence of the Lord Mayor of London, Sir Matthew Wood, though Sebastian doubted even the Prince Regent's accommodations could compare to such grandeur. If they could, he decided, then England had far greater difficulties than a mad king.

Sebastian's grandmother had been right. Everyone of consequence seemed to be in attendance. Seated near the head of the first table, as he was, he would never find *her* in the crowd. Especially since he'd barely had a glimpse of the miss. No, unless his Enchantress of the Night wore a wine-stained blue gown to the dinner, his chances of finding her were slim at best.

The guests were packed cheek by jowl at four long dining tables, each seating nearly one hundred, stretching the length of house's grand Egyptian Hall. Footmen hurried steaming dishes of every conceivable variety to the tables for the guests' dining pleasure.

But Sebastian had no appetite this night. He had a mission. To find the woman he had wronged in the library before his grandmother did.

He stirred the food on his plate, leaving gaps in places so as to avoid drawing his grandmother's attention to untouched food. He speared a wedge of beef and forced it into his mouth. As he chewed, he peered across several tables at the massive fluted columns that braced the lofty, vaulted ceiling so heavily ornamented with decorative moldings. Why would the Lord Mayor require all of this?

He glanced up and squinted at an enormous chandelier positioned above the table. Like all the others in the hall, it was weighted with hundreds of sparkling crystals, casting bright light on the soaring Egyptian-patterned walls and the hundreds of guests supping noisily below.

It happened then.

Again.

He started thinking about his grandfather, father, and brother dying in improbable accidents. His grandfather, the first Duke of Exeter, had decided to walk the length of his dukedom in gratitude for the land he'd been granted. A day later, a footman returned with his charred remains, claiming that a ball of lightning shot from the sky and struck the duke when he was only strides from the border.

The second duke perished in the London Beer Flood. When vats at the Meux and Company Brewery burst, sending three hundred thousand gallons of beers into the street, eight people drowned. The duke died the next day of beer poisoning, when on a lark, he and his friends swam into a beer-flooded basement to frolic in the foam and drink their fill.

And then there was his brother Quinn, the third Duke of Exeter. He shuddered at the memory.

But then he had led Quinn to his horrid death, hadn't he?

A breeze from one of the windows set crystals tinkling about his head, drawing his gaze. Quickly, he forced his gaze away from the heavy chandelier above, trying to block from his mind the image of crystal monster crashing down atop him. The curse of the Duke of Exeter, *The Times* would call it, and note that what a blessing it was that His Grace had no heirs, and the curse would end with the extinction of the last Duke of Exeter.

"Ages us all, does it not?" came a rich male voice from behind him. He turned to see a rather tall, grayish-haired gentleman wearing ceremonial garb of ermine. "I asked that we reserve the candles and cast a kinder glow on our ladyfolk, but have they listened? No." He chuckled.

Good God, Sir Matthew Wood was addressing him directly! Sebastian abruptly pushed up from his chair. "I beg your pardon, my lord. I should not have had my back to you."

Sir Matthew laughed aloud. "Then how would you eat, Sebastian . . ." Sir Matthew paused then and peered at him, almost as if he was waiting for something.

Sebastian—he used my Christian name. There

was something very familiar about the man. Not something he might have read in the newspaper, or heard. Something he . . . should *remember*. "Do forgive me. It is Your Grace now, is it not?"

"I fear, Sir Matthew, that I am at a disadvantage. My eyes and my mind assert that we have met— though as I am only just arrived in London from Exeter, this is an impossibility." The Lord Mayor chuckled.

The shaking of his grandmother's shoulders caught his notice. Good God, now she was laughing at him too. Heat rose in Sebastian's cheeks. He felt every bit the fool of the moment.

"Your Grace"—Sir Matthew clapped Sebastian's shoulder—"we have met, many times over."

"How can this be?" Sebastian sieved through his memory, but nothing occurred to him. "I confess, though your face is known to me, I cannot fathom when or where we might have been introduced—though I know it was not in London."

"No, it was not," the Lord Mayor said. "It was in Exeter."

"Exeter?"

His grandmother turned in her chair. She smiled at the Lord Mayor. "Shall we release him from his confusion?" Sir Matthew replied with a wink. She turned to look at Sebastian. "My dear, you do not remember because you were but a small child when Sir Matthew came to visit."

"When I was fourteen, I was apprenticed to my uncle, a chemist and druggist in Exeter. I met your father that August. We were mates of the best sort from that day—until he left for London when he became the second Duke of Exeter twenty years ago."

Realization dawned on Sebastian. "You are . . . *Matty*."

His laughter burst forth in such an undignified manner that he feigned a cough to conceal his amusement.

"Yes, dear," his grandmother interjected, "though most refer to him as Lord Mayor of London."

"I do beg your forgiveness." The eyes of everyone nearby were fixed upon him. Some gazed in horror, others in sheer amusement.

The Lord Mayor turned when a distinguished-looking gentleman neared. "Ah, there you are Aster. This is the lad I was so desirous that you meet, Sebastian Beaufort, Duke of Exeter."

Lord Aster studied Sebastian, almost critically, then smiled and offered a quick bow. "Your Grace, I am honored to finally meet you."

"Finally, Lord Aster?" Sebastian looked quizzically at the man.

"Yes, the crowd at your gala prevented me, and my daughter, Delilah, from being introduced. Though, as a miss just out, she employed every stratagem possible to reach you." He winked at the Lord Mayor, and the two men laughed.

Sebastian was a little late in understanding the ribbing. "Lord Aster, it is a privilege to know you now, and I would greatly enjoy meeting your daughter when the opportunity presents itself."

"She is a fair child, I have no doubt you would." The Lord Mayor chuckled softly as he grasped Sebastian's hand and shook it. "Good to see you again, Your Grace."

Lord Aster echoed the sentiment.

Sebastian exhaled with relief.

The Lord Mayor was about to depart when he turned back to Sebastian. "Before you leave this night, I should be desirous that you speak with my Sword-bearer." He inclined his chin to a portly fellow, standing several strides to his left. "I would like to discuss a committee that greatly interests me and Lord Aster . . . and I would think you might be interested in it, as well."

Sebastian bowed again. "It would be my honor, Lord Mayor." When he straightened, he saw a

fleeting smile of appreciation cross his grandmother's lips. The Lord Mayor tipped his head to
them both as he bid them good eve.

"Not in London a week and already you have
the support of the Lord Mayor." He turned his
head to see a well turned-out gentleman with
casually swept ginger hair and thick, ruddy eyebrows taking the vacant seat beside him. "Didn't
mean to eavesdrop, Your Grace, but I had neared
with great hope of catching the Lord Mayor's
notice myself. But you did, so now I vow I must
become your best mate." He grinned. "Mr. Basil
Redbane." He snatched Sebastian's hand and enthusiastically shook it. "Actually, we met, though
only in passing, at your gala."

"Yes, of course." Sebastian hesitantly returned
the smile. The fact that they had supposedly met,
though he had no recollection of it, relieved him
of the need for a gentleman to properly introduce
them. Such a *faux pas* would have distressed his
grandmother since she had made abundantly
clear that he must not follow his father's example of correct behavior—but the first Duke of
Exeter's. He shifted his gaze to her, but she had
already drifted away from the table with two
older ladies. He looked back at the gentleman.
"Redbane, I am—"

The other man laughed. "Good heavens, I know. *Everyone* knows, Your Grace. You are the fourth Duke of Exeter. One would think you were royalty given the way people queue up just to meet the bachelor duke. Did I hear correctly that Lord Aster's daughter has sought an introduction?"

"So it would seem." Sebastian saw Redbane's cheek muscles tighten, but then what almost appeared a sneer transformed into a grin.

"She's a fine one, that chit. Fair as Helen of Troy, but not too bright. Ripe for the plucking, I'd say, if you get my meaning."

Sebastian struggled for a well-mannered response to Redbane's rudeness. "I understand she is very young. Only just out. I am sure, given her father's standing in the House of Lords, that she is quite intelligent."

"Mayhap you are right, Your Grace. She is no doubt naïve because of her young age. Though she is out . . . and as I said, ripe for the plucking." He laughed and clapped Sebastian's back good-naturedly. "Shall we adjourn and chat about our future friendship?"

Sebastian thought to resist the invitation for several reasons, but the most important was so that he might search for the Scottish lass.

Before he could refuse, Redbane spoke again.

"Come along, Your Grace, the whole of table one, save the two of us, has withdrawn into the next room."

Unfortunately, he was quite correct. A packed crowd funneled like sand through the pinch of an hourglass as they made their way through a large doorway then flared into the room beyond.

Redbane raised his hand, gesturing for Sebastian to pass. "After you, *Your Grace.*"

Why did it seem that there was slightly mocking edge to his tone?

Inside, an orchestra hurriedly settled on a narrow dais at one end of the room, while liveried and bewigged footmen passed through the guests with salvers of sloshing crystal goblets holding crimson wine.

Sebastian availed himself of a goblet, thinking to drink it down quickly and excuse himself for another, and thereby purchase himself a few minutes alone to search for his Scottish miss. But Redbane, who seemed oblivious to manners, lifted three goblets from the tray, setting one in Sebastian's free hand.

"With this horde, another waiter mightn't pass by for an hour—best to be prepared, eh?" He waggled his eyebrows, and Sebastian could not disagree. In the few minutes he'd known Redbane, Sebastian had found him to be an entirely like-able, and occasionally uncouth, chap. He seemed at ease here, in the company of aristocrats, politi-cians, and liverymen—an elected group of power-ful merchants to which Sebastian assumed from his manner that Redbane belonged.

Redbane leaned close, as if not wishing to be overheard. "Fancy all these bluebloods in one room." He nudged Sebastian's arm with his elbow, nearly causing his wine to spill. "Not like you though, eh?" He chuckled, but as if forced.

Sebastian was exhausted from lack of sleep and was sure that Redbane was not intentionally insulting him. It only seemed to his tired mind that he was. "I confess, I do not take your mean-ing, Redbane." Sebastian straightened to his full height and cast his gaze downward at Redbane, challenging the man to clarify his statement.

"Come now. Everyone knows your grandfather bought the title from the king." Sebastian winced at that. Redbane's misstep was purely intentional. "You're no more a nobleman than the commoners in the other two rooms."

Sebastian bristled. "I truly do not understand you, Redbane. You claim to wish my friendship, and yet you intentionally offend me."

Redbane widened his eyes. "Surely you do not believe my intent was to insult you—I only meant for you to understand how we're the same, you and I. Far closer than you know. Though I didn't earn my status as warden through servitude; I bought it. Nothing wrong with that if one has the means. I reckon being cut of the same homespun, we might be able to help each other if the need came about. That's all, mate."

"My grandfather earned his patent through service to His Majesty King George III. The Duke of Exeter's title is one of honor." Sebastian shifted abruptly to slam both his goblets onto a passing footman's tray.

Redbane stepped before Sebastian before he could leave him. "Is that so? Is that why you are trying so desperately to fit into his robes? Your father didn't even try. He knew what he was and accepted it."

"I am *not* my father." His fingers coiled up into a fist, and his temples pounded as he envisioned Redbane's pulpy mug in one minute's time.

"Excellent vintage, dinna ye agree, Grant?"

Sebastian dropped his fist and listened.

"Weel, I wouldn't use the word excellent . . . yet. It's a wee bit early to free it from the bottle. Another year," said a second man.

Sebastian knew those voices. He had heard them amongst the elms at Vauxhall Gardens. And now he was hearing them again, not far behind him. He spun around, instantly forgetting Redbane. There, just on the other side of a circle of ladies, were three extraordinarily large men—who were taller than even himself. The lady's brothers. They could be none other.

Redbane clutched Sebastian's coat sleeve. "I vow, Your Grace"—Basil Redbane gently turned him so that they faced each other again—"I admit my language is too coarse. I only wished to establish our similarities when outwardly there may seem to exist none at all."

He had no time for this, especially when Redbane had shown himself for the ill-mannered lout he was. He'd have to be as mad as the king to desire any sort of alliance with him. "Redbane, sharing a glass of wine with you was most enlightening. But if you will excuse me, there is someone I must speak with about an important matter. Good evening, Redbane."

With a quick bob of his head, Sebastian spun around in the direction of the Scotsmen—but they were no longer there. He looked this way and that around the room, stretching his neck to allow a more elevated view. Nothing.

"Looking for the Sinclairs?" Redbane asked from behind.

Whipping his head around, Sebastian snared his gaze. "The Scots? Sinclair is the family name?"

"If you mean the statuesque family quitting the room at this moment, yes, they are the infamous Sinclairs."

Sebastian's eyes flashed to the door. He just glimpsed the crowd closing behind a tall, ebony-locked woman and several gentlemen as they disappeared through the doorway to the Egyptian Hall.

"Their father is a Scottish duke—from one of the oldest noble families in the realm," Redbane added. "Have you a connection to the family?"

Sebastian started after them but turned back to Redbane for one last question. "The woman with them, a Sinclair as well?"

Redbane shrugged. "I confess, I did not see her, but there are several sisters and brothers. Seven, all told, I've heard. Don't know for certain though."

Sebastian lobbed a parting scowl at Redbane, then headed for the doorway.

Redbane trotted behind uninvited, chattering on, as Sebastian passed quickly through Egyptian Hall. Footmen busily collected plates, crystal, and cutlery from the deserted tables. Redbane's breath was becoming ragged. "I h-hope you don't have it in your mind to woo one of the Sinclair misses. They are true noblewomen. Not of your ilk, chap. Give up the thought."

Liveried footmen opened the outer door, and Sebastian stepped into the night, stopping to scan the line of carriages on the road for the Sinclairs. They could be inside any of them, even three yards away, and he'd miss them.

Suddenly, Redbane, who evidently had not noticed that Sebastian had stilled, careened into his back.

"Waiting for me, are you? I knew you would eventually see the truth of me words," Redbane prattled on.

Sebastian turned around and glared. "*Do* leave me alone, Redbane."

"Why? I can help you. I know London, if nothing else. If you fancy a skirt, we can head on down to Hooker Street. No complications. Unlike *these* ladies, none of the Maryannes on the street expect a bloody ring for quick poke of her quim."

Sebastian thrust his palm against Redbane's chest, meaning only to prevent him from coming closer. Instead, the force knocked him back a step. "I am serious; go, before I make sure you cannot follow me."

Redbane threw a punch, pulling it back at the last moment and laughing.

Sebastian took a step forward, scowling.

Sudden panic widened Redbane's eyes, and he scuffled backward. "Here now. See, we are more alike than you admit. You're just a common rough-and-tumble scoundrel like me—and your father."

Priscilla lowered the cab window as the Sinclair family's hired carriage drew away from Mansion House. Something had caught her interest. "Siusan, look there. Quickly!"

Siusan had just closed her eyes and was leaning against the leather squab. "What is it now?"

"Only the most gorgeous man I have ever seen!" Priscilla tugged at her sister's arm but did not remove her gaze from the men on the pavers. "*And* he's about to throttle some red-haired fellow. Who do you think he is, Siusan? Do you know?"

Killian pulled Priscilla away from the window and leaned out himself. "He's got some size on him. The ginger hasn't a chance. What say you, Grant?"

Grant waited for Killian to slide away, then he rose and peered out the window. "Ginger's got a lower center, canna discount that—but aye, a pounder on the tall lad."

He looked back inside the cab. "What, no takers?"

Siusan opened her eyes only to glare at her brother. "The money belongs to all of us, Grant. What good would wagering against each other do?"

This climbing about the cab to peer out of the window was all quite ridiculous to Siusan's way of thinking. Still, the night's event had been so numbingly dull that any diversion was welcome. "Move aside please, let me see." By time she poked her head through the open window, it was too late. She could see nothing but the muscular silhouette of a large man reaching down to help a squat fellow up from the ground. "Humph."

"Och, I suppose I should take a look as weel." Lachlan had imbibed quite a lot of the wine served that night and was moving very slowly.

"Nay, you needn't bother yourself." Siusan leaned back against the seat cushion and closed her eyes. "The tall man is the victor."

Chapter 5

To be idle and poor have always been reproaches, and therefore every man endeavors with his utmost care to hide his poverty from others, and his idleness from himself.

Dr. Samuel Johnson

The Sinclair residence
Mayfair

It was still quite crisp for the noon hour, but the sun felt warm on Sebastian's back as he stood before the door of the Sinclair residence. No, he hadn't had many confirmations, if any, that the shapely miss he'd known in the library was indeed a Sinclair. Still, something in his gut assured him that he was standing before the correct house.

He did not hesitate in slamming the brass door knocker to its rest three times in rapid succession. He heard footsteps, but the door did not open. He knocked again. And then a third time.

His toes fidgeted inside his boots, and his fingers twitched. *Be patient. Wait a minute more.*

But he couldn't wait any longer. Damn it all, he'd been waiting here for more than a handful of moments and was growing more than a little impatient.

Someone was at home and bloody well knew he was at the door. He glanced at the windows above. The curtains on the second floor had fluttered suspiciously each time he knocked though he could see that the window was not open to the breeze.

No, he would not leave until the door was answered and his assumption that his lady lived here was either confirmed or laid to rest.

Gritting his teeth, Sebastian slammed down the brass knocker upon its rest twice more, then stepped back and gazed upward at the window to await the peeper above. But this time the curtain didn't flutter. Instead, he heard the click of the lock being released and, within a moment, a small, balding servant opened the door. The little man blinked in the bright afternoon sun. "Yes, my lord?"

"I have come to call upon the Sinclair family." Sebastian waited for the man to reply in some manner, but he didn't. Only peered up at him, his countenance drawn in confusion. "Are they at home this day?"

"Aye, my lord, they are." The little man turned to the sound of hurried footfall behind him and a flurry of hushed whispers. He stepped forward and closed the door a little as if to conceal whatever might be going on inside. "Though it is only just past twelve of the clock, and I regret to inform you that the Sinclair family does not accept callers until four in the afternoon."

Sebastian exhaled and turned his head up to the window again before looking back to the butler. "And you are—?"

"Poplin, my lord." His watering blue eyes were almost slits now as he stepped completely into the sun.

"I am greatly saddened then, for I shall be unable to return something that one of the ladies left behind at the gala held in my honor a few days ago." He reached into his pocket and absently caressed the smooth stocking ribbon he'd found in his grandmother's library.

The door opened slightly at that moment and Poplin ducked his head inside as though he were listening to someone speaking softly from the other side of the door.

"V-very well, then. Perhaps another day." Something damned odd was going on inside. Sebastian certainly wasn't about to leave, and yet it occurred to him that pretending he was might coax whoever was hiding behind the door into the light. He sighed loudly to convey disappointment, then turned and started down the steps toward his carriage, waiting on the street below.

"Uh . . . oh dear . . . one moment, please, my lord." Poplin scurried out the door and down two steps. "Who shall I say has called?"

Sebastian concealed a smile before he turned around. "You needn't, Poplin, for I shall simply call another day. No need to bother the family with a caller who was not polite enough to send a card announcing his intended visit." He nodded to the man. "Shan't happen again, I assure you." He peered up at the window and grinned, then tipped his hat and turned for the carriage.

"Please, my lord," pleaded a lilting feminine voice as sweet as Highland heather. "My brother and I will receive you."

The woman in the doorway was tall and lithe, her dark hair swept up on each side with pearl-tipped pins, while the rest tumbled down her back in loose waves.

There was a tall, broadly built man standing just behind her, with auburn hair. His coat was finely cut but certainly meant for evening, though his riding boots, also of the highest quality, suggested a casual outing might be planned. Still, Sebastian knew him at once. He was one of the men he'd seen at the Lord Mayor's dinner the night before.

The gentleman beckoned him. "Do come inside, lad." He shot Sebastian a wink then. "As long as you dinna have another scuffle in mind—as ye did outside Mansion House. I've only just risen, ye ken. Wouldn't be fair."

Sebastian grinned. So, they had seen him at the Lord Mayor's dinner, and outside as well. Interesting.

Sebastian quickly took the steps. "Please forgive my impertinence. We have not been introduced formally, and I fear there is no remedy, though I can tell you that our paths have crossed more than once. And therefore, because my time in London is abbreviated, I beg that you forgive my lack of manners and accept my introduction." His words shot forth as rapidly and impatiently as his knocks had upon the door.

The gentleman raised his eyebrows expectantly, then, squinting against the sunlight, peered past him to the Exeter carriage waiting on the street below.

"I am—" Sebastian began.

"The Duke of Exeter," the gentleman interjected. "Damn me," he added beneath his breath.

A tiny squeal escaped the girl's lips, and she went rigid, glancing worriedly at her brother. His visage, however, displayed no hint of surprise. "Duke," he said calmly, "since, as you say, your time is short, and we have no other remedy, allow me to introduce myself. I am Lord Grant Sinclair, younger son of the Duke of Sinclair. And may I present to you my sister?"

"I shall be honored. Please do." Sebastian turned to fully face the young woman.

"Lady Priscilla Sinclair, daughter of the Duke of Sinclair." Lord Grant nodded to his sister.

The miss honored him with a deep curtsy though she flashed a coquettish glance as she arose. "Duke."

"Duke, will ye come this way? I vow the parlor is far superior for entertaining than the doorstep."

Sebastian bowed and followed the Sinclairs into the graciously outfitted parlor. Lady Priscilla primly took her place before the tea table, where her brother joined her, while Sebastian was directed to a tufted chair nearby.

Poplin hurried into the room and quickly set the tea service, while a round-faced older woman laid a plate of cakes nearest Lady Priscilla, who took the role of hostess and silently began to serve the tea.

"What handsome set of circumstance has brought you to our door this fine day, Duke?" Lord Grant asked.

"Nothing but a very small act of chivalry, I assure you." Sebastian gazed intently upon Lady Priscilla, looking for any sort of a reaction. Yes, her hair was lustrous ebony, and her skin was white as the moon, but it wasn't *her*. Worse still, he couldn't pin down what it was about Lady Priscilla that made him sure she was not the woman who had shared a wholly passionate encounter with him in the library. He just *knew*. She simply could not have been the one.

"Duke, I have noticed your study of my sister," Lord Grant said most casually. At first, Sebastian thought to protest the assertion, but before he could fashion an appropriate reply, Lord Grant continued. "Dinna fash yourself over it. She is a beautiful woman and snares the eye of many." A mischievous look crept into his eyes. "Though, if you are thinking to offer for her, I fear you will have to take your position in a long queue of admirers."

"Grant!" Lady Priscilla's hand jerked, and tea sloshed from the cup in her hand. She righted the cup just in time to avoid scalding her brother's lap with steaming tea. She turned her stunning blue eyes to him. "My brother jests, Duke." Her gaze shifted, and she narrowed her eyes at Lord Grant, but the expression had vanished in a blink, leaving Sebastian to wonder if he had imagined it. "If you would like to court me, I am *sure* my brother has no reservations."

A laugh burst forth, along with a sprinkling of tea, from Grant's mouth. He dabbed a napkin to his lips, but he could not seem to wipe away the smile despite his prolonged attempt to do so. "Do forgive my sister, Duke. Since her sister Ivy wed, she has convinced herself that she must as well—as soon as possible. I've thought to take out an advertisement in *The Morning Post* to warn off all unmarried gentlemen of the *ton*. What do you think of my idea, Duke? Too much? A town crier might be more effective, come to think of it, though certainly more expensive."

"Grant." She narrowed her eyes as she spoke.

"There is nothing wrong with a woman wishing to marry. It is a noble institution and one I wish to observe myself. Even my sister Ivy is married, Duke—and her hair is practically the color of an orange! Why should I, with no visible imperfections such as red hair to impede me, not marry? Wait too long, and every desirable gentleman will be plucked off the market." She smiled prettily at him.

Sebastian glanced down at his tea, hoping that the rising steam might mask the disappointment that surely was visible upon his face. He had been so very wrong. Lady Priscilla clearly was not the woman he sought. Had she been, she would have tracked him down and promptly forced him before a minister for leg-shackling. He sighed inwardly as he raised the dish of tea to his mouth and sipped.

Lord Grant rolled his eyes, then promptly attempted to change the subject. "Duke, you mentioned your visit this day was a matter of chivalry." He leaned forward over his knees expectantly.

"Ah, yes." He plunged his hand into his pocket to collect the stocking ribbon, but stilled.

Lady Priscilla's eyes went wide and slowly rose and clasped her hands just beneath her chin.

"What have you there, Duke? A betrothal ring perhaps?"

The ribbon did not belong to Lady Priscilla, this he knew, and yet, he was now compelled to show it to her. Reluctantly, he withdrew the ribbon from his pocket and dangled it in the air. "I suppose I am on a fairy-tale mission to find the woman who lost this ribbon during my grandmother's gala celebration." He heard a stirring in the passage just then, and, expecting someone to enter the parlor, he turned his head toward the door. No one was there. He waited a moment longer but, finally deciding he hadn't heard anything at all, returned to his host and hostess.

Lady Priscilla stepped forward to eye the ribbon, and for the briefest instant, she excitedly reached for it, but her brother pulled her back. "If it is not *yours*, Priscilla, then we ought not waste the duke's time. His time in London is short."

Her smile fell from her lips. "While we did attend the gala, Duke, I confess the ribbon is not mine." Then, a brightness lit her vibrant blue eyes. "Though . . . I could pretend that it is, if it would shorten your quest, so that you may leave Town when planned."

Sebastian didn't at first know how to reply, but

then he saw that both she and Lord Grant were quietly laughing. Ah, a joke. Sebastian rose. "I thank you for your kind offer, Lady Priscilla, and . . . I shall let you know if it becomes necessary to accept it." With that, he bowed to them both and followed Poplin to the door.

He had traveled this road to its end and found nothing. He had no notion where he would turn next.

Siusan had just flung her portmanteau atop her pallet and opened it when Priscilla and Grant raced into her bedchamber.

Priscilla bent and rested her hands on her knees to catch her breath. "Oh—oh my God, Su, the Duke of Exeter—" She shoved the portmanteau aside and sat down on the bed, still panting from her race up the staircase.

"I know," Siusan replied. She tossed a pair of walking boots into the case. "I peeked out the window when I heard knocking at the door and saw that we had a gentleman caller."

"Then you must agree with me, he is certainly the most handsome gentleman in all of London," Priscilla said.

"Actually, I only saw the top of his hat, and,

when he was sitting in the parlor, his back."
Though, lud, she wished she had seen him. The
man who had made love to her. The man she
must avoid at all costs.

Siusan rolled her silk stockings and put them
inside one of the walking boots.

"Thankfully, you didn't come into the parlor,"
Grant began.

Siusan whirled around. "But I very nearly did!
I paused at the mirror in the passageway to tuck
back a loose hair, when I heard Grant identify
him as the Duke of Exeter." Even now, the
stress of the near meeting set moisture beading
across her brow. She pressed a cooling palm to
her forehead. Lud, her heart was still pounding
madly in her chest. "What if I had walked in?
What if he recognized me?"

"I daresay, he likely would have. Out of the hundreds of women at the gala that night, *something*
led him here. But it also led him away again."
Grant paced before the pallet. "And I think that
something may be that, at this moment, he believes there are only two Sinclair sisters."

"What do you mean?" Siusan settled her brush
and pin box inside the leather case, then moved
around the pallet to Grant.

Priscilla grabbed her arm urgently. "He had your blue garter, Su. He showed it to us." Priscilla's eyes were wide.

Siusan looked at Grant, horrified.

"Aye, he did, and yet, he somehow knew it did not belong to Priscilla and that she is not the woman he seeks."

"I purposely mentioned that Ivy's hair is red, in hopes that the charming duke would rule my sister out as his *Critheanach* who'd lost her slipper," Priscilla added, "though I am sure I made a great goose of myself trying to wedge our own red herring into the conversation!"

Grant took Siusan's shoulders in his hands and squeezed gently. "The question remains. How did he know Priscilla was not the woman he sought? He made it as far as our home, so we must assume he noticed your height."

Siusan stilled. "I-I said something to him in the library. He heard my voice—and likely determined that I am a Scot."

"Aye, that would be enough to bring him to our door. There are few Scots in London Society, fewer still that remained in Town after the Season."

"And none possessing our height," Priscilla said slowly.

"Still, I am confused," Grant said. "You and

Priscilla greatly resemble each another. Many, even those who have encountered you a number of times, have mistaken each of you for the other. How could he know the difference . . . when he only met you in the dark?"

Siusan blanched, and her eyes slowly sought out Priscilla's. She opened her mouth to reply, but she was too mortified to utter a word.

Priscilla set her right hand on her narrow hip and gestured to Siusan with her left. "Because Siusan has breasts and hips." Priscilla looked down at her more girlish form, then averted her gaze, not wishing to draw a comparison. "Fully dressed, the difference between us mightn't be so evident."

"But in the dark . . ." Grant turned his gaze to Siusan.

Siusan crossed her arms over her chest. "Oh, please do not look at me that way!" She spun around, flung open her wardrobe, and snatched a mantle from one of the pegs. "My course is clear. I must leave London before he learns there are more than two Sinclair sisters, which I am sure will not take long."

"But where would you go? We haven't the money to send you anywhere." Priscilla shook her head. "Stay. He said his time is short in London.

You only need to refrain from attending events until he has departed. You needn't leave Town."

"Priscilla, how can you utter such nonsense?" Siusan snapped. "He knows where we live! He is bound to return. Nay, the only thing to do is leave for a time—that way when you tell him you are the only Sinclair sister in London, you will be telling the truth. And you, at least, will be spared Da's anger if he learns of this."

"Now, Su, dinna be hasty." Grant rubbed his face with his palms. "We have to hide you, 'tis all. For a short time."

Mrs. Wimpole, the Sinclair's cook and maid of all things, cleared her throat to announce her presence at the door. How long she'd been standing there, Siusan did not know.

The cook stood in the doorway with tea tray and plate of something green and round. "Thought you might be wantin' something to eat, Lady Siusan, since you missed your meal. Brought sea-kelp biscuits to take with your tea."

Siusan looked at the green treats and covered her mouth. "Thank you, Mrs. Wimpole, but tea will be fine this noon. I do not think I could manage to eat one bite just now."

"Beggin' your pardon, Lady Siusan, but I overheard the goings-on in the parlor, and here . . . and

I am sorry for listening—but if you'll be needin' a place to stay for a time, my cousin Mrs. Huddleston has a school for young ladies in Bath."

"How could she hide in a school?" Priscilla shook her hands in the air. "Su's hardly a miss. Someone would notice," she added, her voice dripping with sarcasm.

"Well, she's recently lost an instructor," Mrs. Wimpole replied. "The girl suddenly ran off to marry without so much as a word of warning or thanks. Maybe you, Lady Siusan, could take her place for a time?"

"But I am not a teacher," Siusan replied. "I have no training whatsoever."

"Again, beggin' your pardon, my lady, but you do."

Grant laughed. "Dancing, dressing, choosing menus, singing—aye, she is very skilled in the art of doing nothing of consequence."

"Exactly, my lord," Mrs. Wimpole said. "She has been trained in the social graces." She settled the tea service on the dressing table, knocking over a candlestick and righting it again before turning back to face them all. "She needs an instructor, and you, Lady Siusan, need a place to hide and a few quid in your pocket."

Siusan looked quizzically at Grant, then Priscilla. "I've never worked a day in my life. For God's sake, I am the daughter of a duke."

"Aye, but we haven't the coin to send you off to a fine hotel or country house until the Duke of Exeter leaves London," Grant reminded her. "In order to leave London, you must work to pay your way."

Mrs. Wimpole nodded, setting both her chins to jiggling. "I can write a letter of introduction now. Take it with you to Bath. Liddy Huddleston will not turn you away. She wouldn't have the school at all had it not been for yours truly."

"What do you mean, Mrs. Wimpole?" Priscilla asked.

"Oh, nothin' at all. Done her a few favors over the years is all, and I know she is grateful." Mrs. Wimpole looked at Siusan expectantly. "So, shall I pen the letter?"

Siusan gazed at Grant and Priscilla, hoping one of them would interject with a resounding "nay!" but both were nodding in agreement. "Aye, Mrs. Wimpole. Please do." She walked over and gave the older woman a hug. "I do so appreciate this."

"I know you do." Mrs. Wimpole started for the door. "I will pack you a basket of food for the journey. Oh, I am so glad I baked a few extra sea-kelp biscuits. They'll keep your belly full enough." She was still talking as she waddled into the passage.

"I'll set Killian off to the mews to purchase a ticket for transport, and send Lachlan out to gather a few supplies for your trip . . . since I would not wish for the driver to open the carriage and find you dead with a telltale sea-kelp biscuit in your hand." Grant chuckled as he turned to leave. He stopped as he reached the door and looked back at Siusan, his mood suddenly somber. "I was opposed to the idea of your leaving before, Su, but I can see now that it is the only way. I am sorry."

Siusan nodded. "I know."

"And, since it is for just a short time, I will let you take the blue satin slippers," Priscilla said happily.

"I will be an instructor at a girls' school, Priscilla. When will I have an opportunity to wear them?"

Priscilla shrugged. "I am sure you will find an occasion." With that, her sister hurried from the room to fetch the shoes.

Siusan looked down at her portmanteau, then sank down onto the pallet beside it. Good God, Lady Siusan Sinclair, the eldest daughter of the Duke of Sinclair, was actually going to have to work for her bread.

Chapter 6

Efficiency is intelligent laziness.
David Dunham

Three days later
Mrs. Huddleston's School of Virtues
Bath

ere are your quarters," Mrs. Huddleston told Siusan, gesturing through the door at a room not much larger than the cabin of a carriage. "Not much, but it should be comfortable enough." She turned a key in a small worktable beside a tiny bed and removed a half-spent candle, which she inserted into a dented iron hogscraper candlestick. "Candles are dear, so take care to remember to remove the taper from the candlestick and lock it in the drawer during the day. The girls will snatch it if it's left out."

"Why would they do that?" Siusan asked, peering at the stub.

"To light their way when they are up to no good in the middle of the night, that's why." She shook her head. "You haven't a notion what you are in for, do you, miss? Oh, but you will learn soon enough. These little ladies are sent here for a good reason, I tell you, and it isn't for a proper education. They are hoydens, every last one of them, and it is our task to stifle their boisterous natures and shape them into virtuous ladies."

Siusan entered the room fully, set her portmanteau on the narrow bed, and took a closer look at her new home. The room was lit, with a single narrow window looking out at the street below. Three hooks on the back of the door served as a wardrobe. A white basin and ewer were perched atop a small pine writing table, and one linen towel was folded on the plank chair beside it.

Hmm. Just like home.

"Mrs. Wimpole's letter made it quite clear that you are in hiding and that the length of your stay is undetermined. She did not deem it necessary to share any other details." Mrs. Huddleston paused

then, as if waiting for Siusan to explain her circumstances, which she was not about to do. The
fewer people who knew of her predicament, the
better.

As if determining herself that Siusan was not
going to explain anything, the older woman's features tightened, and she swallowed hard. "She assured me that you were a woman of breeding and
that you are skilled in the social graces. That is the
only reason I agreed to allow you into the School
of Virtues."

That, and you are short one teacher. Siusan nodded.

"Nevertheless, while you are here, you will obey
the same rules as our students. Candles are to be
extinguished by nine of the clock. No exceptions.
The doors will be locked at that time as well, and
no one will be permitted to leave or enter until
morn." Mrs. Huddleston grimaced suddenly and
bent to straighten the towel so that it aligned perfectly with the table's edge.

*Wait a moment. What did she say? No one may leave
or enter? Impossible.* She must have simply misun-
derstood Mrs. Huddleston. Best to clarify. "Certainly I will have a key so that I may leave once
the girls are asleep."

"No exceptions!" The skin around her eyes
cinched like a reticule drawstring. "Relax the

rules, and the next thing I know my instructors are out cavorting, getting themselves heavy with child, then running off to marry."

"I assure you, that will not be the case for me. I am here to hide, nothing more, though I would enjoy touring Bath while I am here."

"Oh, would you? Then you shall have to make do with lecture outings with the students. *No exceptions.*" Mrs. Huddleston lifted her chatelaine. "If you require supplies of any sort, you must ask me for them. I hold the keys. Our budget here is limited, you understand, and I maintain tight control over the inventory."

Siusan shuddered. *Good God*, she couldn't stay here, even for a few days. This wasn't a school—it was a prison! *Nay. Nay.* She couldn't stay. Dizziness dimmed her vision, and she sat down on the bed.

"I was speaking to you, miss. Stop daydreaming." Mrs. Huddleston loomed over her and peered down her nose.

"I am sorry. What did you say, Mrs. Huddleston?"

"The girls will address you as Mistress."

I am no miss and shall not be treated as if I were! "Nay, if I am to teach them the ways of the ladies in Society, they will refer to me properly—as Lady Siusan."

Mrs. Huddleston's thick gray-flecked eyebrows lifted. "*Lady* Siusan, is it? La-de-da."

"Aye. Lady Siusan. The girls must learn respect, I am sure you agree, so I will be addressed as Lady Siusan."

A queer amused smile lifted Mrs. Huddleston's thin lips. "Very well." She lifted the letter of introduction Mrs. Wimpole had penned to her and poked her finger at it. "But I will address you as *Miss Bonnet*, as it says in the letter of introduction. You can pretend to be a lady while you teach the girls manners, they might even enjoy the game, but I will address you by your proper name—Miss Bonnet."

Miss Bonnet? Who is . . . oh dear. "Um, may I see the letter of introduction?" Siusan reached up for it.

Mrs. Huddleston whisked it behind her back. "No you may not. This is a private correspondence between me and my cousin." She turned and stalked toward the door, tossing glares back at Siusan.

"I beg your pardon, Mrs. Huddleston." Siusan gritted her teeth as she lowered her head obediently. "Of course, the letter is private."

"Dinner is at six o'clock in the dining room."

Without looking back, Mrs. Huddleston quit the room and slammed the plank door behind her.

Siusan buried her face in her hands. Oh, dear God. How would she ever survive here? She knew she couldn't, and yet she must.

Pressing her hands together, she dropped to her knees and closed her eyes. "May God have mercy on my wicked soul—and send the Duke of Exeter far from London . . . with all expediency. Amen."

Six o'clock in the evening

Siusan had meant to arrive a few minutes early, but belatedly decided to spend a little extra time with her appearance. It would be her first introduction to the girls, and she wished to make a striking first impression. Donning her crimson gown, she pinned her hair with brilliants and fastened a small pearl necklace around her neck. She turned to leave but dashed back and snatched up the tiny mirror from the table and practiced a dignified smile to offer her students. Then, feeling prepared, she left the room and descended the stairs in search of the dining room.

Just as the clock struck the first bell of the hour,

Siusan found her way to the dining room. As she slid open the pocket door, she was completely taken aback. Unlike her stark bedchamber, the walls were covered with French patterned paper and the table was set with fine linen, crystal, and gleaming silver cutlery. On the sideboard sat several serving dishes filled with meat, potatoes, soup, and vegetables.

Two young women dressed in gray frocks and twelve girls sat around a long table lit with two large silver candelabra filled with a dozen tapers each. A dozen each—and yet *she* was expected to light her chamber with a stub. It was at that moment that she noticed that everyone in the dining room was staring at her.

Siusan smiled embarrassedly. "I apologize. I-I had not realized I was late." She spied a single empty chair at the head of the table and hurried over to it. The girls sat silently, still peering expectantly at her. "Where is Mrs. Huddleston?" Siusan finally asked.

A small golden-locked girl, who sat next to her, replied. "Mrs. Huddleston never takes her meals with us. Only the mistresses do." Her eyes were wide and wary. "Are you the new mistress?"

Siusan laughed and waved the comment away

as she settled her linen napkin in her lap. "Oh heaven forbid. I am Lady Siusan. And what is your name, lass?"

"Miss S-sarah Seton."

"Well, Miss Seton, I am pleased to make your acquaintance." She looked up from the girl, then swept the table with her gaze. "We shall learn about the rules of introduction on the morrow, which is most important, but tonight we shall just enjoy each other's company."

One of the young women at the far end of the table spoke. "I am Mistress Grassley. I fear I am somewhat confused, Lady Siusan. You are not a mistress, but . . . you are an instructor?"

"Aye, I am." Siusan glanced about for a footman or maid to serve the dinner. The food was rapidly losing its heat just sitting on the sideboard as it was.

"Your gown . . ." A girl with auburn hair and a smattering of freckles across her nose and cheeks pointed at Siusan's crimson evening gown. "It's not gray."

Siusan focused her eyes on the girl.

"My apologies, Lady Siusan. I am Miss Gemma Gentree."

"You are correct, Miss Gentree." Siusan looked

down at her dress. "It isn't. I never wear gray, Miss Gemma. The color doesn't flatter anyone."

"All of the instructors wear gray," Gemma muttered. Siusan noticed that this appeared to be true. The mistresses shifted uncomfortably in their chairs.

"Well, I do not." Siusan turned to little Miss Seton beside her. "I see no footman. Is it customary to serve ourselves from the sideboard?"

"No, my lady," the girl replied. She worked her throat and swallowed hard. "*You* are to serve, Lady Siusan. You . . . and the mistresses."

Surprised, Siusan looked down the table at the other instructors. "Is this so?" They nodded.

"Well, this won't do at all." Siusan rose from the table, then circled around it, tapping four girls on their shoulders. "Please stand up, you four. Come along."

The girls, looking rather nervous, rose from their chairs.

"Since I am here to teach you how to be a lady, we shall begin our first lesson. In a new household, it is often a sad truth that a lady must train her staff to meet her expectations. Tonight, you will each take turns serving the courses."

The girls' mouths fell agape. "But Lady Siusan, we never serve."

"Do you know how dinner is served?"

"I do!" Miss Seton brightened immediately. "The mistresses put the food on our plates, and we eat it."

Oh dear Lord. "Allow me to rephrase my question. Does anyone know dinner should be served—properly?" Siusan looked around the table and at the four girls standing. None replied. "Then tonight you shall learn how it is done in Society." Siusan returned to her chair. "Now then, we shall begin with filling the crystal."

The mistresses lowered their heads and smiled demurely into their laps.

Siusan leaned back in her chair, feeling very pleased with herself, as the girls listened to her instruction and began filling the glasses like proper footmen.

"Most excellent, girls. How quickly you learn." Siusan was actually quite proud of herself for having the task completed for her while teaching the girls how things were to be done in the dining room. The girls were quite proud of themselves as well, for they were actually beaming.

Maybe *working* for her bed and bread wouldn't be so taxing after all. She seemed to have a real knack for it.

* * *

It was no use.

Sebastian had attended dinners, musicales, routs, balls until his face ached from the false smile he wore as an essential part of his evening attire. And though the weather had changed, and his breath floated in white puffs in the air, he strolled through Hyde Park and searched the paths of Vauxhall Gardens . . . hoping to catch a glimpse of *her*.

But he never did.

He had encountered the Sinclairs on two instances. Three brothers and Lady Priscilla. Never was another added to their number, and so he allowed himself to believe what Lord Grant and Lady Priscilla had claimed—the rest of their siblings were not in London—and his lover in the library was not one of their noble number.

Reaching into his pocket, he fingered the stocking ribbon she'd left behind. Here, in the library. It was all he had to remind him that it had not been a dream. That she was real.

"There you are." He looked up from his seat on the sofa to see his grandmother standing just inside the library door. In her shaking hand was a letter. "You must go for her."

Sebastian hurried to his feet and went to her. "What is wrong? Is it Gemma?"

She nodded. "The other girls' taunting has become unbearable. She admits to crying herself to sleep every night."

"Certainly I will collect her if that is what you wish, but if Gemma is anything like her father, she is strong."

"If teasing were my only concern, I would bite my tongue, but there is more . . . a new instructor. A woman filling her head with the nonsensical idea that she ought to set aside her arithmetic and literature for learning in favor of lessons in leisure."

"I do not understand, Grandmother." He took the letter from her hand and led her to sit down on the sofa.

"What use is learning to plan menus and how to greet royalty? She is a bastard. She will never marry beyond her lot in life. The best she can do for herself is to learn as much as possible—so that one day she might become a governess. It is the most we can hope for her."

Sebastian nodded. As much as he wished it wasn't true, the circumstances of her birth made it virtually impossible for her to marry into a genteel family. His grandmother was right. An education was vital to her future. "If this is true—"

"Read the letter!" Her voice became higher as she became more upset. She took his wrist in her frail hand and raised the letter before his eyes. "It is all here."

Sebastian fixed his gaze to the inked words on the page. He read Gemma's letter in its entirety, hoping that his grandmother was wrong. Needing for her to be in error.

But it was true. His ward—his niece—who loved nothing more than to read, was practicing promenading and curtsying instead of studying. She was focusing on trivialities instead of the proper education so essential to her future.

"Where is she?" He came to his feet. "I will go to this school and observe the situation. If this teacher is truly promoting leisure over education, I will take matters into my own hands and either remove her . . . or Gemma from the school immediately."

His grandmother's body instantly relaxed and she exhaled. "She is at Mrs. Huddleston's School of Virtues in Bath."

Sebastian started for the door. "I shall have my man pack this evening. I will leave on the morrow."

One week later
The Pump Room

After a full sennight in Bath, Siusan had very nearly grown accustomed to rising with the sun instead of at noon.

Bath was a health-focused town, and, from what she'd been able to glean from the *Bath Herald*, for indeed, Mrs. Huddleston had remained true to her word and locked the school promptly at nine in the evening, even the balls at the Bath Assembly Rooms concluded well before midnight.

Had someone suggested to her a month ago that she would be promenading through the Pump Room at nine in the morn, she would have accused him of being mad. Still, here she was and with no less than one dozen students, ranging in age from six to fifteen, and Miss Grassley, one of the teaching mistresses, trailing behind her.

Glory be, why hadn't she seriously considered a lecture trip into Bath proper before? True, her first choice would have been an afternoon outing, but nine, it seemed, was the most fashionable hour to stroll through the Pump Room, tasting the warm, foul-smelling mineral water, with all of Bath society.

Crowds of elegantly dressed people passed in and out of the grand room, some old and infirm, others in the bloom of youth, attended, breathlessly seeking out proper introductions to those of the opposite gender.

Her eyes began to tear at the sight. Finally, after so many days and nights of living in the school, teaching children and socializing with young women with whom she had nothing whatsoever in common, Siusan felt she had come home.

"Should we not sign the visitors' book, Lady Siusan?" Miss Gentree, one of her older charges, suggested. Her green eyes glittered with excitement as her gaze fixed upon the large book set prominently upon a podium displaying the names of all who visited the establishment.

Siusan tensed. Aye, to do so was expected, but she was meant to be in hiding. Recording her name would be ill-advised. "We oughtn't crowd about the visitors' book. The eldest two students may sign." A disappointed groan welled up from the rest of her charges, drawing attention from several well-dressed ladies and gentlemen standing nearby. "The rest of you will join me at the King's Pump to sample the water." This offering was met with wrinkled noses and puckered mouths. "Now, now. A true lady takes the water to sustain her as she parades the room. Those who do not drain their cups falter and must soon sit down, wrinkling their gowns."

The girls seemed to accept this explanation, which actually was true to some extent. Without a maid of any sort, Siusan would be required to iron the wrinkles from her own gown, and since she'd never attempted such a daring feat, she knew it was best simply to avoid sitting. After all, her frock was a walking gown and fashioned to look most fetching while moving. So promenade they would, but first, they would sample the water.

Siusan crossed the King's Pump and pressed several shillings into the attendant's hand. "Ladies, you may each come forward and collect a cup of water." Her students, repelled by the strong sulfur odor coming from the pump, stood mulishly in a clump, ignoring Siusan's instructions. She gave her satin reticule to one of the girls, and passed a cup of water to the girls standing nearest her.

Accepting a cup herself, she raised it to her mouth, sniffing it first to prepare her palate for the vile liquid to follow—a trick she'd learned from her sister Ivy to avoid retching when eating

Mrs. Wimpole's cooking. And then, she forced the thick, salty water down her throat. Her stomach lurched as she returned her cup to the collecting tray.

"It smells of boiled egg," Miss Sarah Seton said, louder than was necessary to be heard over the musicians playing in the gallery above. "Boiled rotten eggs!"

Siusan bent her knees slightly and counseled the child in a hushed tone. "A lady does not complain, she simply bites her tongue, does what she must, and remains visibly gracious."

"Ouch!" Miss Sarah Seton clapped her hand over her mouth.

"Dear, I meant that figuratively." Siusan straightened. "You do not need to actually bite your tongue."

She retrieved her reticule and removed another coin for the pump attendant. Three pence for a cup of swill was ridiculous, but when she had requested the coin from the school treasury, Mrs. Huddleston had surprisingly approved the expense. It seemed more than one student's parents had expressed their great pleasure at the change in their daughter's training.

Siusan bounced her coin-heavy reticule in her

hand, and an idea, glittering with brilliance, lit her mind.

Why must she live like a prisoner when there are so many other training opportunities for her students in Bath. She fought to restrain an excited laugh. She had opportunities to live like a lady—financed in full by Mrs. Huddleston's School of Virtues. Why, there were the theater, concerts, art exhibits, fine restaurants, shopping, and balls.

She was nearly giddy at the expanse of teaching opportunities in Bath.

"Next, I shall instruct you how to promenade like a true lady, moving demurely yet confidently, drawing only *desired* attention. Like this." Siusan raised her head, extending her throat gracefully, then peered across the room at a young man. The man's eyes immediately lifted, and he met her gaze. Siusan smiled primly, then looked away. At once, the young man started across the room toward her.

"Now, gather round, my little ladies." She raised her arms, and they encircled her. The gentleman stopped midstride in the center of the Pump Room. "Aye, attention is as easy to control as that." The girls giggled softly, eager to begin rehearsing. "I fear most of you are too young to attempt drawing desired attention, but I recommend that you understand its value to a lady, for it is an important skill."

She palmed the weight of her reticule again. "Before we practice our promenade, who else wishes to take the water? Remember, a true lady must never allow herself to wilt. Doing so ruins the line of your gown."

Four of the girls rushed forward for a cup of salty swill.

Siusan watched them eagerly drink the water down as she considered her next outing with the students. Would tomorrow be too soon? she wondered.

Chapter 7

Laziness is nothing more than the habit of resting before you get tired.

Edgar Bergen

Three days later
Mrs. Huddleston's School of Virtues

ray, just what do you think you are doing lying about in bed when you have a class in session, Miss Bonnet?"

"W-what?" Siusan slowly opened her eyes only to see Mrs. Huddleston standing over her huffing and glaring like a bull readying to charge. Oh, that's right. The girls.

"I heard clapping and laughter from a lecture

room and what did I see when I entered—a man."
She wedged her fists onto her hips.

Siusan pushed up from the bed and hastily
tucked a few pillow mussed locks into place. "Aye,
the dancing master I engaged to teach the girls the
latest dances . . . appropriate in polite society."

Mrs. Huddleston narrowed her eyes, something she seemed to do an awful lot in Siusan's
company. "Exactly. He is teaching the students,
and my instructor is sleeping."

"Napping, actually." She looked down at her
gown and grimaced at the fine wrinkles that had
appeared there despite her effort to remain flat
on her back, gown smooth beneath her whilst
she slept. "I have been adequately trained in the
steps of all of the dances, Mrs. Huddleston. So I
thought it wise to conserve my energy for our lecture outing this evening."

"Another outing?" Mrs. Huddleston sputtered.
"Just how much will this frivolous adventure cost
the school?"

"The outing is not frivolous. It is an important
part of the girls' education." Siusan lifted her eyebrows and looked down into Mrs. Huddleston's
eyes. "And you will be pleased to learn that it will
not cost the school anything."

"Come now, a cotillion at the Upper Assembly

Rooms? Why the subscription alone must cost—"

"Nothing. Lord and Lady Philamont were so pleased with their daughter's progress in finally comporting herself as a lady that they made special arrangements with the Master of Ceremonies to provide tickets for their daughter and the next eldest student and myself. I should inform you now, if you were not already aware, that the cotillion will end promptly at eleven this evening."

"Too late." Mrs. Huddleston crossed her arms over her chest. "You are aware of the rules, Miss Bonnet."

"Aye, which is why Lady Philamont has agreed to speak with you herself about a special exception for her daughter's first cotillion. She is quite persuasive, and I have little doubt you will come to understand the importance of this event to her daughter."

Mrs. Huddleston shook a long, pointy finger before Siusan's nose, muttering silently to herself for several moments. "I knew you were trouble from the first we met, Miss Bonnet, and you have done nothing to change that impression of you.

"Except bring praise to the school . . . as well as two new students."

Snatching up her chatelaine from her belt, she twisted off the key to the school's front door. "Take it. But do not lose it, and be sure to lock the door behind you when you return tonight."

Siusan accepted the key, then gestured to her bedchamber door. "After you, Mrs. Huddleston. I must return to my class, after all."

As Siusan walked down the passage, she wanted to shout with joy. At last, she was going to a ball in Bath! Life resumes.

The Upper Assembly Rooms

One thing Siusan hadn't considered was how she and her charges, Miss Gentree and Lady Penelope, would arrive at the Upper Assembly Rooms . . . the other was the weather.

The school was not so very far from the Upper Assembly Rooms, no more than a brisk walk up the hill, but the ground was still wet with a recent rain, and a sudden cold spell had coated the pavers with sporadic crystals of ice. There was no possible way they could reach the cotillion on foot, especially in blue satin, heeled slippers.

Mrs. Huddleston, feeling forced to relaxing her stringent rules, held Siusan at her word that the school needn't pay a single penny for tonight's lecture outing. Siusan had no choice but to pay from her own reticule for a hackney to transport herself and the girls to the Upper Rooms. But the cost was worth it. She was going to be back in Society, even if only superficially.

"The footmen will take your wraps," she told the two girls, who were entirely possessed by nerves as they passed through the columned entryway to the Upper Assembly Rooms.

Siusan knew exactly how they felt. She had to assume it was possible that some members of London Society would be in attendance tonight.

After all, when Parliament was not in session, no one wished to remain in London if any other more exciting options were to be had. And though, in Siusan's limited opinion, Bath was quite staid in comparison to London, there were those of Society who came to take the healing waters and bathe in the hot mineral pools as a respite from the grueling Season.

Siusan squinted in the bright lights of the octagonal entrance. Crowds became momentarily caught in the too-narrow entry before pushing through the double doors and spilling out into the grand ballroom.

The girls, neither having ever attended a public ball, gaped at the spectacle of Bath Society. Even Siusan was impressed. Bath seemed so different from Edinburgh and London that she had not anticipated the sheer numbers of elegant ladies and gentlemen of Bath Society there tonight.

Massive crystal chandeliers cast a magical glow over the dancers in the center of the floor. Miss Gentree's eyes were glistening.

"What is it? Is something amiss?" Siusan asked her.

She shook her head. "No, everything is perfect. It is just I never imagined myself at a real ball."

"Nay?" How queer. Her white muslin gown was smartly embroidered and well tailored to her form. Hers was no doubt a family of privilege else Miss Gentree would not be wearing such a fine gown and attending such a very expensive school for girls. "Well, we have Lord and Lady Philamont to thank for this night. There they are now." Siusan nodded to two rows of cushioned settees beneath a deep-set balcony, where nearly a dozen musicians played.

Lady Penelope waved madly at her parents before glancing up at Siusan and remembering that tonight was a demonstration of her manners and maturity. Recovering, she tipped her head to acknowledge them, then curtsied in greeting when they all arrived before them.

"Miss Bonnet . . . or, this evening shall I address

you as Lady Siusan?" Lady Philamont's eyes brightened with the witticism.

Siusan did not falter. "As you wish, Lady Philamont. Since I am not known in Bath Society, I vow no one would know the difference."

Lady Philamont laughed, taking Siusan's words as a joke. Little did she know how truthful Siusan had been. "You are so very diverting, Miss Bonnet, and I am so happy that you and Miss Gentree were able to attend the cotillion as our guests with our daughter. Our Penelope has written of nothing but your lecture tours, Miss Bonnet. No reading, writing, or ciphers—"

"Except as they pertain to a lady's life," Siusan added.

"Yes, yes, quite right!" Lady Philamont shot her husband a knowing glance. "The entire tone of Penelope's letter has matured and become more elegant. The change was so great in such a short time that we were compelled to come in from the country this night to see if our daughter's transformation from child to a woman is as complete as her letters would indicate."

Lord Philamont smiled approvingly at his daughter. "I must say, she appears quite the lady this eve."

Lady Penelope blushed becomingly, then looked

to Siusan for encouragement. Siusan glanced at her charge's white muslin gown as a prompt. "Mother, I vow you will be so proud when you learn that I directed the mantua-maker in the construction of this gown myself. I am honored that I am able to wear it before my parents to my very first public ball—even if I am not yet out."

"My dear, that glorious day may arrive sooner than you imagine," her mother said, adding, "thanks to Miss Bonnet's clever lessons."

Lord Philamont wasted no time excusing himself to enter the card room, leaving the ladies to their own devices. Unfortunately, that meant leaving Siusan and her charges sitting on the benches, while Lady Philamont chatted with anyone who would listen to the tale of her daughter's miraculous transformation under the tutelage of Miss Bonnet.

Siusan watched the couples on the dance floor with no little amount of envy. It was so long since she had danced that she was sure her legs had gone stiff with lack of proper use. Mayhap a lecture tour to the baths themselves would be advisable, though, after taking the water in the Pump Room, she was not certain she could withstand the sulfur fumes in such abundance.

"I know, since I am not yet come out, I cannot

dance this night. But why are you not dancing, Lady Siusan?" Lady Penelope asked. "A notable number of gentlemen have sought your notice."

"The cotillion is a public ball, my dear. Were this is a private ball, I would be free to dance with any gentleman who requests the set. Here, I may only dance with someone I have been formally introduced to— and since I have no acquaintances in Bath, except your mother, who is entirely engaged with her friends, I am forced to remain a wallflower."

"Oh." Miss Gentree sighed. "Then shall the three of us stroll the perimeter as a diversion?"

Siusan echoed Miss Gentree's bored sigh. "The crush is too much. I think it best that I remain here and protect my gown, but the two of you may rehearse your promenade. Remember, though, do not allow your eyes to stray to the few young gentlemen in attendance. Neither of you is out."

The two girls jumped to their feet, giggling in their excitement to begin their promenade around the room.

Siusan calmed them instantly with a scolding look. "But mind your manners. You are elegant young ladies."

The girls nodded and, to Siusan's surprise, honored her with suitable curtsies before beginning their stroll around the ballroom.

Siusan sighed. This was not what she had hoped for. Not at all. She glanced around the crowded room, then pinned her gaze on the double doors, wishing someone she knew from the London *ton* would enter, looking for a diversion after a day spent at the baths. But she knew her wish was futile. The weather was too miserable to hope a refined member of the London *ton* would make the trek to the Upper Rooms.

She sighed again, feeling very sorry for herself.

Then, something snared her notice. She straightened her back and focused. A tall, broad-shouldered gentleman entered the room through the double doors and stopped, as if looking for someone.

The music seemed to stop along with him. Or perhaps Siusan was too distracted to hear it any longer, for the dancers were still swaying. Slowly she came to her feet. His dark hair was thick with a slight wave to it. Though he was dressed in a smart coat cut for dancing, he wore boots rather than slippers. There was a sprinkling of growth on his angular jaw, too, as though he had decided to attend the cotillion only belatedly.

Then his eyes met hers. The suddenness of his attention sent a jolt through her, but she did not withdraw her gaze. Lord above, but he was a handsome devil of a man.

From the distance, she could not discern the color of eyes. Were they blue . . . or green? Honestly, it didn't matter. It was that all-encompassing way he studied her that did.

A warm quiver shook through body. She didn't know him, but lud, everything about him made her want to. His gaze alone awakened her womanly desires, sending a flush of warmth into her cheeks.

"Lady Siusan?" Someone was shaking her arm. "Forgive me, Miss Bonnet?"

Emerging from her daze, she looked to her side and saw her two students standing beside her.

"Oh Miss Bonnet, I am all aquiver. My new guardian has come!" Miss Gentree told her. "This is so unexpected, I am at a loss as to what to do. And yet, there he is! What a surprise." She nodded toward the door. "My word, you do not think he has come to take me from the school? I shall die if that is his plan."

Siusan followed her gaze to the very gentleman who had so engaged her own attentions. "*He* is your new guardian?"

"Yes. Oh, do come with me, Miss Bonnet. You too, Penelope—you *must* meet him."

At last, there was his ward. Sebastian exhaled in relief. From Gemma's letter, the one that practically left his grandmother wilting beneath a vinaigrette, he'd half expected to find the young miss dancing the waltz with some wasp-waisted pink of the *ton* and her bag packed for a lecture tour to Gretna Green. Instead, she was standing with another demure young miss beside a proper lady.

A very beautiful woman, one, if he had his wish, he would gaze upon all evening.

He reined in his straying gaze and focused on Gemma. Where was this Miss Bonnet creature mentioned endlessly in the letter—the mistress responsible for stripping the innocence from a young girl's mind and replacing it with altogether womanly wiles? When he stopped by the school, Mrs. Huddleston had told him Miss Bonnet was here . . . with Gemma.

Well, he'd soon find out where she was. Sebastian had just started across the ballroom toward them when he saw the goddess shake her head before bending and whispering something into Gemma's ear. Gemma lowered her head momentarily, then raised it again and lifted her hem an inch from the floor as she glided toward him.

"Lord Sebastian—I beg your pardon, your ascension is still so new. Allow me to begin again. *Your Grace,* I was not expecting you in Bath." Gemma's eyes sparkled.

"There is no need to beg pardon. In truth, Lord Sebastian is preferable—as long as I remain in Bath." He cast a serious gaze. "I do not expect you to understand, but I have learned that people are far more guarded when in the presence of a duke, and I would like our visit to be as comfortable for everyone as possible."

She nodded, though he could see she was dubious about his explanation. "Lord Sebastian, I haven't seen you since—" The light suddenly drained from her smiling face.

Since Quinn's funeral.

"My visit was somewhat unexpected, that is true, but your letter to my grandmother suggested great changes at school," he told her as calmly as he might given the fact that, if her letters were truthful, he would ensure this Miss Bonnet was promptly set to the street. "When I called for you at the school, I was informed by Mrs. Huddleston, herself, that you were here—with Miss Bonnet."

"Oh, yes, she is here. I have learned ever so much from her lecture tours especially."

"I have heard of these lecture tours. And that though tonight you are guests of Lord and Lady Philamont, the ball is one of Miss Bonnet's so-called lecture tours."

"Yes, but tonight is a special experience, for

Lady Penelope is nearly out." Gemma smiled. "And because I am next eldest. Miss Bonnet is teaching us *everything*."

"Everything?" Sebastian tried to clarify.

"Well, not history or French, or anything so trivial. She is teaching us what is important in life—how to be a lady."

"And how does one go about being a lady?"

"By learning . . ." She paused, searching for the right words. "By having others do everything for you."

Sebastian's jaw tightened. His grandmother was right in her urgent request that he retrieve Gemma from Mrs. Huddleston's School of Virtues. Only he wasn't going to inform her of this while standing in a public place. It was clear she greatly admired this Miss Bonnet.

"Gemma, I should like to make Miss Bonnet's acquaintance. Perhaps I shall visit the school tomorrow morning," he said, affixing a warm smile to his lips.

"She would like to meet you as well, Lord Sebastian—only she cannot." Her earlier buoyant expression sank.

"Is that so? How do you know?"

"Because when I informed her that you were here, and I expressed my wish that she know you, she told me that she had no acquaintances in Bath who might introduce you to her—except me, and well, I am not permitted."

Sebastian straightened and scanned the room for a teaching mistress. "Where is she, Gemma? Perhaps I have an acquaintance who can facilitate a proper introduction."

Gemma looked dubious. "Do you?"

Sebastian was surprised by her quick question. He glanced about the ballroom, withholding his negative reply until the Master of Ceremonies finished announcing the next set. "Gemma, I—" He held his next words. Because, though he did not see a soul he recognized, there was one person whom he might coax into making an introduction to appease a new duke in want of a dance partner—the Master of Ceremonies. "Actually, I believe there is a gentleman who may be able to assist us. Now, where may I find Miss Bonnet?"

Gemma was beaming with excitement. She placed her hand on his arm and turned him until he was facing the point where he first saw her. "There, in the peacock changeable silk gown. She is beautiful, is she not?"

Dear God. There was the beguiling woman he'd noticed when he first entered the ballroom. *She is the reprehensible Miss Bonnet?*

Her shining hair was dark as jet, her skin as smooth and pale as porcelain. She was beautiful beyond compare, that much was obvious to everyone in the ballroom judging by the numerous glances cast her way. But as he drew closer, what most drew his notice, and nearly robbed him of breath, was her remarkable resemblance to Lady Priscilla Sinclair.

Yes, he had to meet this woman, but he had to arrange the introduction very carefully. "Do allow me a moment longer, Gemma. I must fetch my acquaintance." She nodded and started back toward Miss Bonnet. "Gemma—"

She came back to him. "Yes, Lord Sebastian?"

"Please do not mention the introduction just yet."

He shot her a sheepish grin. "I should like to request that she dance with me, and I do not want to lend her any time to fashion an elegant refusal."

"Very well." Gemma laughed softly, then turned and made her careful, studied promenade back to Miss Bonnet.

Chapter 8

Natural amiableness is too often seen in company with sloth, uselessness, with the vanity of the fashionable.

William Ellery Channing

Siusan's gaze threaded through the crowd. Drat it all, the only gentleman with any potential, Miss Gentree's new guardian, had disappeared into the mingling masses. Odd that she hadn't known the girl was a ward, but now that she considered it, she realized that she had never asked her or any of the girls, about their families. In fact, aside from Lady Penelope, who had secured from her titled parents admission to the ball this night, Siusan realized she knew nothing about any of her students at all.

There was the great pity. The girls were separated from their families, just as she was. How alone they must feel. Why had she never considered that before? Her own family was everything to her. She missed her brothers and sisters terribly, even her great silly goose of a sister, Priscilla.

And so must her students.

Well, she would correct her omission beginning tonight. She would endeavor to know them all. "Miss Gentree, where is your guardian? I do not see him." She let her gaze flit over the ballroom.

Miss Gentree's eyes glittered as brilliantly as the chandeliers above. "He believes he may have an acquaintance in attendance tonight." She sucked the seam of her lips into her mouth and glanced over her shoulder.

"Oh, how fortunate for him." *Well, why should he not?* For all Siusan knew, he resided nearby. Mayhap she should ask. She had made a vow to herself to know her students, after all. She would not be prying. "He came to the cotillion. He must reside in the region. How splendid for you."

Miss Gentree shook her head. "No, my lady, he is not from this region but rather from Devonshire . . . as I am." Miss Gentree seemed rather agitated. She twisted her fan in her hands, and her feet could not seem to remain still.

"Devonshire, really?" Siusan snapped open her own fan and waved it before her face to conceal her continued search for Miss Gentree's guardian.

When he entered the ballroom, he had been looking directly at her. She had little doubt he would coax an introduction to her. A smile fluttered upon her lips. Mayhap he would even ask her to dance. "His arrival at this particular ball is quite fortuitous. How delightful he happened upon your very first ball."

Miss Gentree's gaze darted about the crowded ballroom. "That he happened upon this ball, in Bath, is what I fear," she muttered. Her eyes were glistening as if she was about to cry. "Mrs. Huddleston told him I was here when he called for me at the school this night."

"Dear Lord." Siusan bent her knees and offered her a lace handkerchief from her reticule. She leaned closer to the girl. "Is something amiss, Miss Gentree?"

"My dear Miss Bonnet," crooned a sophisticated male voice from behind her. She straightened and whirled around.

There stood Mr. John Charles, the Upper Rooms' new acting Master of Ceremonies—and Miss Gentree's knee-weakeningly handsome guardian.

"Miss Bonnet, it would be a great honor if you

will allow me to present Sebastian Beaufort, the Marquess of Wentworth." Mr. Charles gestured to Lord Wentworth, who bowed graciously before her.

Miss Gentree was blinking madly, but Siusan did not think the display was to drive back her tears. She looked positively dumbfounded. "Lord *Wentworth* . . . is m-my guardian," she added.

"And may I present to you, Lord Wentworth, Miss Siusan Bonnet."

Siusan dropped into an overlong curtsy to conceal the amused smile itching at her lips.

"I confess, until but a moment earlier I had no acquaintances in Bath," Lord Wentworth admitted, "except my ward, of course, but I could not endure listening to such exceptional music without dancing."

Siusan didn't believe this for a moment.

"And so I begged the Master of Ceremonies the honor of an introduction to my ward's favorite instructor, trusting she enjoys dancing as much as I." He smiled down at Miss Gentree, who was still blinking confusedly, then, looking proud as a peacock, back at Siusan.

How clever of the man to have arranged their introduction through the Master of Ceremonies. Why, she doubted she would have thought of it though she was certainly grateful that he had. Now they would be required to step onto the dance floor together.

"Shall we dance then, Miss Bonnet?" Sebastian asked her. "I fear it is the cost of our introduction."

The Master of Ceremonies laughed heartily, sending his wig bouncing on his head. "Oh, indeed it is."

"Alas, there is no escaping our responsibility. Everyone is watching. Miss Bonnet?" Sebastian offered his arm to the wide-eyed beauty, and to his surprise, she took it and allowed herself to be led to the center of the ballroom.

"A waltz has been called." She looked into his eyes quizzically. "It is very new."

"If you prefer, we can wait for a contradance." Truth to tell, he actually hoped she would choose to do just that. It would be very telling. What sort of instructor of the art of being a lady would be without training in the waltz, one of the most fashionable new dances in all of England? He awaited her reply with bated breath.

She tilted her head to the side and flicked up an eyebrow. "I confess, I *adore* the waltz. Forgive me, my lord, I only wondered if you were comfortable. It has only recently been performed in court."

"Quite comfortable, I assure you." An adequate

reply, but the true test would be her skill. "Shall we dance?"

Miss Bonnet tilted her head and smiled as she moved into position.

He flashed a bright smile in response.

The Master of Ceremonies deserved Sebastian's great thanks for not only arranging an introduction to Miss Bonnet but for using his position to convince the reluctant woman to dance with him. And a waltz, no less. The intimate position would allow conversation, as well as a much nearer study of the infamous Miss Bonnet.

The music began and within a moment she was in his arms staring directly into his eyes as they turned.

This was no shy-and-retiring instructor. There was an elegance about her, as well as an attractive assurance he'd never witnessed in a young woman. *This, from an instructor at a school for young ladies?*

It hardly seemed possible. From the moment they were introduced, he had noted her complete ease in what to most would be a very uncomfortable situation. There were too many incongruities. He definitely required further study.

As they turned to the closed position again, he gazed at her face. Her wide eyes, delicate nose, and high cheekbones were nearly identical to those of Lady Priscilla Sinclair. But there were differences too, and the longer he examined those, the less convinced he was that she was a relation.

Her top lip was deliciously plumper than the lower, and for a fleeting moment, he wondered how those lips might feel moving over his. And her jaw was stronger, alluringly feminine, but more square than oval. Her form, well, it was far more womanly.

Her cheeks flushed becomingly, pinking her ivory face. Damn, she knew he was studying her.

"Y-you are Scottish, Miss Bonnet," he noted awkwardly, feeling a need to say something.

"Aye." Her mouth twitched upward before she schooled her features once more. "You are tall."

"As are you."

"My, you are very observant, my lord." She was more graceful and fluid in her movements than any other on the dance floor, and though his intent might well see her removed from her teaching position at Gemma's school, he simply could not take his eyes off her. "What other startling skills have you to recommend yourself?" she asked.

Had he not seen the flash of amusement on her

lips a moment before, he might have misread her question as derisive instead of intriguingly flirtatious.

"I can claim a clutch of accomplishments that might impress one such as you, Miss Bonnet." He studied her very expensive gown, which so perfectly accentuated the soft curves of her body. "Though I confess," he added, "dressing well is not one of them I possess."

"Nay, it is not." She shot a glance at his riding boots, then at the slippered feet of the gentleman dancing beside them. "It is a *learned* skill, however, and it is my belief that it is never too late to practice dressing *à la mode*."

That was a pinch, but also his opening to confront her about her curriculum. "Is it a skill you are teaching my charge?"

"Aye, among many others essential to my students' development as ladies."

As they turned, he misstepped and moved against her, his chest momentarily pressing against her full breasts. *Bloody hell.* From the twitch of her eyebrow he was sure she believed he had misstepped intentionally. "So sorry."

"Everyone makes mistakes when learning, Lord Wentworth." She looked directly up into his eyes and instantly set him worrying that beneath her scrutiny, he would err again.

"Miss Bonnet." Now it was his turn to unsettle her. "Do you not believe French, history, literature, and art more appropriate subjects for the young ladies?"

Without realizing it, he had tightened his grip on her gloved hand and her waist, drawing her closer. Though her wit and tongue were sharp, her body was soft . . . the feel of her against him pleasing.

"My lord." She cast her gaze at their clasped hands. "I assure you, I will not fall. You may loosen your grasp unless you are concerned that you may misstep again and tumble to the floor."

Suddenly he was all too aware of how close he'd drawn her body to his. "I beg your forgiveness, Miss Bonnet. My experience waltzing may be somewhat less than I led you to believe."

"Evidently." When he increased the space between them, she seemed to relax. "To answer your question regarding the students, I do believe in a well-rounded education rich in all of the subjects you mentioned. However, an education lacking in etiquette and the social graces is incomplete." A slow smile slid across her rose-hued lips. "How fortuitous for your ward that I am here to offer an opportunity to complete her education."

"Indeed. Mayhap I shall visit the school tomorrow to better understand the value of your instruction." He cast down the gauntlet.

And she instantly snatched it up. "Mayhap you should, my lord." She dropped her head back, and a low, entirely seductive laugh welled up from her middle as he spun them around a little too fast. She raised her head up, and as they came to rest, there was a challenging gleam in her eyes. "You may find that you learn something of value."

His pulse quickened as his gaze silently accepted the dare they both knew had nothing to do with school. The music ended, and as the dancers applauded, he leaned his mouth to her ear and whispered hotly into it. "I may already have, my dear Miss Bonnet."

The next morning
Mrs. Huddleston's School of Virtues

The clatter of plates and teacups met Sebastian's ears too late, for he was already standing before the open door of the schoolroom.

In synchronized pairs, the girls looked up at

him with matched stares of disapproval. He'd intruded upon their breakfast, it seemed. He stepped back quietly, meaning to wait in the ante-parlor until their instruction resumed, but Miss Bonnet caught notice of him before he could escape and called out to him.

"Do come in, Lord Wentworth." She gestured for him to enter and take a seat before two petite tea tables surrounded by a dozen pupils. "How lovely that we have a guest, ladies. What better way to practice the art of serving tea, eh?"

"Practice?" Sebastian hadn't meant to say it aloud and certainly not in such a scoffing tone, but he could not seem to stifle his words. "You are *teaching* them to serve tea? Haven't they been drinking it nearly all their short lives?"

Miss Bonnet carefully set the teapot upon the table and a fist atop the swell of her hip. "Aye, they have, but as children, how many opportunities have they had to take the role of mother?"

He readied a sarcastic retort on his tongue but then noticed the other misses in the room staring aghast at poor Gemma. His ward's pleading eyes were pinned on him while she mouthed the word *please*. Sebastian withheld the comment and waved Miss Bonnet onward.

"Look this way, ladies." Miss Bonnet remained

silent until every eye was trained on her. "Before your guests arrive, arrange with your maid or manservant to dress the table with a cloth, lace is preferable, and a posy of fresh flowers or greenery when available." Miss Bonnet turned and lifted a large tray from a desk near the window. "It is important that Cook has taken care to warm the pot near the cooking fire or oven. Omit this precaution, and your teapot may well crack when the boiling water is later added. The tea will also remain warm longer in an already warmed pot." She looked pointedly at each girl as if to impart the great importance of this step.

Sebastian leaned forward over his knees, feigning interest in the tea instruction. Gemma, on the other hand, was genuinely transfixed.

"While, because of staffing limitations, you may be required to add the tea and the boiling water yourself, I find it preferable to bestow this honor upon Cook." The girls exchanged worried glances. "If you are *required* to fill the pot with boiling water yourself, add one teaspoon of tea per cup desired to the pot." She opened the tea caddy and added several teaspoons to the teapot. "Only then do you add the boiling water. And it must be boiling, else the tea will not steep properly."

The students were wholly captivated. Why,

anyone watching would think she'd performed a feat of pure alchemy.

Miss Bonnet's gaze next fixed upon Gemma. "Will you please pour the water into the teapot, Miss Gentree?"

Gemma rose and carried the hot kettle from the desk to the teapot on the table. Her hands were shaking, and when she opened the lid of the teapot and began to pour, she spilled nearly a half cup on the tablecloth. The other girls began to laugh.

"Perfect, Gemma. This is exactly what I wished for all of you to see." She took the kettle from Gemma's hands and returned it to the desk. "A full kettle is often heavier than you might expect, and the steam may leak up and lick your hands. I do not know any lady, highborn or not, to have escaped this experience." She patted Gemma's shoulder gently. "I vow, it has happened to me a number of times, which is why I prefer Cook to do this for me." She grinned at Gemma, whose relief was plain on her face. "Miss Gentree, you did very well. Much better than I am able with such a full kettle of boiling water."

"Shall I pour the water into the teapot, Miss Bonnet?" Sebastian asked. An attempt at humor to relieve Gemma from her embarrassment—

which failed miserably. Gemma's visage had shifted from smiling to cringing within the span of his question.

"While it would be helpful, Lord Wentworth, I do require the girls to practice." She looked at the students. "Queue up. Quickly now, before the water cools. Each of you will pour one half cup of boiling water into the teapot. Do not be over-concerned about spills. We have plenty of tea and boiling water in the kitchen."

Sebastian watched as Miss Bonnet patiently tutored each girl in each step of making and serving the tea, bestowing the skill the same import as mastering Latin. *Ridiculous.*

If he allowed his mind to dwell on her farcical instruction, he would certainly say or do something to further embarrass Gemma. And so he kept his lips tightly sealed and continued his study with his eyes alone.

Aside from the physical similarities to the Sinclair family, the more he watched her, the more convinced he was that she was no relation at all. No, she was simply a bright and patient teacher who had confused education with the inconsequential. A misstep he would correct given the opportunity.

Gemma had just finished her instruction when

Miss Bonnet bent and spoke softly into her ear. Gemma lifted the dish of tea she'd just poured and carried it to Sebastian, proudly serving him his tea.

There was a light in her eyes he'd never seen before, a confidence she'd never revealed. He thanked Gemma and tasted the tea, complimenting her skill.

Miss Bonnet smiled proudly at Gemma.

The muscles he'd held tight during his entire study of the teacher this morning instantly relaxed.

Mayhap he was judging Miss Bonnet too harshly.

While reading literature and quizzing ciphers was obviously paramount to education, he could see how the simple act of learning social graces was helpful in developing his ward's confidence in herself.

Of course, more observation would be required before making the decision to allow Gemma to remain at this school. It was the girl's education—and her future—after all.

For five days, Lord Wentworth attended his ward's daily lessons. Or rather, Miss Gentree's lessons with *her*. It seemed he had no concern with the content of his ward's other classes, for neither of the other mistresses had the pleasure of his company during their instruction hours.

One day, Lord Wentworth's unfortunate timing required her—upon Mrs. Huddleston's firm order—to invite him along on her planned education outing with the students to Milsom Street for a lesson on how to assess quality millinery and to select ribbons that vary the look of even the most simple of bonnets.

Expecting a first-rate assortment of spiteful comments from Lord Wentworth, Siusan rejected the order. At least she objected until Mrs. Huddleston agreed to finance the purchase of three ribbons for each of the students—and three for herself as well, for demonstration purposes.

Seeing that this arrangement might be rather beneficial, Siusan agreed to allow him join them, hastily arranging another outing the next day to select fans.

Now she was onto something grand. The ease with which she secured funds to buy a fan for both students and teacher was almost comical. All it took was a hint that Lord Wentworth suggested he might join his ward on the outing, and Mrs. Huddleston provided funds.

Siusan did not feel even a twinge of guilt. She simply needed the proper supplies to teach her class—just as the other mistresses required foolscap, ink, books, and maps.

Nay, the outlay of coin from the school would not be great after all, for the girls only required very simple neoclassical fans without color or ornamentation to flatter their maidenly white muslin gowns. Her fan, however, ivory sticks and guard topped with painted silk leaves, would be more costly—but essential for demonstrating basic fan communication and practical drills.

Securing the fans during a return class visit to Milsom Street was entirely uneventful, even with Lord Wentworth trailing behind.

It was her class about how to properly command a fan that was her undoing.

"A lady may spend her lifetime perfecting her fan technique," she began. Lord Wentworth cleared his throat in what might have been mistaken for a disapproving groan. She paused a moment, until she was satisfied he would not interrupt again. "However, in only three days, I will have imparted the basic movements and a rudimentary understanding of the language of the fan."

Lord Wentworth snorted. Siusan angrily discharged her fan, sending a thunderous crack through the small schoolroom. Lord Wentworth's mouth fell open. "Oh, first lesson will be opening your fan. But this action must be considered, for a fan is an extension of yourself, and it communicates your emotion as clearly as your face. Please, pick up your fans."

Several of the students snatched their fans from their laps, while others raised them as carefully as they might a baby bird.

"Depending on your location, you may choose to discharge your fan demurely or instantly command the attention of all around you by cracking it—though it requires quite a lot of practice to achieve without damaging a delicate fan such as mine."

The girls sat still, too petrified to attempt opening their fans for fear of breaking them. Siusan collapsed her fan and touched it to Lady Penelope's shoulder. "Discharge your fan, please."

Without delay, Lady Penelope snapped her fan open, so obviously pleased with herself that she produced no sound at all. Siusan touched her fan to Miss Seton's shoulder, who let her fan's leaves fall from the guard as slowly and silently as a maple leaf tumbling through the air to the ground. "Very good, Sarah, though a wee more force next time. Please try again."

Lord Wentworth's eyes were merry with amusement. She handed him a fan. "Let us *all* try," she said, suppressing a chuckle. "Then we will move along to fluttering."

"Very well." Lord Wentworth grinned cockily and stood. He raised his fan and snapped it open with such force that it ripped down the middle, cracking two leaves.

"Oh dear. I see you will require more than three days' practice, Lord Wentworth." She picked up another fan to hand to him, but he waved it away and quickly sat down.

The girls laughed uproariously.

Lord Wentworth groaned again.

"On second thought, we will address fluttering another day and instead move on to *language*." Siusan raised her brow at Lord Wentworth, whose softened features showed his relief that she was at last teaching the girls something he considered worthy of their time. Her lips twitched with mischief. ". . . the language of the fan."

Rather than quitting the school after her session, Lord Wentworth paced the passageway outside the schoolroom until the students had departed. "Miss Bonnet, your lesson today, or rather your training camp for coquettes, was entirely inappropriate."

Siusan pinned him with her gaze. "I beg to disagree, Lord Wentworth. My lesson was entirely factual. If the truth intrudes upon your morality, then mayhap you should withdraw to a monastery."

"The truth?" Lord Wentworth laughed. "Opening and shutting your fan communicates *kiss me*?"

"Aye," Siusan replied without hesitation. "Though the length of time between opening and closing it conveys the meaning." She opened her fan and fluttered it before her face for several long moments before snapping it abruptly closed. "That means *I hate you*. Some difference, do you not agree?"

Lord Wentworth's reply was very nearly a growl. "This is not something in which a young girl should be schooled."

"I disagree, my lord. If Miss Gentree, for instance, is not schooled in the use of a fan, what message might she accidentally impart to an interested but more worldly young gentleman?"

Lord Wentworth had certainly readied a retort, but instead of speaking, his mouth dropped open. Clearly he had not been prepared for such a thought-provoking and important question.

"Lord Wentworth, unless the miss is destined to live a life in the seclusion of the country, never to move about in public, let alone in elevated circles, then the instruction I provide is essential to her education."

"Oh, really?" He was nearly huffing in his disagreement.

"Aye, Lord Wentworth, *really*." Siusan raised her chin.

"And where did *you* learn such lessons, Miss Bonnet?"

Siusan paused, drawing her lower lip into her mouth and biting it. She could not admit that she had learned all she knew as a consequence of error and ridicule. That she and her sisters had been forced by need to learn the proper ways to be ladies when all of Edinburgh Society believed her and her sisters to be hoydens.

Or that she was driven to always act the lady by a desire to be like her mother—the duchess everyone in Society admired and emulated. The woman who would have taught her and her sisters what it meant to be a true lady had she not died giving birth to Killian and Priscilla, leaving her and her siblings alone.

Blast. She felt the backs of her eyes begin to burn and knew she had to separate herself from Lord Wentworth before she made a soggy cake of herself. She squeezed by him and charged down the passage.

"Ah, I thought so," he called out, mockingly.

She whirled back around and glared at him. "I know the value of what I teach. I know, too, every girl in Great Britain requires this knowledge, these skills, if she is to elevate herself beyond the scullery." Her voice sounded thin, reedy.

"Is that so, Miss Bonnet?" His eyes were blazing, but there was no obvious reason for his expression.

"Aye, it is. It is essential knowledge for *every* female!"

He laughed at her comment. "If that is so, then mayhap you should write a manual so that all females should have the benefit of your knowledge!"

He was mocking her. But he did not know how disadvantaged and ill prepared a girl would be if thrust into the world without this knowledge.

But she knew. She knew exactly what was required for a wayward hoyden to become a lady true. All too well. "Forgive me, Lord Wentworth. I fear you do not understand what I seek to impart to my charges, and I am quite sure you never will. Good day, my lord."

Siusan dropped him a curtsy, though he did not deserve the honor, and hurried down the passage to her bedchamber.

* * *

Tears of frustration filled her eyes by the time she returned to her nun's cell of a bedchamber after her morning instruction hours. She was so angry and hurt that she could hardly catch her breath. But it wasn't Lord Wentworth she was angry with—it was herself. She had given him the power to wound her to her core. This was what happened when she shed her sin of sloth, lifted her mask, and showed the world her true self. She became vulnerable. And her heart ached.

When she sat down on her pallet, her gaze was drawn to a letter sitting on her bedside table. She tore open the red wax wafer and carefully released the letter from its folds.

Instantly, she recognized the dainty, overslanted hand as Priscilla's and laughed in blessed relief. She needed this letter so very much. She needed her family.

Dearest Siusan,

I cannot believe I actually miss you terribly, and yet I do. I simply cannot endure another month without you—and indications are that I may not have to. The Duke of Exeter has not been observed in Society for nearly a sennight.

I would herald a message to you to come back to London now, except for an article in _The Times_ that briefly mentioned his name as part of the Lord Mayor's special committee on food shortages in the wake of the wars with the French.

It is possible that the Duke of Exeter is simply too busy to attend social affairs, for it has been reported that food riots have broken out all around London, and grain warehouses have been looted. Because of the heavy rains, flooding, and early frosts, fall harvests have been all but lost.

Our own family worries over the rising costs of food. Grant even told me I am forbidden to spend so much as a shilling without discussing it with him first. I will write to you again as soon as I learn more about the whereabouts of the Duke of Exeter—once I swipe a coin for postage from Grant's purse.

I miss you, sister.

Yours,
Priscilla

"I miss you too, Priscilla." Siusan rested her face in her hands, and the tears she'd tried to hold back puddled in her palms.

She rose from the bed and deposited Priscilla's letter in the table drawer. Inside, she caught notice of the small Bible her mother had given to her when she was a very small child. She lifted it from the drawer and pressed it to her chest, patting it, the way her mother used to pat her back when she was very young to soothe her when she was upset.

A sob welled up inside her and burst into the air. "Please, God, forgive me my wicked indiscretion and send me home soon. Allow me to return to my family." Lowering the Bible to the table, she scrubbed the tears from her cheeks with the back of her hand. "I need them. Until now, I didn't know how very much."

Chapter 9

I don't think necessity is the mother of invention. Invention, in my opinion, arises directly from idleness, possibly also from laziness—to save oneself trouble.
Agatha Christie

Sebastian watched Miss Bonnet hurry down the passageway and out of sight. *Damn me!* He hadn't meant to taunt her and certainly not to aggravate her to the verge of tears . . . and yet he had. While it was true that her notions of education and his differed, he did not need to insult her person.

The more he studied the proud woman, he saw the image that she presented the world was naught but a cleverly crafted blind. While her elegant clothing was fashioned of silks and satins, their styles *à la mode*, they appeared somewhat worn. He would not doubt it if he learned she owned but three frocks, all of which he'd seen her wear multiple times over the five days he'd visited the school. Save one.

The only gown he hadn't seen again was the peacock blue confection she'd worn at the Upper Rooms when they had first met. Even then, he could have sworn she was wearing blue satin walking shoes rather than tissue-thin flat slippers, which were more appropriate for dancing. Even he knew that.

Now, as the pieces of her identity began to come together in his mind, he felt quite the lout. Her clothing, as well as her training in the ways of Society ladies had all probably been passed along to her from a generous former employer. Perhaps a daughterless mistress from some grand family, who, as a diversion from the tedium of her days, trained her maid in the ways of the *ton*, but then passed away unexpectedly.

It was possible. Hell, it even likely. Why else would someone so skilled in the leisure arts take a position as a teacher? No, the reason was becoming increasingly transparent. She had no other choice.

But he did. His course was all too clear. He had

to shove his damnable pride down his gullet and find some way to apologize for insulting her.

Sebastian slammed the school's heavy front door behind him and stalked out to the pavers, more confused by then than ever. Bloody hell, he wished he was certain about what he should do about Gemma. His grandmother had been so startled by the change in the girl, and her descriptions of Miss Bonnet's teaching methods, that she had nearly demanded that Sebastian remove her from the school and immediately engage a governess for her.

Admittedly, that was his first inclination as well. Now, he wasn't so sure.

He'd observed Gemma withdrawing into herself when in the presence of Mrs. Huddleston or even the other students. Not so when she was in the presence of Miss Bonnet. There, she blossomed. But more, each day she seemed to display a little more of the confidence she'd gleaned from Miss Bonnet's lecture tours in the other hours of her day. Even with him. She was maturing.

No, he would set aside the decision about removing Gemma from the school for the moment. He'd bring his thoughts back with him on the morrow, when he returned to London for the

Lord Mayor's committee meetings. Discuss his resolution, whatever it might be, with his grandmother, then return to Bath come Michaelmas to fetch Gemma for the holiday.

That night

The moon was still high in the sky when Siusan awoke with a pain in her belly. She rolled from her pallet and sat on its edge, her hands pressed to her stomach, as she rocked, hoping to ease the cramping.

In her sleepy state, it took several moments for her to notice the slight wetness between her legs, but when she did, she pulled away her coverlet and stood in the moonlight cascading through her window. There, stark against the snowy white of her night dress, was a dark, wet bloom. At once she recognized the aching in her belly, the familiar cramping, for what it was.

Her eyes widened, and she cupped a shaking hand over her mouth to stifle her exuberant gasp. Her courses had not arrived when expected, and she had feared the worst. But it wasn't so. Tears of relief collected in her eyes.

She was not with child.

The next morning

Her mood as bright as the morning sun, Siusan herded the other two teachers into her bedchamber before classes, then quietly pressed the door closed behind her.

"I must tell you what Lord Wentworth said yesterday after class." A flush of heat rose up in Siusan's cheeks just thinking about it.

"Do you not recall? You already informed us yesterday afternoon, Miss Bonnet," Miss Hopkins replied. There was a hint of annoyance in her voice.

Siusan heard a buzzing in her ears and knew the other teacher had replied. She wasn't really listening for a response anyway. Though she did catch notice of the slanted glance Miss Hopkins cast in Mistress Grassley's direction. Clearly they could not endure suspense any longer.

Well, she wouldn't make them suffer a moment longer. "He said that if my lessons were so important, perhaps I should write a manual about it for the benefit of all! Can you believe it?" Siusan was huffing with relived anger.

Miss Grassley closed the novel she'd seemingly been unable to put down all day. "Perhaps you should, Miss Bonnet."

Siusan whipped her head around at the other teacher. "What did you say? I am certain I misheard you. He was mocking me." She crossed her arms over her chest.

Miss Grassley looked Siusan straight in the eye. "I agree with him. I only wish I had been trained in the ways of being a lady when I was younger. It might have changed my course in life."

Siusan looked to Miss Hopkins, waiting for her to chastise the other teacher for teasing her so cruelly. Only she didn't.

"I confess, I agree with Lord Wentworth and Miss Grassley as well," Miss Hopkins admitted. "When I accompanied you and the girls to the draper, I vow I learned more about dressing and fashion than I have after years of reading *La Belle Assemblé.*" She stood and nodded slowly. "The next day, I found myself standing outside of your door whenever possible, listening to your lesson, knowing that the more refined and skilled I became, the better my chances of making a good match someday."

Siusan's eyes went wide. She reached out behind her and caught the back of a wooden chair and guided herself into it. "Can this be true?" she demanded.

They both nodded, with nary a glimmer of

humor twitching at their lips. Gorblimey, they *were* telling the truth. "Assuming I do this, do you believe the manual might actually have enough interest to secure a publisher?" Siusan could scarcely manage the words.

Miss Hopkins grinned. "My brother is engaged as a typesetter at G. G. and J. Robinson in London. He actually set the second edition of Mrs. Radcliffe's *The Mysteries of Udolpho*. He is very skilled. I will write to him today and ask him if he can help you with this endeavor."

Siusan's heart tightened in her chest. "Oh, what shall I do?" She waved her hands in the air as if shaking droplets of water from them.

The notion of writing a manual frightened her. And aye, such a huge endeavor ought to, but God above, if Miss Hopkins was correct, she had an undeniable duty to the females of Great Britain!

She leaped to her feet. "I will do it. I will!" She hurried over and grasped the other teachers' hands and drew them a step toward the door. "But I will need your help. I cannot do it without the two of you."

"*Ours?*" Miss Grassley flashed a nerve-shot glance at Miss Hopkins. "How can we assist?"

"Can either of you slip the key from Mrs. Huddleston . . . unnoticed?"

Miss Hopkins gulped. "She is at the baths now. Her knees are paining her again. Probably from all her stooping to peer into keyholes." She grinned then, though Siusan knew her words were not said in jest.

"She very likely left the chatelaine in her bedchamber . . . but we could never—" Miss Grassley peered warily at Siusan.

Siusan arched an eyebrow. "Aye, we can if we are quick about it. I will fetch the keys and open the storage room." Siusan patted Miss. Hopkins's shoulder soothingly. "Of course, I will need foolscap, and plenty of ink." She turned her gaze on the other teacher. "Most importantly, Miss Grassley, I will require someone to watch the passageway for Mrs. Huddleston whilst I slip into her bedchamber." She grinned at the promise of adventure. "Come along. We have much to do before the old wretch returns."

The other teachers exchanged worried looks for a brief moment, then squealed with nervous laughter, and the three of them rushed for the door.

One week later

Miss Hopkins and Miss Grassley stood before the desk in Siusan's bedchamber as she read the letter she had just received. Disappointment tugged heavily at her shoulders. "All is lost."

"What do you mean, Miss Bonnet? My brother claims his publisher is very interested in your manual."

"The publisher may be." Siusan sighed. "But, Miss Hopkins, while I do thank you for your assistance, I cannot wait six months, at least, for the manual to be published—assuming the publisher finds it suitable." Siusan dropped the letter on the bed and paced her bedchamber.

This wasn't at all what she expected. She had spent every free minute of her days and nights transcribing her lessons in the art of being a lady . . . and now this delay?

"Miss Bonnet, each individual letter must be placed as type, and while my brother will do anything to assist me in this endeavor, including seeing to the typesetting himself, the process does take time." Miss Hopkins bowed her head, her face looking as though she had failed Siusan.

"I apologize, Miss Hopkins. I have written nearly twenty lessons, and I had hoped to see this manual in print much sooner." She patted the other teacher's shoulder.

After all, she'd be leaving Bath soon enough—

or so she hoped—and she did so want to depart knowing she had made a difference there.

"There is another option," Miss Grassley broke in. She'd always been a clever one, and Siusan's hope glimmered once more.

Siusan shifted her gaze. "Do you know of another publisher—a faster one?"

"Well, no, not a publisher of books . . ." Miss Grassley raised a finger, then dashed from Siusan's bedchamber. She returned a moment later with a newspaper in her grip.

"A newspaper?" Siusan squinted at it, not understanding what Miss Grassley was about.

"A newspaper—exactly. Perhaps, to generate interest in your forthcoming manual, you publish an instructional column in the *Bath Herald*?"

Siusan stared at the paper Miss Grassley fluttered in her hand like a silk fan. "But why would the newspaper publish my lessons?"

Miss Grassley smiled. "For the very same reason the publisher will print your manual— *public interest.* I am certain, if at the conclusion of each shortened lesson you mention ordering the manual and the direction of your potential publisher, you would certainly drive the publisher's interest and purchase of your book."

"Are you suggesting I promote the sale of the book before the publisher has yet agreed to see it into print?"

Miss Grassley didn't need to reply. It was exactly what she meant. And utterly brilliant.

Siusan laced her fingers and once again began to pace the short distance between her pallet and the door. "Very well, I shall deliver my first lesson to the *Bath Herald* today. And, please, pray for me that they accept it." Siusan was giddy at the idea of her work—*her work*—being presented to the public in print. Any money they offered her, while needed, wasn't her motivation for sharing her knowledge with the less privileged females of Bath.

She would change lives.

If the newspaper would accept her abbreviated lessons, she would be doing the females of Bath a great service.

And maybe, just maybe, this service would be enough to do the impossible . . . make her father proud of her.

By the end of the day, Siusan had sent not one, but two abbreviated lessons to Bath's most widely read newspapers. She'd submitted a very timely lesson on creating the perfect menu for a Michaelmas dinner to the *Bath Chronicle*. To the *Bath Herald*, a publication she preferred because of the quirky yet informative *on-dit* column, the Strange But True column, she'd sent an indispensable step-by-step lesson on transforming last year's fashions into gowns that are positively *à la mode*.

Most certainly she had not expected either newspaper to reply to her query and sample column so quickly, but to her astonishment, by nine of the clock the very next morning, both newspapers had sent letters with astounding offers to *pay* her for any columns she would choose to submit. If she had an archive, the *Bath Chronicle* offered to publish one per day, except on Sunday.

Both, too, agreed to close each column with the direction of the publisher of her manual. Of course, she had not informed either publication that she had yet to be made an offer for her manual, but that was of little concern to her. Letters with offers of payment would be enticement enough for the London publisher to hurry her manual to press. Or so she believed.

She also agreed to submit her columns to both newspapers. She had some scruples, however, and would give each newspaper a different lesson with each submission, for neither had required exclusivity, and well, what sane woman in want of funds—and a wish to do a good deed—would do otherwise?

Two days later

Putting her spare time to use writing lessons made the days pass quickly, though not so quickly that she hadn't noticed that Lord Wentworth had not visited the school so much as once in over a sennight.

Sometimes she absently glanced out of the schoolroom window for him, and, when she escorted the girls on their lecture tours of Bath, she took care to glance down the streets and into the stores, secretly hoping their paths might cross again soon.

Siusan peered down into a steaming cup of tea, remembering the one time they had danced at the Upper Rooms.

"Ah, so you already know." Miss Hopkins had suddenly appeared at her right.

Siusan peered blankly up at her. "Miss Hopkins, whatever do you mean?"

"Oh! Then you haven't seen them." She bent close to whisper in Siusan's ear. "I left two newspapers on your bed."

Siusan stared up at her, silently quizzing the other teacher. "Y-you do not mean that my lessons . . ."

Miss Hopkins bobbed her head. Within an instant, Siusan was racing from the dining room to her bedchamber. She slammed the door behind and nearly spilled the dish of tea still clutched in her hands as she reached out for the first paper. The *Bath Herald*!

Where? Where was her column? She settled the teacup to the desk, but her hands were still shaking so badly that turning the pages was nearly impossible. At last her eyes met the words she'd searched for.

Excerpts from The Handbook of Elegance
By Miss Siusan Bonnet

Lud, there it is. Tears of pride budded in her eyes. Ladies and misses of Bath and Cheltenham were reading her lessons, gaining experience in living a life of elegance and graciousness. All because of Lord Wentworth's suggestion that she publish her lessons for the good of all.

How horrid she had been to Lord Wentworth. Why had it taken her so long to realize this? He had not been mocking her at all. In truth, he *had* seen the value of her work and the potential in her—when she had never seen it herself.

He had had faith in her. Lord Wentworth, when no one else in her world did.

Next, she snatched up the *Bath Chronicle*, trying to blink away the ridiculous tears that blurred her vision as she scanned the front page.

She saw it then, and a shudder shook through her body. It wasn't her column, but rather a report from London. It detailed the riots over shortages and the immediate selection of a committee chosen from the House of Lords to draw up legislation and establish penalties to stop this violence and breaking of machinery. But the paragraph that truly snared her attention was the questioning of the experience of one newly appointed committee member—*the Duke of Exeter*.

Siusan slapped her hand to her chest. Lord above, he was still in London and, judging from the seriousness of the insurrections, was not about to return to Exeter soon. A chill prickled her skin, and she dropped the newspapers on the bed in order to tighten her mantle around her shoulders.

Oh, Priscilla, what shall I do now? I canna stay in Bath forever, but what choice have I?

At least I have my work.

* * *

The very day the lessons were published in the Bath
newspapers, three students' mothers came to visit
the school. Mothers, who, though living within the
area, had *never* condescended to visit their daughters before—or so Miss Grassley claimed.

Over the next three days, six more parents came
to visit their darlings and observe the lecture
tours, which, at Mrs. Huddleston's urging, had
become more frequent.

To Siusan's disappointment, Lord Wentworth
was not included in this number, and though
it was great folly even to entertain the notion
that she might never see him again, the thought
nagged at her mind constantly.

"Miss Bonnet?" *Oh dear.* It seemed that Mrs.
Huddleston had crept up the passage to stand
behind her like a spider ready to pounce on its
prey.

Siusan whirled around. "Aye, Mrs. Huddleston?"

"I would have a moment of your time. In my
office, if you do not mind." Mrs. Huddleston
pointed a felt-tipped walking stick in the opposite
direction. The stick was padded, and Siusan bet
the older woman's shoes were as well. She narrowed her eyes at Mrs. Huddleston. No wonder
she had not heard her approach!

"Certainly." Had the parents complained about her methods of teaching? Of her growing notoriety? She fervently hoped not. From the girls' chatter, she thought it more likely that the parents' meetings with Mrs. Huddleston were highly complimentary.

Still, she could not help feeling like Marie Antoinette being marched to the guillotine. She paused at the open door of Mrs. Huddleston's office. *How odd.* Her office door was always closed and locked.

"Enter, Miss Bonnet." She tapped the handle of her walking stick on the door. "Sit."

Siusan slowly moved inside and took the chair nearest the door. "How might I assist you, Mrs. Huddleston? Is there something wrong?"

Mrs. Huddleston chuckled as she sat down at her desk. The door remained wide open.

Siusan was more than a little anxious now. Just then, Siusan saw her eyes track to a bulging leather purse tied to Mrs. Huddleston's chatelaine, one that had never been there before.

The instant Mrs. Huddleston realized that her own eyes had betrayed her, she slipped the cording free and stuffed the weighty bag into her desk drawer. "Miss Bonnet," she began, "you should have spoken with me before publishing your lessons in the newspapers."

The blood in her veins seemed to chill. "I th-thought I had. Nay?"

"No." Mrs. Huddleston manufactured a purely unconvincing smile and fastened it to her lips. "But never mind. I am pleased that the school is being put in such glowing light. Already, I have received correspondence from six other families wishing to install their daughters in my School of Virtues."

"Oh, how lovely for the school." *Is that all—a subtle thank-you? May I leave now?*

"There is quite a lot of interest in *you* too, Miss Bonnet, apart from your unique way of teaching your lessons." Her smile remained in place, but her lips went flat. "Not only from the parents of students or potential students."

Why was she baiting her? "I am sure I canna imagine who else might be interested in me."

"Can you not?" She narrowed her eyes. "According to a columnist from the *Bath Herald*, Bath Society is drooling with anticipation of learning your *true* identity."

"M-my true identity?" *Oh dear. Stay calm. Do not react.*

"No one believes you are of common birth or circumstance." Mrs. Huddleston paused. She stared at Siusan, but then her gaze lifted to the door for the briefest of instants.

Siusan didn't dare reply or turn around. Too dangerous. And so, she simply shrugged.

"I told the columnist all I know. That your name, as far as I know is Miss Siusan Bonnet and that you are Scottish. Though he offered me coin as enticement for anything else I might recall over the next few days."

Siusan's feet began to twitch. She wanted to run. She wanted to throw her clothes into her portmanteau and take the first mail coach back to London.

"And I have remembered one or two tidbits that might interest him." She licked her thin lips. "That fact that you have a connection with Mrs. Wimpole of Mayfair, who sent you to me to hide you from a looming threat—of a man."

Anger crested over her fear. "You would not share that information. You owe Mrs. Wimpole a great debt." Siusan only wished she knew what that debt was—to lend weight to her own counter-threat!

"I do, but I do not owe *you* anything. You with your fine ways and clever wit, making everyone else feel inadequate." Mrs. Huddleston was seething.

"That is not my intent." Siusan rose from the chair. "My goal is build confidence in the girls—in women. That is why I am writing the lessons!"

Mrs. Huddleston snickered at that. "So your lessons are to provide the community with a great good? You do not write them for the money the newspapers pay you?"

Och. Here it is. The real reason I am here in this room. "You are saying you want me to *pay* you for your silence with the money I receive from the newspapers."

Mrs. Huddleston chuckled softly. "You mistake me, Miss Bonnet, I do not believe I said anything remotely like that." She winked at her. "However, it is something to ponder, is it not?"

Siusan turned to leave. She'd made for the doorway when Mrs. Huddleston called out to her.

"The school will be closed over Michaelmas. All of the students will be with their families, or elsewhere, so I am shutting down the school." Mrs. Huddleston's gaze was deliberately cruel as she delivered her plan.

"But you know that I have nowhere to go." Siusan's stomach clenched.

"You can always rent a room if you have no family."

But I do have family. And I want to return to them, she screamed inside her head. "But why should I when my bedchamber remains vacant?"

"Why waste coal, tapers, and food when none of the misses will be in residence?" The corner of her lip pulled upward.

"Because I will be here."

"No, you will not. Miss Bonnet, I suggest you make arrangements to take a room for the three days, or else go back to wherever you came from." She pushed her spectacles to the bridge of her long nose and turned her gaze at a stack of papers on her desk. "Good afternoon, Miss Bonnet."

Movement just outside the doorway caught Siusan's notice. It was Miss Gentree. Siusan flapped her hand outside the doorway and waved her away.

She cast a parting glare at Mrs. Huddleston, then silently turned and headed for her bedchamber.

Miss Gentree was waiting for her at her door.

"Lady Siusan—I mean Miss Bonnet, may I speak with you?"

Siusan wearily welcomed the girl into her chamber. "How can I help you, Miss Gentree?"

She doubted she could help her with anything, not with Mrs. Huddleston's threats floating over her head.

"I-I heard what Mrs. Huddleston said . . . about Michaelmas. I apologize, for I did not mean to eavesdrop. There was a little man standing outside the door, but when he saw me he disappeared. I was going to report this to Mrs. Huddleston, but when I neared, I heard your voice."

A little man? Could he be the columnist Mrs. Huddleston mentioned?

Miss Gentree bowed her head as if in shame.

"Look at me, Miss Gentree. The door was left open, and Mrs. Huddleston made no attempt to lower her voice. I do not think you ill-mannered at all." Siusan patted her small pallet for the girl to come and sit down. "Now, how may I assist you?"

"I received a letter from my . . . my guardian's grandmother. I had requested that you be invited to spend Michaelmas with us at her country house outside Bath."

Dear God. "You did what?" Siusan leaped from the bed.

"I did not know what else to do. I fear that my guardian is planning to remove me from the school. I know that if he and his grandmother came to know you better, as I do, he will not entertain such an idea. I do not wish to leave the school, Miss Bonnet. I cannot leave." Tears budded in her eyes. "You and this school are all I have."

Siusan hugged the girl to her. "Your guardian cares deeply for you. I am sure he will do what is best for your interests."

"Remaining here is what is best, but I fear he will not realize that until it is too late." Miss Gentree hugged Siusan around her middle. "Please, come. Say you will."

Siusan's eyes began to burn. "Dear, Gemma, I cannot. I have not been invited."

Miss Gentree peered up at her through tear-filled eyes. "But if you are asked formally, you will come? *Please.*"

Siusan knew it was wrong, for spending Michaelmas with Lord Wentworth and his grandmother was naught but a worried girl's wish. But it would give her a few days away from Bath—and the columnist Mrs. Huddleston told her was investigating her.

And then, there was also Lord Wentworth, to whom she owed so much. If she spent Michaelmas with . . . *the family,* she would at last have an opportunity to thank him.

It was selfish, she knew, but she nodded her assent anyway. "If I am *formally* invited to spend the holiday with you, certainly I will accept, Miss Gentree."

Gemma jumped to her feet, but then remembered herself and curtsied like a proper lady. "My guardian arrives on the morrow. I will secure a proper invitation for you then." She dropped another curtsy, then dashed from the room.

Lord Wentworth will be in Bath tomorrow. Tomorrow.

Siusan snatched up one of the newspapers, then lay back on the pallet and tented the paper over her face. What would she say to him?

Och, life is so much easier in Scotland.

Chapter 10

The time will come when Winter will ask you what you were doing all Summer.
Henry Clay

The change in the weather had come without clear notice. Though a dark line traced the horizon that morning, the sun shone brightly, and the air was as crisp as the dried leaves tumbling across the ground. By afternoon, the sky was heavy with angry dark clouds, and the wind bit viciously at exposed skin.

Siusan sat before her window, feeling forlorn as she watched the last of the students happily herded into family carriages and wheeled from the school.

Even Miss Gentree had been collected. Or so

she'd been told. The teachers had each been tasked with making arrangements for the closing of the school. Miss Hopkins was positioned like a sentry at the front door to assist families with the collection of their daughters. Miss Grassley saw to washing the morning's dishes, while Siusan had been sent to the bakery to cancel the school's order for the coming days.

Though Siusan had dutifully packed in anticipation of an invitation to spend the holiday with Miss Gentree and her family, it hadn't been offered.

Now she was in a pickle. What would she do? She'd made no arrangements for lodging. Sighing, she looked up at the menacing sky and shivered. If she did not leave the school to find a place to stay now, she'd be walking in sleeting rain.

She pushed up from the chair, already weary from the thought of having to venture out of doors again, then turned around and closed the leather bag sitting atop her pallet.

"Lord Wentworth has come to collect you." Siusan wrenched her head around. Mrs. Huddleston was standing in the doorway, leaning on her walking stick.

"I beg your pardon?" Siusan folded her arms

over her chest and crossed the small room in three strides. "Did you say that Lord Wentworth is here . . . for me?"

"You have been invited to stay at Clover Hall over the holiday." Mrs. Huddleston snickered.

"Miss Gentree did speak of an invitation, but I was never formally asked." Confusion loomed as heavily as the gray clouds brushing the rooftops.

"Of course you were. Why, I accepted the letter myself from Lord Wentworth's man of affairs." Mrs. Huddleston shook her head. "Tsk, tsk. If you did not intend to accept, you should have at the very least sent a card to the family in response. It would have been the proper thing for a lady to do."

"Mrs. Huddleston, you *never* presented me with a letter." Siusan narrowed her eyes.

"Oh, but I did. I distinctly recall you taking it from me and placing it in your drawer." Jabbing her walking stick into the old pine-floor planks, she caned her way to the desk near the window. Tugging open the drawer, she reached inside and withdrew a letter.

Siusan peered at it, confused. Indeed, there was a letter—one she'd never seen before—though the wax wafer had been broken. It was clear that while she had not, someone else had already read the letter.

"Here it is. And, I think it quite evident that you read it. See here?" She shook the letter from its folds and flicked the broken wax seal with a ragged fingernail.

"I never saw that letter," Siusan protested.

"And yet, here it was, in your drawer."

Siusan winced. She'd been warned to keep the drawer locked, though she never had. She trusted the students completely, never once considering that Mrs. Huddleston herself might invade the drawer, for whatever reason. She stalked forward and snatched the letter from Mrs. Huddleston's hand and quickly read it.

It was an invitation, conveyed by Lord Wentworth's man of affairs, to spend three nights at Clover Hall. Her hands shook with anger as she lowered the letter to her side.

"When you did not come down to the carriage when you were summoned and could not be found anywhere in the school, I suggested to the driver that it would probably be best to outpace the coming storm and deliver Miss Gentree to Clover Hall safely." The edges of her withered lips quivered. "Who would have guessed that Lord Wentworth, himself, would return to collect you? Certainly not I."

"Mrs. Huddleston, you sent me to the bakery

to cancel the school's orders during the holiday. Though when I arrived, I was informed that those arrangements had already been made a week ago." Siusan stuffed the letter in her portmanteau, then whirled around. "You deliberately sent me away so I would not be present when Miss Gentree was looking for me."

Mrs. Huddleston's eyebrows crept toward her nose, but the smile that only teased her lips before spread across her mouth. "Such an accusation, Miss Bonnet!"

Siusan turned, meaning to leave Mrs. Huddleston, find Lord Wentworth, and explain everything to him, when she remembered the open drawer . . . and the letter from Priscilla inside of it. She squeezed past her employer and felt inside the drawer. Nothing but a stub of candle. Her heart clenched as she bent and wrenched the drawer off its runners. *Empty.* She felt inside the cavern left behind, hoping that maybe the letter had been caught up inside. Nothing.

She let the wooden drawer drop to the floor. The candle stub rolled beneath her pallet. "Where is it? Where is the letter from my sister?"

"Why, Miss Bonnet—or shall I say Lady Siusan Sinclair?—I fear I do not know what you mean." A low chuckle rolled off her tongue.

Dear God. She knows who I am. She knows I am Lady Siusan Sinclair!

Siusan scurried to her pallet, dug deep in her portmanteau, and drew out her reticule. She fumbled inside it, but thinking further, cinched it closed again. "Here, take the money. All of it." She shoved the reticule toward the older woman.

"Now, now, *my lady,* we both know it will take more than a few pounds to hush me, knowing what I do about you . . . and the gentleman who threatens you." She chuckled nastily. "The Duke of Exeter, is it? I rather guessed as much. I only needed more proof."

The reticule in her hand suddenly became too weighty for her to hold out to Mrs. Huddleston, and she lowered it to her side. "What is it that you want from me?"

"Well now, that I do not know. Yet." She started from the room, talking as she walked, not bothering to turn around. "Mayhap I will think about it over the holiday. Yes, I think that is what I shall do. We will speak of this again upon your return. Of that, *Miss Bonnet*, you can be certain."

Siusan's mind was caught in a dizzying whirl. What could she do? God above, what could she do now? She paced across the bedchamber several times but came no closer to grasping a solution.

All she could think to do was run. Just as she had before. Leave Bath and never come back. But the idea was nonsensical.

Her heart thudded in her chest. If the columnist learned her true name, it was only a matter of time before her connection with the Duke of Exeter became known in London as well. And then . . . her father's man would report it to her father and—"

"Miss Bonnet." Lord Wentworth was standing just outside the doorway. For how long, she did not know. "I waited, but when you did not come down to the entry hall I thought perhaps you required assistance with your bag."

"L-lord Wentworth." She could barely find her voice. "I beg your pardon, but I confess I only learned of your family's kind invitation minutes ago."

He smiled at her. "I thought as much. When my man of affairs did not receive a response to my invitation, I knew something was amiss. A fine lady, such as you, would not have neglected to acknowledge the invitation."

At the moment, Siusan didn't quite know if his comment was a compliment or jibe, and his expression gave no clue. "But Miss Gentree left several hours ago—early this morning."

"And when you were not with her, she was so very disappointed that I decided to come myself and do whatever I must to convince you to grace Clover Hall with your esteemed presence." He flashed a charming smile at her. Just then, he caught notice of the packed bag on her pallet and gestured to it. "I hope this means you have decided to accept our invitation, belated though its delivery may be?"

She nodded and smiled brightly at him. "Aye, my lord. I am greatly honored. For if not for your family, I would certainly be spending Michaelmas alone." Grabbing the leather handle, she whisked the bag from the pallet and carried it easily to the doorway, where she set it down before Lord Wentworth. She closed the door behind her and locked it with the turn of a key.

Lord Wentworth looked positively stunned that she had carried the bag so easily. "How very kind of you to offer assistance with my portmanteau." She rubbed her shoulder briskly. "I fear it is heavier than I realized. Already my arm is sore." She smiled demurely at him, feeling quite missish as she fluttered her lashes at him like a fan.

He hoisted the portmanteau. "We had best hurry, Miss Bonnet. The journey this evening is not a brief one, and the sky smells of snow."

"Snow? So soon as this?"

"The Avon is already crusting with ice." He gave her his arm, which she graciously accepted. A tingle swept through her body.

Had the circumstances been different, had the invitation to Clover Hall not been merely a convenient means of escape, how welcome a party at a country house would be. Especially with a devilishly handsome gentleman as host.

Though Lord Wentworth had thought to carry several blankets and an oilskin, with only the carriage header to protect them against the elements, Siusan was shivering within minutes. Freezing rain made travel treacherous and slow on the road toward Bristol, and already it was growing dark.

Though she knew it improper, for shared warmth, she moved closer to Lord Wentworth as he drove the phaeton. Drawing a blanket tightly around her shoulders, she buried her face in it to claim the warmth of her own breath.

Admittedly, her muslin dress was entirely inappropriate for severe weather. She was a Scot, and, aye, she did own a woolen cape, but in Town, a fashionable lady never wore more than a mantle, no matter the conditions. And, too, there was the fact that when she left London for Bath, she had had no notion she would be staying for more than a fortnight. Even if she had, this weather was extreme for autumn, and would have been even north in Edinburgh. But excuses for her dress were not going to keep her warm. Perhaps she ought write a lesson about extreme circumstances superseding fashion. A bone-deep shiver shook her body. Aye, she would write the lesson. Most definitely.

The horse's breath was white against the freezing twilight sky, and several times its hooves slipped on the ice-slickened road, causing it to falter.

"How much farther?" Siusan asked, hoping he would tell her Clover Hall was just a mile down the lane.

He sighed. "We've been driving nearly two hours, which would normally put us halfway."

"But the weather . . ." Siusan fought back a whimper.

"We are no more than a quarter of the way to Clover Hall, and with the worsening conditions, I honestly cannot gauge the length of our journey." He glanced across at her but quickly returned his gaze to the road. "We should never have left Bath this afternoon. I should have followed my instincts and insisted we remain in Bath until the storm passed. I am truly sorry, Miss Bonnet. I hope you will forgive me."

"Neither of us expected the weather to become extreme." Siusan felt her heart sink. "Should we . . . return to Bath?" She cursed her words. She had no place to stay were they to return. Nowhere to go.

He paused for a long while before replying. "I fear our only choice is to push on for another five miles or so and secure lodging at the Crux Inn . . . assuming there is a room to be let on such a needful night."

She shifted her numb knees beneath the blankets. A thin crust of ice crackled on the oilskin. She'd be frozen to his side in another rotation of the minute hand.

To her surprise, he passed her a flask of brandy. "Medicinal purposes. It will help warm you."

Unflinchingly, Siusan accepted it and took several draughts.

"No protests at all, eh?" Lord Wentworth chuckled.

"Lord Wentworth, ye're aware I am Scottish." Siusan played up her burr as the slightest bit of warmth flushed her cheeks. "And, I have four brothers, mind you."

"Four, eh?"

"Och, aye. And I understand the medicinal purposes of strong spirits quite weel." She smiled, but in the darkness, she knew he could not see her.

Freezing to death with a bachelor. What a lovely ending Mrs. Huddleston's columnist would have for his expository story about Miss Bonnet . . . more widely known as the scandalous Lady Siusan Sinclair.

Another shiver rattled her entire body.

Without a word, Lord Wentworth, most inadvisedly, took the reins into one hand and reached around her and pulled her closer to him.

She slipped her arm around his waist and snuggled against his chest. What did she care what the columnist or anyone else thought. They were alone in the middle of nowhere—freezing.

But he was warm. And caring.

And so ridiculously handsome. Siusan closed her eyes.

Driving snow spat in Sebastian's face. He squinted against the onslaught, desperately struggling to focus on the road. His entire body tensed.

Disaster flashed in Sebastian's mind. The carriage sliding from an icy bridge and plunging into the freezing stream below. His hands tangled in the reins, holding him just inches beneath the rushing surface. Water filling his mouth. His lungs burning. Drowning.

The tragic death of the fourth Duke of Exeter.

He blinked hard and shook his head. *No, no. There is no bridge for miles. Do not think such thoughts. Just watch the road. Slow the horse. All will be well.*

Miss Bonnet clung to him in her sleep. Her shivering had stopped, which he hoped meant she had warmed against his body, not simply fallen senseless from the cold, though he greatly feared the latter.

In the distance ahead, he could just make out the straight lines of a structure. He focused hard. Shook his head and tried to blink the snow from his lashes. There were no lights, but something was there. Shelter.

Rein in the horse.

His heart pounded with excitement, and he yanked hard on the reins. Too hard. The horse faltered, its front hooves slipping, failing to make purchase on the road. A cry screamed up from the beast as it began to fall.

The carriage lurched forward for an instant, then

jerked to the side, twisting as it overturned. The world seemed to slow as if in a dream—a nightmare. His body floated in the air for a moment, and he frantically reached out for Miss Bonnet, who was clinging to a hoop stick as the vehicle flipped.

He couldn't reach her. Couldn't help her.

He was on his back, but moving over lumpy terrain. His head was spinning as he ventured to open his eyes. He could see his legs and feet, dark forms against the snow, and realized he was being slowly dragged up a slope. Then, a wave of dizziness overwhelmed him, and he closed his eyes and gave in to the darkness once more.

When he opened his eyes again, he was no longer moving. He could hear the wind shrieking and howling its fury, but he was somehow protected from it.

"Och, you are awake now." Though he could not see her, he recognized Miss Bonnet's lilting voice. "You gave me quite a fright, you know. You ought to be thanking the heavens you were born a hardheaded Englishman. But I reckon you will be just fine."

"The carriage—" Sebastian was shaking with cold.

"Weel, it did not fare as well, I am afraid. I untethered the horse because her attempts to stand kept moving the carriage overtop of you. Once I freed her, she bolted across the road. I suppose that was a good sign. She seemed unhurt. Mayhap we can find her in the morning. Eh?"

He felt her fumbling at his clothes. He caught her hand, stilling it. "Cold."

"Aye, so I am. I am taking care of that, if you will permit me." He felt something against his mouth. "Drink a little of this. For medicinal purposes. Go on. There's not much left. I'll finish the last drops if you cannot. It will help us both *feel* a little warmer at least."

He released her hand and drank down what he could, then closed his eyes.

When he opened his eyes this time, he was no longer dizzy but was oddly disoriented. He didn't know where he was or why. All he knew was that he was naked. And that he wasn't alone.

The weight of several blankets . . . and a woman wrapped him in delicious warmth. He did not know who she was, or how they had come to be in some sort of corn crib or shed, unclothed, but he really didn't care at this moment. She felt too good lying half atop of him, pressed against him this way.

Beneath the blankets, he rode his hands down

the slope of her back and cupped his hands over the swells of her bottom. He pulled up, and she stirred in her sleep as he dragged her body over his. So soft.

As her full breasts crossed the crisp hair of his chest, her nipples hardened. The tiny curls between her legs caressed his shaft, and it twitched, awakening fully to her.

He raised a hand to her jaw and her mouth up to his and kissed her gently. A sleepy sigh of pleasure escaped her lips.

Sebastian rolled to his side, taking her along with him. He felt her lashes flutter. He brushed her hair from eyes and kissed her again. This time, she responded, and moved her lips over his.

God, how he wanted to touch every inch of her soft body.

He raised his hand and cupped her breast, letting his fingers linger over her ripe nipple. She moaned softly against his mouth, opening her own to him, allowing his tongue to slip inside.

This was maddening. He desired her—this woman he could not see, did not know—with a ferocity that startled him. He skimmed his hand down her body to the curls between her legs. His fingers grazed her moist folds, strumming her center.

She ran her fingers around the back of his neck, pulling him closer, his tongue deeper inside of the slickness of her mouth.

She was arching into his touch, pressing hard against his hand. He skimmed his thumb over her heat, then slipped his finger into her sheath, sliding it slowly in and out. She gasped, bearing down on it. He moved a second finger inside her, curling them slightly forward, easing them in and out, arousing her, making her so hot, so wet. Her gasp became a moan and she bucked against him.

He could not delay much longer. He needed to feel his cock deep within her.

Sebastian pressed her gently onto her back, breaking the bond of their mouths. He slid down inside their blanket cocoon until his mouth reached her breasts. He flicked her nipples, one after the other, with the tip of his tongue, before kissing a trail lower and lower still.

She did not stop him. Instead, she set her hand on his shoulder, pushing him lower. He thrilled at this and let himself imagine that her passion this night rivaled his own.

He centered his mouth over the bud between her swelling folds, sucking her, lashing her with his tongue as he pumped her with his fingers.

Her body arched and shook. Her body rocked as though she thrashed her head from side to side above. He knew he'd brought her so close. Just a moment more.

Her fingers scrabbled at his back. Frenetically, she hooked her fingers through his hair and pulled him upward. His forehead hit her ribs momentarily. Not hard at all, but as agonizing pain ripped through his head and shot down his spine, he gasped. Dizziness assailed him yet again, and, for moment, his body slumped atop her.

"Sebastian!" He felt her arms slip under his shoulders, gripping him. "Dear God, Sebastian, answer me, *please!*"

He tried to answer her. She sounded so frightened. *I am all right.* He said the words, heard them in his head, but he recognized nothing but the wind howling.

He couldn't move. He was stunned and began to worry that something was very, very wrong with him.

"Sebastian, *please*, say something."

He drew a deep breath and gradually felt his strength flowing back into him and a moment later, he slowly emerged from the blankets, blinking.

Though he stared in the direction of her face,

she was still cloaked in the icy darkness, but suddenly he really didn't need to see her face to know the truth.

He'd been so wrong. He *did* know this woman. How had he not realized this? Knew every curve beneath him. Knew her kiss. Her taste.

"Bloody hell. I *know* you. Don't I?"

Chapter 11

Diligence overcomes all difficulties, sloth makes them.
Benjamin Franklin

Siusan cringed the moment Lord Wentworth fell motionless atop her. How addlepated she was! In the throes of their passionate exchange, she had completely forgotten about his injury. He was hurt, and perhaps even dying for all she knew. Tears budded in her eyes.

Aye, he had *seemed* fully recovered. Strong. Willful. But he *had* received a substantial blow to his head, one hard enough to render him senseless. He had not bled, so far as she could tell in the darkness with only her fingertips to assess the seriousness of his injury, but a bump the size of quail's egg had risen just below his hairline. And, quite obviously, it was painful to the touch.

"I know you," he said weakly.

"I-I beg your pardon. What did you say?" Her words sounded too loud, so completely out of place in the intimacy of the previous moment. She decided to say nothing more. Instead, she looped her hands under his arms and carefully guided him higher as he moved toward her face. She listened for his breath.

His raised his head from her chest and held the position for some moments, and she knew he was looking at her intently, though he did not say a word. She gently placed her hands on the sides of his cheeks, angling his chin down so that she might kiss his forehead softly, just beside the bump. Calming. Soothing.

Again, she felt his chin lift. Felt his eyes burning down upon her even in the cold black of night.

"I *know* you." His voice was deep and husky, strained. Still unsure.

"Aye, you do." Confusion clouded Siusan's mind. He seemed to have recovered after the carriage crash, and yet something was very, very wrong.

"Though . . . I do not know your name." He leaned his face closer and nipped at her bottom lip.

Lack of her name didn't seem to reduce his passion. Now. However, she was sure something was dreadfully wrong. Siusan pressed up on his shoulder, straightening her arms like braces. A flood of icy air flowed between then, stinging the moistness between her spread thighs. "Aye, you do know me, my lord, but my name is unknown to you? Can you not remember?" Her temples throbbed with concern. *Dear God*.

"I remember *you*. I remember everything about you." She heard him swallow. Was he beginning to realize the inconsistency too? "I remember everything, except your name. Though, I never knew it, did I?"

Were it light, he would have seen Siusan's eyes widen in shock until they stung. She wasn't sure if he was being nonsensical, or if somehow he had learned that in truth her name was not Miss Bonnet.

Gooseflesh prickled his skin, and he began to shiver violently. Siusan bent her arms and drew him back to her, nestling him against her skin and tightening the blankets around them both.

The moment he was pressed to her, it was as though nothing had changed. He began kissing her throat, and he wedged a hand beneath her in the small of her back. She felt his hardened sex pressing against her belly. Felt him move his hips lower, seeking and finding the damp folds between her legs.

She wanted him, this much was true, but not now. Hot tears sprang up in her eyes. She hadn't the brandy to blame for her wanton behavior this time. She hadn't had more than a few nips, only enough to make her feel a little warmer.

She could not even blame her lust on missing Simon. Now that she really pondered it, since the moment Lord Wentworth came to Bath, she hadn't even considered her late fiancé. Och, she was as sinful as everyone claimed.

There was nothing to blame except herself—her weak, smitten-with-Lord-Wentworth self, nothing more. All it took was to feel his naked, muscled body against hers, and she ached for him. Urgently wanted to feel him inside her, moving, pleasing, claiming her, no matter the circumstance.

And she thought he felt the same thing for her.

Apparently, he did. She felt his sex twitch, waiting for her to spread her knees wider. To invite him deep into her sheath. It was clear he wanted her.

Och, this was all so wrong. He'd hit his head and was not in his right mind. "Aye, I want you too. But not like this. Not when you do not even know my—" She closed her mouth and, instead of speaking, caressed his cheek, soothing him, whispering hushing sounds in his ear. "You only need my warmth. We need each other's heat to-night. That is all." She guided his head to rest in the crook of her neck and shoulder, then wrapped her arms around him. "Go to sleep, my love," she whispered, belatedly startled by her own words.

My love. Where had that come from? Even in the chill night, she felt hot blood rise into her cheeks.

"Go to sleep. All will be well in the morning."

She felt him nod, his muscles relax, but his hand moved over her breast and rested there. Maddeningly, his erect sex remained poised at her moist opening. And in that position, he drifted off to sleep. She tried to nudge him back, just a bit, but he moved back into place.

Oh, good God. There would be no more sleep for her. Not as aroused as he'd made her, not with him touching her so intimately even now.

Nay, there'd likely be no rest for the wicked this night.

The light cutting through the plank walls of where Sebastian found himself was glaringly white and sparkling in the morning sun. He closed his eyes again. *Too bright.* And, damn, how his head throbbed.

He moved his hand to bring it to his eyes, when he felt something warm and soft beneath it give and pebble as the icy air touched it. He opened his eyes to mere slits and gazed across pale smooth skin. A breast. His face was wedged against a long neck, and, from the welcoming, familiar sensation, he was lying between a woman's silken thighs.

Sebastian leaned up just enough to look at his partner's face. *Hell's blazes!* His eyes widened as he realized the identity of the naked woman beneath him. He rolled to his side and from the blankets and staggered to his feet. "Miss Bonnet!"

She brushed her long ebony locks from her face and lazily peered up him, but within an instant her eyes were wide. "Och, thank heaven you remember me and are well. I was so worried about you last night after the accident."

Sebastian blinked again. He raised his fingers to his pounding temples. Dark images flashed in his mind. Being dragged up a hill. A voice in the darkness, soothing him. His clothes being removed. At the thought, he glanced down at his naked body and shivered uncontrollably. He was standing before Miss Bonnet without a stitch of clothing.

"Unless you prefer to freeze, I think it best you come back under the blankets while we discuss all that happened."

"But Miss Bonnet, I am naked. We cannot—"

Siusan laughed. "Dear sir, I am naked as well, as we were all through the night—sharing our warmth. Our clothes were wet and covered with ice. We would have died if I had not acted logically and removed them." She gestured to their clothing piled in a heap a few feet away.

Sebastian turned and snatched up his trousers, but they were stiff as the plank walls. Casting them aside, he paced, fiercely shaking with cold. He had to think. What the hell had happened?

"We were too cold. Warmth was necessary for our survival. You were injured. I will think no less of you if you return to the warmth of the blankets . . . I will not look upon your body, and you need not gaze upon mine. But if you continue to pace, I shall be forced to stand against you, for my own warmth is quickly waning."

He started for the blankets but stopped abruptly, recalling the position of his body when he awoke. "Forgive, Miss Bonnet, but I must know. Did we . . . that is to say did I—" He covered his penis with his hands.

"Make love?" Miss Bonnet's face betrayed nothing. She sat fully upright, and the edge of the blankets fell to her lap revealing a pale, full breast. She nonchalantly covered herself. "Nay." She reached a hand to him. "Come, let us stay warm while we think of a solution to our very grave problem."

Still he resisted.

"Come now, Lord Wentworth, I would not have imagined you to be so concerned with propriety that you would rather lose your . . . extremities to the frost than to share my warmth."

"Propriety is not my concern." Not quite. His concern was more of humiliating himself the moment his body touched hers with a hard, bouncing cock. Standing there, the cold would prevent embarrassment.

Fine granules of snow seeped in between gaps in the lowest two feet of the planks. The air was so cold he could not draw enough of it into his lungs. No one would be coming for them in so much snow, in such freezing weather. Miss Bonnet was right. They would have to come up with their own solution, and quickly.

He started toward her. Miss Bonnet lifted the blankets, exposing her own porcelain body to him, as he climbed underneath. Without delay, she rolled against him, and, instinctively, his body pressed tightly against hers.

After several minutes, his shivering had subsided. His teeth no longer chattered. But without the cold, he was now forced to fight with everything he was not to react to the soft, warm body pressed so intimately against him. He had to ignore the feel of her nipples hardening the second his cold chest pressed against her breasts. Pretend that the curls between her legs were not tickling his cock.

How long, though, would the remnant cold mask his desire? How long could he rein in his body's fierce arousal when all he could think about was sinking deep into her ultimate warmth?

"Who would have ever imagined this?" Miss Bonnet said softly, moving her arm tighter around Sebastian's body, pressing her full breasts against his side.

"What? Do not tell me you never imagined this." His mouth twitched in want of a smile. "I know I have."

"Och, well to be truthful, I have to admit, during the drive from Bath, I considered it many times," she admitted.

Sebastian tensed. He had been only teasing her with his question. And yet, she admitted it without reserve. "Not until we left Bath, did you have . . . this thought?"

"Och, good heavens, nay," she replied as if the notion was distasteful. "Why would I?" She raised her thigh higher over his legs.

He squeezed his eyes shut. How could he endure this sweet torture any longer?

"I confess," she added, "we were hardly three miles from Bath when I first imagined the risk of freezing to death."

Sebastian opened his eyes and could not restrain the chuckle welling up inside of him.

Miss Bonnet leaned up and peered at his face. "You were speaking of freezing, were you not?"

Sebastian schooled his features. "Of course, I was."

Miss Bonnet turned to lie down again, pausing briefly as she did so. "I only wondered because of your . . . tent." She glanced down, and he followed her gaze.

Gorblimey. His engorged cock was standing straight out from his body beneath the blankets . . . exactly like a tent pole. "I beg your pardon, Miss Bonnet." He swallowed. "It is morning."

"Oh, is that it?" He glimpsed a smile on her

mouth as she lay down on her side, this time with her back against him. "I thought you fancied me."

"Well, I . . . um . . . I—" Yes, he did, but she was his ward's teacher. He could hardly admit that he would like nothing more than to bury himself inside of her that very moment.

"It is still very early. I think it advisable if we sleep for a while and store our strength. The sun will surely warm the air, and perhaps we can venture from our blankets then and figure out some means for rescue."

"Very good, Miss Bonnet." Sebastian closed his eyes, but his wicked mind imagined her full breasts bouncing as he thrust into her.

That image made him harder still, the skin of his shaft stretched painfully taut. He could not lie there, beside her like that. He needed to stop this throbbing ache, and yet he could not seek relief.

Withdrawing his hand from the warmth, he angrily palmed his erection down through the blankets. A pained gasp hissed through his clenched teeth.

Miss Bonnet rolled over, facing him again. He hurriedly slid his hand from his erection and held his breath, willing it to relent. "I beg your pardon."

Suddenly, he felt her soft hand move beneath the

blankets and grip his member. His eyes flashed open, and he saw that she was looking intently into his eyes.

"Miss Bonnet—"

"Siusan." Her hand slid down to his base, then back up, palming then ringing his crown. "The morning had nothing to do with this. But I did." Her hand tightened around his shaft and mercifully pumped him twice, three times.

Damn it all, this is worse. It only made him want to have her more.

She looked up at him, moistening her lips with her tongue as she continued to move her hand.

"Siusan, I want to—-oh, Christ." He cupped her face in both hands and angled her mouth to his, kissing her harder than he meant to.

When he lifted his mouth from hers, she pressed her lips down upon his, resuming their kiss. Ringing his crown with her fingers, she concentrated her touch, her movements, *there.* Bloody hell, he could not take it any longer.

He turned and rolled on top of her, making her release him. Sebastian wedged his knees between her thighs as he pinned her with his gaze. "I need you, Siusan. I have to be with you. *Now.*"

She stared back into his eyes, then cupped his cheeks and kissed his lips with a stirring passion that matched his own. Her thighs opened wider, and she wriggled lower, until his marble-hard erection touched her moistness.

He thrust into her, burying himself to the hilt. Gasping with pleasure, she spasmed and jerked, her body tightened with passionate force around him. He pumped into her, lost in the pleasure of her softness, of her scorching heat.

Slipping his hand between them, his circled her core, sending her into a fierce, bucking climax. He circled again, quieting her moan with his mouth.

She nipped at his lips as she clutched him to her, urging him forward.

Semen welled at his base. He tried to pull back, but Siusan wrapped her legs around his back and held tight. "No!"

But it was too late.

He pounded deep into her sheath. He pumped forcefully into her, then collapsed atop her, panting.

His head was throbbing again from the exertion, but as his heart slowed, somewhere in the recesses of his mind he recalled the one other time in his life when he hadn't been able to stop. Hadn't wanted to.

Soft, silken thighs wrapping around his back, holding him inside of her.

Devil take me. The library. The night of the gala.

Could she be the woman he'd been searching for these weeks?

He lifted his head and gazed down into Miss Bonnet's drowsy eyes. "Siusan," he whispered. "Who are you—really?"

Chapter 12

Siusan shuddered inwardly. Somehow, Lord Wentworth had realized she was not the person she claimed to be. Thankfully, though, he hadn't yet discovered that she was Lady Siusan Sinclair . . . hiding in Bath to avoid crossing paths with another man, the Duke of Exeter.

How long could she conceal this? Word of her world in London had already come creeping into Bath in the guise of an *on-dit* columnist. Already her untrustworthy employer knew too much, enough to force Siusan into leaving Bath the instant she returned from Clover Hall.

That is, if they ever arrived at all.

"I am Siusan, your ward's teacher." She reached out and caressed his forehead, carefully avoiding the red-and-blue bump at his hairline. "I fear your injury is looking worse. Does your head ache? Are you feeling light-headed or nauseous? How do you feel, Lord Wentworth?"

He caught her wrist and drew it from his head. "Call me Sebastian. After all we have been through together, rattling titles seems wholly unnatural."

She blinked at him, worried that he would assail her with another string of questions.

He lowered his head. "I am sorry, Miss Bonnet . . . Siusan. I know this cannot make sense to you. Memories, like flashes of lightning, keep appearing in my head, and I cannot ignore them."

Siusan shifted against him, gulping back the ball of nerves rising in her throat. "W-what sort of memories? And, are you sure that is what they are? Perhaps they are glimpses of dreams. You were struck in the head with such force that you lost your senses for a long while."

"They are not dreams. The flashes are real. I do not know how I know, but I do." He gazed upon her. "You and I were making love."

"Aye." She turned her gaze away, feeling somewhat embarrassed. "Well, we . . . did."

"I do not mean now—*before*." He turned her face toward him, forcing her to meet his gaze. "Shards of memories keep coming back. Not always visions. Physical sensations. Emotions. I know you cannot understand this."

"Sebastian." Siusan's cheeks heated. "When you awoke this morning, lying with me as you were, you asked me if we made love."

"And you told me we had not." His eyes began to squint with growing confusion.

"I was not being entirely truthful." She bit into her lower lip. "During the night, we touched, kissed, caressed each other most intimately. And, we very nearly made love. I do not know why. It was as though we were driven to do it. Aye, we were unclothed, but what compelled us went far deeper than that."

"You are right. Though I cannot explain why we were so driven."

"We were nearly frozen to death." Siusan angled her face to look at Sebastian. "I believe it was because we both feared death . . . and were grasping for life. Does that make sense to you?"

"Indeed, it does." Sebastian pondered her theory for a moment more. "Several members of my family died unexpectedly, tragically." He stared upward, instead of at her, his eyes blank as though lost in memories of the past. "Their deaths . . . well, they changed my life in ways you cannot imagine."

Siusan's head lolled back, and she peered upward too. "My mother died when I was but a wee lass. And in a blink, nothing was ever the same again. So, aye, I do understand what you mean." She turned her head to the side to look at him. "As the reality of death loomed over us, we had to fight it. What is more life-affirming than making love?"

He turned his head to look at her, caressing her cheek with the tips of his fingers. "Siusan, when we made love moments ago, it had nothing to do with fear of death." A trace of a smile touched his lips. "It was undeniable attraction. Passion. Emotion. *Need*." Suddenly, the smile fell away, and his eyes widened as if something occurred to him. "Before, when we were about to make love, why did we stop? You didn't mention why."

Shame forced Siusan to bow her head against his chest. "I stopped you . . . the moment I realized you did not know who I was. I knew then that you had not recovered from the blow even though you were conscious and lively."

He turned her face to his. It was different when he stared into her eyes then. Almost as though he was seeing her in a new shaft of light.

"I will tell you the truth." She swallowed deeply before making her admission. "I wanted to be with you, Sebastian, wanton as this may sound to you."

Still he said nothing, but only peered intently at her.

Siusan knew there was no need to lie any longer. She had shamed herself freely and should admit it in the same manner. "Though we constantly argue, and can agree on nothing at all, I have felt a great esteem for you since the moment we met at the Upper Rooms. I daren't attempt to explain an attraction of such strength."

"Siusan . . . there is something more. Something that greatly confuses me." Sebastian set his large hand on her shoulder and drew her tight against him. He didn't say anything more for a long while. "When I said we had made love before . . . I . . . damn it all . . . this cannot be and will sound totally daft to you, but I must say it."

Siusan turned her head on his shoulder, drawing back on his muscled biceps to see his face more fully.

"Over a month ago, I made love to a woman

in London during a gala. It was dark, and I was foxed, and had mistaken her for someone else."

Christ above! Siusan tensed, and her heart thudded as fast as a bird's. *This cannot be! Oh, dear God, help me!*

"I have been searching for her since that night, knowing nothing more than that she was a Scot and had ebony hair. Like yours." He eased his head to the side and peered intently. "Siusan, my hands know you. My body knows you."

"W-what are you saying . . . Sebastian?" She was petrified of what he would say next. Of what each additional word he spoke was informing her, not so much about her identity but confirming his own. *Oh God.*

"That I do not know how Providence led me to you in Bath, or why, but I believe with every fiber of my being, that you, Miss Bonnet, were the innocent I bedded in the library during the gala."

Her heart pounded in her ears, and she could scarcely breathe. Siusan felt as if she didn't run, her lungs would burst from lack of air.

How had this happened? She had fled from London only to fall into his arms. To disgrace herself yet again. Lud, her father would never forgive her for this. *Never!*

"Siusan, Miss Bonnet. I beg you to forgive me

for pretending I was someone else. Truth is very important to me, and yet these past weeks I have found myself being less than truthful again and again. I even lied to you, at least by omission."

Siusan looked away from him, wanting truly to hide her head beneath the blankets. He spoke of lying, and yet his deception could never match her own. Since she had arrived in Bath, lying had become second nature to her.

"While it is true that I am the Marquess of Wentworth, a title I gained only recently, that is only my secondary title, inherited with my real title when my brother died a few months ago." He slipped a hand from the blankets and ran his fingers through his hair. "I had my reasons for not revealing myself, none of which had to do with you. Still, I must offer you my confession now." He paused a long while, drawing in deep inhalations of breath, as if summoning the courage to admit to her what she already knew.

She held her breath. *Please do not say it. Please do not let this be true.*

"Siusan, in truth, I am Sebastian Beaufort, the Duke of Exeter."

Dear heavens. She had wanted to believe that she was fitting the pieces of his memories together incorrectly, but now there was no more pretending. Her heart slammed against her ribs, and she was sure he could hear its pounding.

She had no other recourse. She peered blankly back at the duke and feigned ignorance. He resolutely believed her to be the woman he bedded during his gala. That much was clear, but he still did not know that her name was not Miss Bonnet.

Though, if Mrs. Huddleston was correct, and an *on-dit* columnist was already snooping about, he and everyone else in Bath would learn of her true identity within days—if not sooner.

"I do not know how to respond, Your Grace," she muttered. Truly, she didn't.

"I know you do not." He slid from the blankets and hurried to their frozen clothing. "I reviewed my grandmother's guest list more times than I care to imagine, and I am fairly certain there was no Miss Bonnet upon it."

"Of that, Your Grace, I am already sure."

"As I said, I know this is all confusing to you, but I know what I feel." He turned around, leaving his hard, muscled body silhouetted, edged by a thread of white light coming through the plank walls.

Siusan squeezed her eyes tightly closed. Even knowing what she did now about his identity, her body still yearned for his.

"And, you agreed to call me Sebastian." He smiled at her, wincing slightly as his brow lifted.

"And I am Siusan—even in the daylight." She returned his bright smile as he carried the clothing back to their cocoon and began laying it out beneath the top layer of oilskin. "What are you doing?"

"Our clothing is only ice-slicked. Once that melts, it will not take long for everything to dry. We just need to keep shifting things between the oilskin tarp and hope the wetness is not sufficient to soak through the blankets to our skin."

"Of course. How did I not think of this?"

"You, my beauty, were too busy saving me and keeping me alive." He winked at her, then grinned.

How she wished she could admit everything to him. But that was impossible. The moment he learned that she was Lady Siusan Sinclair, she would be at risk of being cast from her family forever. And being without her brothers and sisters was something she could not bear. They were everything to her. Together they were strong. Unlike everyone else, their love was unconditional, and they would never leave her vulnerable and broken as her parents and Simon had.

Nay, if she and the duke ever escaped their ice shed, she would have to leave him before he learned her identity. There was no other choice. She had to leave before he left her—as he surely would, once he knew the real Siusan.

They'd spent the rest of the morning looking around the corn crib for any means to make a fire. They tried rubbing broken planks over straw, striking two nails together to create a spark, but their efforts were fruitless and left them shivering and fatigued. They hurriedly retreated to the blanket cocoon until their shaking stopped.

By midafternoon, judging from the position of the sun slanting through the planks, Sebastian and Siusan donned their damp shoes and the top oilskin tarp to venture outside the corn crib with an idea to collect enough snow to quench their parched mouths.

As they opened the door, the frigid blast slammed their chests with the force of a charging bull, making them gasp for air.

"We cannot stay outside for more than a few moments." Sebastian folded the edge of the tarp they held around them into a pocket. "Put what snow you can inside. Hurry."

Only Siusan couldn't move. She just stared. More than two feet of snow blanketed the world outside, and had the broken carriage not jutted like a great black boulder from the white drifts, they could not have guessed that there was a road nearby. The backs of her eyes began to sting.

The air was bitingly cold, but the sky was a clear blue, and the sun was bright. Still, the snow showed no signs of melting. She could see no chance of rescue for several days at the very least.

They would not survive for that long.

"Do not worry, Siusan." Beneath the blankets, Sebastian tightened his grip around her shoulder, trying to reassure her. "The sun is strong, and in a day or two, enough of the snow will have melted enough to allow a carriage or a rider to pass through." Though Sebastian managed a slight smile, she could see that the doubt in his eyes matched her own. "Come now. Scoop up a couple handfuls of snow and let us hurry back to the shed."

To their dismay, it was still too cold inside the corn crib for the snow to melt. They tried letting bites of snow melt in their mouths, but after a few minutes they had swallowed only droplets of water, and their bodies had begun to shake again.

Sebastian reached for a husk of dried corn to fill their aching bellies, but the corn was inedible, and even the task of chewing the dried corn exhausted them. By twilight, they could hardly move.

"I heard a h-h-horse." Siusan's words were starting to slur. He pulled her closer and rubbed her body vigorously. Her skin had been cold since they ventured outside, and even though they been together beneath the blankets for hours, she wasn't getting any warmer.

"Hush now, love, it is only the wind." He folded back the top blanket from himself and doubled it over her. "I am sure of it."

"Nay, I heard it clear—clear . . . the horse is near . . ." Her voice trailed off.

Damn it to hell! He had to do something. She was going to die of the cold if he didn't think of some way to get them out of there—and quickly.

It was night when the whinny of the horse woke her. She slid from their blankets, careful not to wake Sebastian, and pulled her clothing from beneath the upper layer of the blanket pile atop them.

Her petticoat and gown were very nearly dry.

She pulled on her stockings, which felt heavenly against her cold legs, then her walking boots. Flinging her pretty mantle around her shoulders, she bent and picked up a handful of dried corn for the horse and walked out into the night, looking, knowing it was near.

She trudged through the knee-deep snow around the corn crib, clicking her tongue and calling out soothingly to the horse.

And there it was. She stilled. The white mare gleamed like the snow in the moonlight. She held out her hand to it, showing the mare the corn. "Come now. This has been hard for you, has it not?" She clicked her tongue again. She rolled the corn around in her hand, hoping the horse would notice it. "Here you go. I know you are hungry." The horse came forward and nibbled the corn from her hand, its bit clinking in its mouth.

She eased her fingers around its bridle and started to guide the horse toward the corn crib, when in the distance, she thought . . . nay, nay, she was sure of it . . . she glimpsed a dull light. She stared until her eyes watered.

Siusan ran her hand down the horse's neck, following the thread of the long carriage reins from its bridle to the snow.

She was shivering again, but the light she saw

was not so far away. It could not be. She could
ride the horse astride and reach the light in less
than half of an hour. She could.

And they would be rescued.

She looked back at the corn crib, thinking to
wake Sebastian before she attempted this, but
quickly rejected the idea. He would only demand
that he ride himself. He, injured from the wreck
of the carriage. Nay, she would do it. She must.
And when he was rescued, he would thank her
for thinking of him.

Siusan held the reins in her teeth and grabbed
the horse's mane and jumped up, trying to balance so that she could throw her leg over its back.
But she was too weak. She tried again, falling
back into the snow.

In the moonlight, she could just make out the
side of the carriage jutting from the snow. A
mounting stool, or at least she could use it as one.
"Come, horse. This way." She would use the carriage to boost herself onto the horse's back.

By the time she reached the carriage, she had fallen
three times, and her skirts and back were sodden
with icy snow. She walked around the turned carriage, trying to assess where she might best step up
and mount the horse, when she noticed the edge of
her portmanteau poking up through the snow. She

led the horse to it, tying the reins to the spoke of the broken wheel as she tugged the bag from the snow and opened it.

Inside was a single change of clothing, cold but dry, a brush, her reticule, and her lesson book of notes. She decided to take the bag with her.

Her hands were completely numb and shaking as she fumbled to tie the bag around her waist, using knotted woolen stockings.

The weight made it even more difficult to hoist herself onto the horse, but finally her foot managed to remain solid on the carriage footboard, tilted as it was, and she flung her leg over the horse's broad back.

It had taken more than a quarter of an hour, and her teeth were chattering so fiercely that her felt as though her skull were rattling too.

Still, she had done it. She was riding toward the light. Dizziness and snowdrifts hampered her progress, and, once or twice, she was almost sure the light was moving away from her. She told herself it was an illusion, a trick of the eyes.

She would reach the light. She would.

And Sebastian would be rescued.

She would not stop, no matter how cold she was, until she was sure he would be safe.

* * *

When Sebastian awoke the next morning, he felt
frozen through. Worse, Siusan was nowhere to be
seen. He told himself that she'd probably gone to
collect some snow, or take care of nature, but when
she did not return after a few minutes, he realized
something was wrong. "Siusan?" He paced the
interior of the corn crib, calling her name repeat-
edly through the gaps between the planks. If she
was nearby at all, she should have heard him.

And then he noticed that her clothing was
missing. His heart skipped a beat. "Bloody hell,
Siusan!" In her delirium, she'd probably gone
looking for that damned horse!

Sebastian threw on his chilled clothes and coat.
They were still damp and had retained the cold
of the night, but they would give him some protection. She could not have gone far.

The sun was still low in the sky, working its
way to its noon perch, making her tracks in the
snow difficult to see. He squinted in the light and
followed the snow wake left by her skirts around
the corn crib. There, his gaze fixed on the tracks of
a horse. "I'll be damned."

She had heard a horse after all. It made sense
that the carriage horse would return after being
spooked during the accident. Why hadn't he believed her?

But Siusan's tracks and those left by the horse were running parallel to one another, confusing him. They did not return to the crib, and it was evident that Siusan was not riding the horse. Instead, it seemed she had led the horse down the slope to the wrecked carriage. He trudged down the slope to the overturned phaeton.

Her tracks ringed the carriage, as if she was looking for something, but then, she eventually mounted the horse, for only one set of tracks set out over the next ridge.

"Siusan!" he called out. "Siusan!" *Damn it all.* Why didn't she stay to the road, as best she could see it? She wasn't in her right mind, he reminded himself, and she had no idea where she was going.

Sebastian paused to listen for any reply. He held his breath, warming it in his lungs before calling out for her again.

He listened again, and he thought he heard the jingling of bridles, followed by rumbling.

"Ho, there!" came a male voice from up the road. "Might you be the Duke of Exeter?" Something was coming over the rise. He could see it now. A farmer atop a dray being pulled by two strong plow horses.

Sebastian raised his hand and tried to call out, but instead a hail of coughs exploded from his lungs. He crumpled forward, fighting to catch his breath.

"Are you injured?" the farmer called out to him.

"I am fair enough, but Miss Bonnet—I fear she's out there." He feebly pointed to the ridge beyond. "Tracks."

"She was, indeed. Made it as far as the Smithsons' last eve." The farmer reined the horses in and stopped the dray just a stride away from Sebastian.

"And is she well?" Sebastian tried to step out of the hole he'd made when he fell forward, but he did not have the strength. "I need you to take me to her. I must see her."

"Well, I have no notion how she is today. Heard she was near frozen through by time she reached the barn. That's where they found her. Sleeping. She'd strapped herself around the horse."

"She will be all right, will she not?" Sebastian searched the farmer's eyes for any hint.

"Honestly, Your Grace, I don't really know." The farmer hitched his team to the carriage wheel, rushed to Sebastian, and pulled him from the snowdrift. "We've got to get you warm. I've got blankets on the dray. It's about the only way to get around with all of this snow. Too deep for a cart or even a sleigh."

"I need to see h-her." Sebastian reached out for the older man's sleeve.

"I am afraid I cannot oblige, Your Grace. The surgeon, Ferguson, is waiting for you at the Crux Inn. I've got my orders to deliver you directly to him."

Though he wanted to argue, say anything to convince the farmer to take him to Siusan first, the moment Sebastian was settled onto the dray, his world fell into darkness.

Chapter 13

Periods of wholesome laziness, after days of energetic effort, will wonderfully tone up the mind and body.
Grenville Kleiser

Two days later

et me go to her," Sebastian demanded. "You did not see her the night she ventured into the snow. She was cold, delirious, I could hardly understand her when she spoke."

The surgeon shook his head and leaned his chair back against the wall so that it balanced on its two hind legs. "I am being paid a goodly sum to see you well again. You were asleep for nearly two days. I'll not risk the coin nor your health by letting you leave just yet." He leaned forward and allowed the chair to return to the floor. "And in case you've got some idea about leaving anyway, I should inform you that I've got a man outside the door . . . for your protection, Your Grace."

Sebastian clenched his fists beneath his blankets. He was still very weak, but the lump on his head was no more than a large blue-and-yellow contusion. The surgeon had told him he was no longer in any danger of dying.

He *was* leaving. That very moment.

Sebastian sat up straight and threw his legs over the edge of the mattress. "Tell me where she is. No one can stop me. I am going to her." A wave of dizziness washed over him, preventing him from standing. But he was fine. He was sure of it. Rose too quickly, that was all.

Just then, the door to the bedchamber opened and Sebastian's grandmother charged inside and set her hand on his shoulder. She pressed him back to his pillow. "What is this, Sebastian? You need your rest."

"I have to go to her." He'd wait a minute more, then try to stand again. "I have to let her know I am well—and I have to see for myself that she is too."

"Dear boy, I visited her last night. She is very weak, as you are, but I assure you that her mind and body are sound." She nodded at Ferguson, who lifted Sebastian's legs and guided them back under the blankets.

"Miss Bonnet knows you are well, dear, and she is very relieved. She wept when I informed her of this." His grandmother's eyes too seemed to well as she recounted the story.

Sebastian slid his legs under the covers and laid his head back against the feather pillow. "Thank God."

"You may, but if you do not mind, I have already thanked Miss Bonnet." His grandmother took her hand in his. "What she did was foolish and dangerous, but had she not possessed the courage to venture out into the night in search of the horse, the two of you would have surely been dead by nightfall."

"I should have been the one." Sebastian lowered his head. Why did he not wake when she left? He should have heard her. Should have stopped her. If he actually believed the horse was near, *he* would have gone.

"No, you were injured, far worse than you knew." A funny little smile lifted her lips then. "She is bold and courageous, and yes, unyielding in her beliefs, but kind and generous with her students, according to Gemma. Your niece adores Miss Bonnet. And, though I have only met her once, I believe I would be very pleased if you were to marry a woman as honest, intelligent, capable, and respectable as Miss Bonnet."

Sebastian returned her smile. All day, he'd been thinking the very same thing. Siusan was everything his grandmother would expect in the bride of the Duke of Exeter. But she was also extraordinarily passionate, desirable . . . and Christ, the way she made him feel when she touched him. Well, she was everything the duke would want in a wife as well.

"Now, I've sent for my carriage. I would prefer that you convalesce at Clover Hall, rather than this straw-bedded, crowded . . . what is it called, the Crux Inn?"

"I must see Miss Bonnet first." Sebastian started from the bed again.

His grandmother chuckled. She sat down in the chair beside the bed. "I thought as much, which is why I have also sent a hackney to collect Miss Bonnet from the farmhouse where she is staying. The hackney will bring her within an hour or two; then we will all travel to Clover Hall together, so you both may recover in warmth and comfort. I owe the dear lady my grandson's life, after all. Sleep well, dear boy. We'll leave just after noon."

A relieved smile eased across Sebastian's mouth as his grandmother rose, and she and the surgeon quit the room, leaving him alone. Sebastian collapsed against the mattress and closed his eyes to sleep for a spell, knowing that, when he awoke, he would be with Siusan again.

Three days later

Siusan had had to forfeit half the coins in her reticule to convince the hackney driver to convey her from the Smithsons' farmhouse to Bath, rather than a few miles down the road to the Crux Inn. The snow on the road had melted to a drivable level, and the driver was eager, after losing several days of pay, to such accept a generous fare.

To ease Sebastian's mind, she left a letter with Mrs. Smithson for him, thanking both him and his grandmother for the kind invitation to Clover Hall, but that overnight she had regained her strength and since the school holiday was at an end, she felt it her duty to return to her teaching responsibilities at Mrs. Huddleston's School of Virtues.

Nay, her reasons for leaving were not those, but her need to put as many miles between herself and the Duke of Exeter demanded that she take advantage of this chance to escape.

Because the snow made travel difficult in Somerset's outlying areas, most of the students still had not returned to school after the Michaelmas break, including Miss Gentree. Classes were officially canceled, and what few girls had managed the trek through the snow to Mrs. Huddleston's School of Virtues were content to simply spend their days reading and chatting with each other.

To Siusan's great surprise, instead of printing her lesson on arranging greenery for the holiday table, the *Bath Times* had instead included a story about the near-fatal carriage accident involving Miss Bonnet and Lord Wentworth. This prompted a number of readers to pen letters to Miss Bonnet, in care of the school, wishing her a rapid recovery and a continuation of her lessons in the newspaper.

Mrs. Huddleston had shoved a massive basketful of these letters into Siusan's hand as she entered the school and advised her that if she desired, she would be permitted to craft her lessons from her bedchamber for the next week.

There was no further word about her threat to expose Siusan's true identity to the *on-dit* columnist. In fact, except for meeting her at the school's front door, Siusan had not seen Mrs. Huddleston. This worried Siusan considerably, for the old woman could not be trusted and was likely out and about investigating the most secret connection between Siusan and the Duke of Exeter. After all, the more interesting her story, the more the *on-dit* columnist might be willing to pay.

Nay, Siusan knew she had much to do and a limited amount of time to do it.

Her first task was to write a letter to Priscilla, telling her all that had occurred between her and the Marquess of Wentworth. Since he was in truth the Duke of Exeter, she had no choice but secretly to leave Bath for London on the Thursday mail coach.

Now that she knew that the Duke of Exeter was recovering at Clover Hall, it would only be a matter of time before he was well enough to escort Miss Gentree to Bath and call upon her at the school.

It was time she knew she did not possess, for Mrs. Huddleston and her columnist were sure to accost her soon enough and reveal to everyone that Miss Bonnet was in truth Lady Siusan Sinclair. Why they had not yet approached her was likely only a matter of the great outpouring of public concern over Bath's etiquette-teaching heroine's near-fatal accident. They were simply biding their time.

Suddenly, her bedchamber door pushed open, and the Misses Grassley and Hopkins rushed inside.

"We heard you were arrived." Miss Hopkins's eyes studied the whole of her critically. "The newspaper said you had nearly died but that you had miraculously recovered after taking Mrs. Smithson's chicken-and-leek soup."

Siusan almost laughed, but guessed that having something inside her stomach had helped her regain her strength, and it was the first bit of sustenance she had been able to keep down. "Aye, it is a recipe every lady should have in her kitchen in the event of illness. I should write to her and request the ingredients."

The two younger women nodded enthusiastically. But there was something more going on. She could see it in their faces. They were bursting with some sort of news.

"All right, what is it? What has happened?" Siusan raised her eyebrows and waited.

Miss Grassley exploded with joyful laughter. "I am getting married!" She squealed like she was one of the students rather than an instructor.

"Married?" Siusan stared at her in disbelief. "But you never leave the school? How?"

Miss Hopkins giggled into her hand, then nudged Miss Grassley. "Tell her. Tell Miss Bonnet that your engagement is all thanks to her."

Oh dear. "Thanks to me?" Siusan gripped Miss Grassley's upper arms. "Do tell."

"While it is true, Mrs. Huddleston does not permit us to leave the school, she has allowed us to chaperone lecture tours with you on several occasions."

Siusan nodded. She could see where this path was taking them, and Mrs. Huddleston would not be pleased when she heard of losing another teacher to marriage.

"Mr. Bolten is a waiter at the tea garden. I met him first when your class took tea there. We started exchanging letters the very next day. We began making arrangements for him to be outside the draper's, or along Trim Street when the class was shopping. Everywhere. And . . . and, well, we fell in love!" She squealed again.

"So q-quickly?" Siusan opened her mouth to expound about the improbability of falling in love in such a short period, but then realized how ridiculous her argument was—because, in truth, she had no argument. Though she hadn't known it at the time, she had fallen in love with Sebastian the very moment they encountered each other.

"And then," Miss Grassley added, "over Michaelmas, he offered for me, and my father accepted!"

Miss Hopkins giggled with excitement. Siusan cupped a hand over her mouth.

"Congratulations, Miss Grassley! I am so happy for you both." She pressed a quick hug to the young teacher, then straightened her arms. "Does Mrs. Huddleston know of this yet?" Siusan stared into Miss Grassley's eyes with all seriousness.

"Not yet, but I will have to inform her. We are to be married at Christmas."

"Whatever you do, please do not inform her just yet." Siusan couldn't tell her that the reason was that *she* was leaving in two days, and Mrs. Huddleston might very well lock the doors from the outside if she knew even one teacher was contemplating leaving. "If you need your position here until the wedding, I would not mention it. The moment she knows you are leaving, she will look to engage another teacher, and if she finds one quickly, you will be dismissed."

Miss Grassley's face went pale. "I had not considered that eventuality."

"Of course you hadn't, dear. You are in love and

bursting with joy." Siusan flattened her smile. "But a lady must use her mind and act logically. Keep your secret for now. Even from the students, if you would like to keep your position—and continue chaperoning my lecture tours."

"You are right." Miss Grassley placed her index finger over her sealed lips, then looked at Miss Hopkins and Siusan to do the same.

"Siusan . . ." A sheepish expression fell across Miss Grassley's features.

"Aye?"

"I have learned so very much from your lessons—la, even how to draw desired attention, a lesson that very likely allowed me to meet Mr. Bolten." She approached Siusan and took her hand. "I wondered if you would tutor me in wedding etiquette, dressing, planning . . . everything."

Siusan smiled at Miss Grassley. She would like nothing more than to assist her friend, but she would be leaving very soon and would not have enough time to plan Miss Grassley's day.

"My mother passed away a few years ago, and I know she would have helped me—"

Siusan lowered her head. Miss Grassley had said exactly the words to prompt her acceptance— her mother had passed away. The poor lass didn't know what to do and had no one to teach her.

She knew how helpless Miss Grassley felt, because she had felt the same way when Simon offered for her, and she had no idea what to do next. "Of course I will, Miss Grassley. In fact, I shall write a lesson on weddings and dedicate it to you!"

"Thank you! Thank you!" Miss Grassley dropped to her knees. "You are a saint."

Siusan laughed. "Do stop being a goose. Stand up, you will wrinkle your frock."

Miss Hopkins was giggling as she pulled Miss Grassley to her feet. "I have the latest edition of *La Belle Assemblé* in my bedchamber. You should take a look at it. Can't very well wear your grays to your own wedding, now can you?"

Siusan shook her head. "Absolutely not. Go, go. Have a look. I fear I must finish some correspondence first."

A few seconds later, the other teachers left the room, shutting the door behind them, but the door bounced open again before it had time to close. Siusan laughed as she glanced up, expecting Miss Grassley had doubled back for additional advice.

A tiny man, with an oddly shaped head and a cane in his hand stood in the doorway. His clothes were worn and dusty, but his boots were of fine quality and polished to a gleam.

Siusan shot to her feet.

The little man, who did not stand any higher than her waist stepped into the room. "May I come in, Miss Bonnet?"

As startled as she was by the appearance of this man, Siusan stepped boldly forward and had begun to raise her finger to the door when he spoke again.

"I beg your pardon. How ill-mannered of me— Lady Siusan . . . Sinclair. I have the right of it, do I not?"

"Who are you?" Siusan ground out, though she already knew. This man was the *on-dit* columnist . . . without a name, without a face.

He removed his hat, revealing his balding head. "Alas, we have not had the pleasure of meeting formally, and, given my position . . . and yours, we never shall—officially. Still, I will tell you my name. It is Mr. Hercule Lestrange." He grinned at her then. "I can see by your expression, you already know my occupation, so I will confirm it. Yes, I am the *on-dit* columnist for the *Bath Times*." He gestured to the wooden chair, silently requesting permission to sit.

Siusan nodded and watched the little man lean on his cane and walk in a slightly twisted manner to the chair. He set his cane down and worked to pull himself up to the seat. Siusan snatched up her portmanteau and hurried over and set it down beside the chair. Then, she walked to her pallet and sat down.

The little man chuckled, then bent and moved the bag aside. He set his large hand on the arm and hoisted himself easily into the chair. "You are already in my favor, Lady Siusan." He peered across the bedchamber at her, smiling in a very pleased manner. "In my lifetime, I have most commonly come across two sorts of people. Those who, knowing they are in my gun-sight, watch me struggle to climb up into a chair. There are also those who try to lift me into it as though I were a child. But once in a very great while, I come across a person who does neither, but instead gives me an arm, allowing me the choice of whether or not to accept it."

"You did not accept it, but I see that is because you never needed my help to begin with—and yet you wanted me to believe that you were unable to climb into the chair yourself." Siusan peered at the interesting fellow. "Perhaps, though, Mr. Lestrange, I knew you had the ability all along. You came to me in a position of power. You would not have forfeited that by demonstrating a weakness. You simply would have chosen to stand. You, sir, were assessing my character."

He chuckled again. "You are so very entertaining and perceptive. *Oui*, Lady Siusan"—he bent at the waist as though bowing—"you are exactly correct."

Siusan nodded her head. When she raised it again, she speared him with her gaze. "I know, too, why you have come. You have assembled my puzzle and are very intrigued with the mystery you have discovered. You are not the sort to accept pay for silence, so I can only assume you are here for clarification on some point and to inform me as to when your column will be published."

"Very good, my lady." His eyes took on a serious cast. "The column has been set and will publish on Saturday."

"My thanks, Mr. Lestrange. I will have my affairs in Bath in order before then." She schooled her features, forcing her eyes, her brow, and her mouth to appear impassive. But she felt her throat working to restrain a sob, and there was no obscuring that.

Truth be told, she did not entirely want to leave Bath. Her friends, the girls, her position, her teaching and writing had all become so important to her. And yet, she'd *always* wanted nothing more than to return to the bosom of her family.

But she could not allow the Duke of Exeter to learn her identity. If she could turn back the hands of the clock and never have slept with him at the gala, she would. That rash decision, made out of loneliness and grief, might have cost her a life of love with the very same man.

That act proved her the wanton, sinful, weak woman she was.

And now, as penance, she would lose both Sebastian, her teaching position, and, in time, her family, too.

"Dear lady, I do not know why you were running from the Duke of Exeter, nor how in your flight, you ran directly into his arms, here at this school. Will you enlighten me?"

Siusan huffed at that. "I will not tell you why I fled London, only that I felt I had no choice, and rather than hurt my family, I left the only people in the world who love me." Siusan bit the inside of her mouth, steeling herself to continue. "And, when I met Lord Wentworth, for that is how he presented himself to me, I did not know who he was, in truth."

"And yet, you nearly died for him. You ventured into the freezing night to save him." He was studying her again.

She tightened her lips. "Did I?" If she said any more, she was fearful Mr. Lestrange would reduce her to tears.

"*Oui.*" He leaned forward over his knees. "You chanced your life to save his—because you love him."

Siusan raised her chin. "Aye, I do. But that changes nothing." *We can never be together*.

Lestrange slid forward on the seat, then turned over onto his belly and lowered himself to the floor. When he came to his feet, he bowed deeply to Siusan, then caned his way to the door. Before leaving, he turned to face her. "My dear lady, that is where you are wrong."

Siusan rose from the bed and looked quizzically at him. "I do not understand."

"Perhaps now . . . you do not understand. But you will in time. What you did, risking your own life because you love him, changes everything . . . for both of you." He replaced his hat upon his head and opened the door. "Oh, did you know your manual is being rushed to press? It seems, since your daily lessons have now been acquired by *The Times of London* as well, orders for the manual are flooding your publisher's offices."

Confusion crowded Siusan's thoughts. How

could this be? "But no one has formally agreed to publish my manual."

He shrugged. "Nevertheless, the manual is being set and will be available before Christmas. Good day . . . *Miss Bonnet*." He disappeared through the doorway.

"Miss Bonnet? What did you mean?" Why did he refer to her that way when he knew she was Lady Siusan Sinclair? But he meant *something* by it. Of this, she was quite certain.

Siusan rushed to the door, pausing for a blink to pull her ribbonless stocking over her knee, but when she reached the passageway, the strange little man was already gone.

Chapter 14

People who throw kisses are hopelessly lazy.
Bob Hope

By noon, Miss Grassley's giddiness had caught the notice of every girl in school. An hour later, it had become clear to everyone, except Mrs. Huddleston, who hadn't been seen all day, that the reason for the mistress's infectious gaiety was that she was in love. From the roots of her pale blond hair to the tip of the toes she danced upon through the passageways—*in love.*

Love.

Aye, Siusan knew it. Remembered it. She sat down and peered out her bedchamber window.

Or, at least she was almost certain she remembered the warmth of the all-encompassing feeling. Aye, she'd thought she had known love when, after a short courtship, Simon asked for her hand, and her father blessedly agreed. The elation. The passion when he took her, his beloved betrothed, to his bed to show her what love meant.

Or, so she had thought at the time. Now, she was not so convinced that what she felt then had been love. Doubt pricked at her memories. She rubbed her temples vigorously.

Everything was different now . . . with Sebastian. Not just the physical act of making love. There was so much more to it. With Sebastian, her mind, heart, and body were fully immersed. There was no separating the emotion and the physical act of making love.

She frowned as she considered this. With Simon, the two were never so intertwined as they were with Sebastian.

With Sebastian, her heart throbbed in time with her body. She could not separate the intense passion she felt for him, as a man, as a lover, from the physical sensation of touching him, feeling him, wanting him inside her.

With Simon, it had been so very different. At the time she had thought what she and Simon shared was love, but that was because she had had nothing against which to compare what she shared with him—until *now*.

She always believed that Simon had loved her. Always. Even when he returned home after Waterloo, torn and raw from his wounds, she would not accept the truth he admitted to her—that he'd never loved her. That he only offered for her because of her family's money and title. That he loved another, and if—if he survived, he would cast Siusan aside for her, for life was short . . . and love was rare, and he would never love her that way, no matter how hard he tried.

She hadn't been able to believe it. Hadn't been able to admit the truth to herself. Her heart would not allow it.

When her mother died and left her children behind, Siusan felt a pain that she did not believe she could endure. And then, when her father cast her and her brothers and sisters aside, choosing whisky instead of their well-being, he had shouted the most terrible things.

Though her heart shattered, her brother Sterling reminded them all that it was the pain of the loss of his wife causing their father to wound them. That it was not what was truly in his heart, for deep inside he still loved them all.

And she had believed her brother. She'd had to in order to survive.

So, when Simon spat the hurtful words to her as he lay on his deathbed, Siusan did not believe them. For they too were engendered of pain, not of truth.

Or so she had convinced herself most completely. Now she wasn't so sure. For what she felt when she was with Sebastian, even as they lay half-dead from the cold, *was love.* Authentic love. A love in which each was willing to die for the other.

Siusan clenched her fist as her realization became clearer still.

She *loved* Sebastian.

She had tasted true love, and yet, because of her past, because of her sinful ways, she could never live the life her heart begged of her.

She had ruined everything. She wrapped her arms around herself and began to rock.

She was too flawed, not worthy of being loved by anyone. She had proved this again and again to herself and to all of Society. And soon, Sebastian would realize it, too.

Siusan stilled, then resting her face in her palms, she began to weep.

* * *

On Thursday morning just before dawn, Siusan boarded the mail coach for London. By night-fall, two days later, she would arrive at Grosvenor Square. The journey would take hours upon hours, but it would permit her plenty of time to reflect on her days in Bath. As she peered out of the crowded coach's window at the snow-encrusted fields, her thoughts fell to Sebastian, and her eyes began to sting.

Since the moment they first encountered one another in the dark library of Blackwood Hall, everything about her life had changed so completely, so fundamentally, that she barely remembered her old self. She was certainly no longer the same person she had been before the gala, and doubted that she would ever be again.

Or ever want to be. She had grown and become a better person.

Siusan marveled at the irony. It had taken a wicked indiscretion—one that, if made public, would disgrace her and her family name forever—to initiate a transformation so profound that she would at last become the daughter her father wished her to be. The woman she wanted to be.

She had learned so much about herself while teaching in Bath. That, too, was ironic. Lud, how her heart ached that she had not been able to say good-bye to Miss Grassley or Miss Hopkins, Miss Gentree, or the other students.

Aye, leaving Bath had been inevitable from the outset, and for weeks she actually prayed for the day of her departure to arrive sooner. But when her immediate exodus suddenly became imperative because of her impending exposure, she was crushed with such sadness that bidding her friends and students farewell in person was impossible. And so, in lieu of a proper leave-taking, she wrote a letter informing them all that she was needed by a family member in Edinburgh who was ailing. It was true, in part.

Her father had succumbed to drink and, though he was gradually recovering, he still fell prey to periodic bouts of drink, resulting in angry letters focusing on the abject worthlessness of his children. His words' sharp edges still scarred her and her brothers and sisters deeply, and she wondered, even if her father truly recovered, would they?

Would they hold true his assertions, and, as Siusan had, believe themselves unworthy of love?

Or would they heed her lesson and shed their wicked ways in time to earn love at last?

Only time would reveal the answer.

It was too late for Siusan. She had dropped her mask of the sin of sloth, but her delay had cost her a life with the man she had come to love with all her heart.

Siusan's homecoming was a quiet one. None of her brothers dared to bring up the ordeal she had shared with the Duke of Exeter in the snow. Instead, they allowed her to pretend that she had never left home at all and that life had not changed for her so completely and irreversibly.

After a late dinner, Priscilla helped Siusan withdraw her meager belongings from her portmanteau and put them away. Her sister, however, was not going to bite her tongue.

"After all that passed between you," Priscilla began, "why did you not admit to him that it was you, Lady Siusan Sinclair, with whom he was intimate in the library during the gala?"

"You do not understand, Priscilla. He values truth, industry, and moral fortitude above all. Admitting I had lied all the while about who I am would have shaken him and destroyed his trust in me."

"You are wrong, Su."

"I am not. Word would seep into Society, and soon enough Da would hear and cast me from the family. That, Priscilla, I could not bear." Siusan exhaled, feeling too keenly her defeat. "Nay, it is better that he believe me to be Miss Bonnet, a schoolteacher who has returned to Scotland."

"But the duke might have accepted you if only you confessed." Priscilla did not seem to be giving up.

Siusan looked away. "That was a risk I could not take. More likely he would think I had taken him for a fool and despise me." Siusan sat down on her bed and covered her face with her hands for a moment before looking up at her sister. "In my life, all I have known for certain is the love of my family—you, and Ivy and our brothers. Nothing more." Siusan felt her armor clamping down around her. She could not talk about Sebastian any longer. Not then. Her pain was too raw. Her emotions hovering just below the surface.

"But Siusan, did not your carriage accident in the snow prove his devotion to you?" Priscilla moved to the bed and hugged Siusan against her.

Siusan squeezed her eyes closed against unbidden tears.

"Nay." Siusan lowered her head until she could contain her emotions. "He was hurt. The devotion was mine. I had to save him, even if it cost my life."

"But what now?" Priscilla shook Siusan.

"What do you mean?" Siusan pulled away from her sister.

"You saved his life. Surely he will come for you. At the very least he deserves an explanation why you left so abruptly."

"I wrote a letter. I gave him an explanation he could believe."

"He deserves the truth."

"Aye, he does deserve to hear the truth, but I will not risk my family just to ease my conscience," Siusan admitted. "Unless the *Bath Times* has reported my identity, he does not know who Miss Bonnet of Mrs. Huddleston's School of Virtues, truly is. And if I can prevent it, he never will."

"But if you love him—and I know you do—"

"Aye, I do. I love him. I admit it!" Siusan rushed to the window and, unable to face her sister, peered out into the night. "Don't you understand, Priscilla? I don't deserve him. Any association with me would destroy his future."

"You said you loved him. If so, then why—"

Siusan whirled around. The tears she'd held back as she stood before the window broke from her lashes and rolled down her cheeks. "I do. I am doing this *because* I love him."

One month later

Priscilla tossed a newspaper onto Siusan's pallet. "It has been weeks, Siusan, and yet there has been no mention of the Duke of Exeter's returning to London." Priscilla turned slowly before the looking-glass, admiring a saffron-hued gown of the finest satin, a gift from Siusan, paid for from her lesson columns, which were now being published weekly in London as well as Bath and Cheltenham.

"He is assigned to the Lord Mayor's special committee on the Condition of England Question. I have no doubt he will return given the increasing unrest of late." Siusan's gaze rolled down the heavily inked columns of the newspaper.

"Still, he has not returned *yet*, which is why Grant is taking us to the Theater Royal Drury Lane tonight." Priscilla grinned. "Hadn't you better dress? You canna venture out looking like . . . a schoolteacher fresh from the classroom."

Siusan didn't dignify her sister's comment with an answer. But Priscilla was correct about one thing. It was time to reappear in Society. Her prolonged absence, more than her attendance at events, was likely to set tongues wagging amongst the ranks of the wellborn if it had not already.

The Theater Royal, Drury Lane

Repositioning her snowy kid gloves over her elbows, Siusan nervously took her seat next to Priscilla and Grant in the private box at the Theater Royal Drury Lane. It was not as grand as the royal box positioned just to the left, but the view of the stage would be magnificent.

Pity the uninformed gentleman who unwisely accepted Grant's bet at White's and lost the use of his family's box during Edmund Kean's special performance in *Othello*. Foolish man. Didn't he know that, since their brother Sterling had returned to Scotland, Grant's skills at cards were unrivaled in London?

Hundreds of candles glowed, but the theater was so cavernous that the chandeliers shed no more than a dull light upon the hundreds of patrons below.

Siusan gazed at the dozens of ladies and gentlemen sitting in the crescent of boxes nearby. Even as her vision gradually adjusted to the low light, she could not discern faces well enough to identify anyone. And this pleased her quite well. For if she could not recognize individuals, then the chance of her being seen was also greatly reduced.

Still, a bout of worry filled her. Though it was highly unlikely that the Duke of Exeter would choose tonight to make his return to Society, she ought to take precautions. Siusan raised her fan before her face until only her eyes peered over it. Much better. Between the hazy gold of the candle-light and her fan, she finally felt able to relax and enjoy the performance.

As the orchestra began to play and the curtains opened to reveal the famous actor, Edmund Kean, Priscilla giggled with excitement. "Thank you for bringing us this eve, Grant."

He leaned forward and peered past Priscilla at Siusan. "I hope *both* of my sisters enjoy the play."

Priscilla nudged Grant back and turned to Siusan. "Put that fan down," she hissed. "You are being a goose. Please, just do as Grant bade you—enjoy Mr. Kean."

"I said to enjoy the *play*," Grant said, snickering.

"To each her own. I plan simply to gaze upon Edmund." Priscilla sighed. "Siusan may enjoy whatever she chooses so long as she retracts that distracting fan."

Siusan snapped her fan closed with a huff. She was not ready to enter Society, not until she was certain that the Duke of Exeter was back in Devonshire for good. Honestly, she preferred to be at home writing a new lesson about attending the theater for her columns.

She sat and forlornly stared across the theater. Lud, she should be happy. She was with her family again. Money was no longer such a concern for her family, and she was proud that she, of all of them, was the one earning their daily bread—and gowns—and whisky.

Who would ever have guessed she had the potential to do anything of consequence? Until she had been forced to leave London and teach, she had never had the inclination to try anything of consequence. And, until she arrived in Bath, her life had been naught but a practiced study of leisure.

Who would ever have imagined that Lady Siusan Sinclair would miss planning her daily lesson plan and spending her day teaching her pupils?

Or that she would miss the one man in the world who could separate her from her family forever?

A thin golden thread suddenly appeared a finger's length before her eyes. She shifted her focus to it and saw that from its end hung a tiny black spider. She gasped, but the draw of air pulled it to her face and at once she felt it crawling on her nose. "Ahh!" Siusan screamed, leaping to her feet and clawing at her face.

Grant was on his feet in a instant. "Hold still." His words were more of a growl than a whisper. His huge hand covered her face, and cinched closed in a quick movement. "I've got it." He squeezed the spider in his fist, then brushed it from his palm to the floor. He smiled, looked very pleased with himself.

"Oh, do sit down, Grant." Priscilla appeared mortified. She glanced sideways at the stage. "*Please.*"

Siusan looked up and saw that Edmund Kean was standing center stage in complete silence. Peering around, she saw, too, that the entire audience had turned to see who had caused the disturbance.

While it was conceivable, evenly likely, that in the low light no one had noticed Lady Siusan Sinclair's return to Society, the opposite was true now. The Sinclair name rushed through the audience toward the stage like a wave crashing on the beach.

If there was a lesson to cope with extreme humiliation, it was one she, herself, had never learned.

With a wave of her gloved hand as apology, she sat down, then promptly snapped open her painted silk fan and fluttered it before her entire face.

As though her fan had become the conductor's baton, the violins tentatively began to play, and Edmund Kean resumed his impassioned oratory.

From the corner of her left eye, she could see Priscilla intermittently glaring at her for causing them all such embarrassment.

Siusan's cheeks burned for several minutes. By degrees, she retracted her fan, stick by stick, until she was sure that no one was staring at her any longer.

And then, she bent forward and crept from the box.

Her slippers barely touched the floor as she hurried down the dim corridor. She turned the corner for the staircase. A hand shot out and grabbed her wrist, another cupping her mouth, stifling her startled scream.

"Good evening, Siusan."

Oh, God. She closed her eyes and stilled. She turned as best she could in his grip and raised her eyes to his.

Sebastian.

Chapter 15

For Satan finds some mischief for idle hands to do.
Isaac Watts

Sebastian's expression was dark and angry. "I need to speak with you. Now, if you please."

Siusan nodded in agreement, and he slowly lowered his hand from her mouth.

"My carriage is just outside the doors. We will speak there." It wasn't a request, and yet, she knew she could not leave with him.

"I must inform my family—" She whirled around toward the corridor, but his grip upon her wrist was still firm.

"The play has just begun. We have plenty of time."

Blast him for being logical.

"Come, my dear." He released his hold on her

wrist then and pointedly offered her his arm. She had no other choice but to take it and go with him.

Several footmen, who had collected wraps earlier, stood near the theater's front doors, but no patrons lingered about, not with the great Kean in the middle of a performance. Sebastian paused and allowed Siusan to retrieve her woolen cloak. He whisked it over her shoulders.

"Do not say a word," she warned, hoping to lighten his mood.

"I wasn't about to." A slip of smile disappeared from his lips.

After the accident, Siusan had set aside the notion of fashion before warmth. And, though Priscilla complained during the entire ride from Grosvenor Square about the spectacle she was making of herself by wearing a heavy cloak to an evening event, Siusan had learned her lesson the hardest way possible, and it was not one she would ever dismiss.

Once outside, Sebastian summoned his driver, and Siusan was quickly ushered into the carriage. He rapped on the front wall. "Drive on, if you will. Anywhere."

Siusan sat across from Sebastian, trying to appear calm. Unfortunately, she was caught up in a whirl of sorrow, regret, and even hope, but his implacable stare was only making her efforts more difficult.

"Why?" His voice cracked, but his expression remained tight with anger.

"You must know now why I had to leave." She gazed down at her hands, unable to look him in the eyes.

"I vow, Miss Bonnet, I do not. None of this makes sense to me. A beautiful woman risks her life to save mine, then leaves without a word. I search for her, finally accepting that I will never see her again when suddenly I find her across a crowded theater in London."

Keeping her eyes lowered, she gazed across at him. His fingers flinched, and he balled them quickly into fists to conceal his agitation. "I had to leave . . . after . . . what passed between us." Her voice was a mere whisper over the rumble of the carriage upon the pavers.

"I do not understand why you left me in the shed—and why you left again after you managed our rescue."

She raised her chin. "I left because I had no choice. I still do not. I have shamed myself and my family."

"No, you have not. We would have died had we not shared our bodies' warmth." He leaned forward and took her hand. "Siusan, I love you. You must know this."

Yanking back her hand, she shook her head furiously. "Nay, you do not love me. You do not even know me, and if you did, if you truly *knew* me, you would never use the word love in the same sentence."

"I do know you."

"Nay, you do not. I am not the respectable, moral, hardworking woman you think I am. I am everything but those things."

"I do not believe it."

She could see in his eyes the truth of his reply. But he would come to believe it in time. Soon he would learn her name. Perhaps as early as tomorrow. Then, he would read all about her and her family in the newspapers, he'd hear the gossip, and he would believe.

And he would leave her. It was inevitable.

Better he hear it now.

Better that she not allow herself to believe someone could love her for who she really is.

"I do love you."

Siusan twisted her fan. "You canna. I am not worthy of your love, Sebastian. Believe me." She peered out of the cab window in an effort to hold back her tears and belatedly realized that they were no more than a block away from the theater. "I am not worthy of anyone's love."

Her words stunned Sebastian, giving her the time she needed to escape. She rapped twice on the wall behind her, and the carriage rolled to a stop.

Pushing down on the door latch, she waited for the lock to release. She turned quickly then and pressed a kiss to Sebastian's mouth, the sad sort of kiss that always means good-bye. "Forget you ever made my acquaintance, *please*. If you love me, as you claim, let me go and do not follow."

He sat immobile with a look of total disbelief on his face.

Siusan opened the door and stepped out onto the pavers and focusing straight ahead, did not allow herself to look back.

The next morning

Sebastian hardly slept all night, and he was sitting before the window at Blackwood Hall waiting for the sun to rise and light the snow-dusted fields below.

How could he sleep when he knew that Siusan was there, in London.

For hours he'd mulled last night over in his

mind again and again, but finding her at the theater made no sense to him. How had she come to be in London?

The only clue he had was that she was sitting with the two Sinclairs he'd met at their residence in Grosvenor Square. She was clearly one of their number. She and Lady Priscilla Sinclair resembled each other so closely that someone might mistake them for twins. And yet, he had convinced himself otherwise . . . because he had wished it to be true.

He had been attracted to her and wanted her to be a simple miss, despite overwhelming evidence that she was a lady.

It was clear to him now that she was one of the sisters they had claimed was not in London. She was not possessed of red hair, so it only stood to reason that she was Lady Siusan Sinclair—not Miss Siusan Bonnet. Hardly a stretch of the imagination. How thick he had been not to have realized this. How easily he'd fooled himself.

What he could not fathom was why the daughter of a duke was posing as a commoner, a teacher at a school for young ladies. Nothing about her seemed to make sense.

He picked up his cup of tea and frowned. It was cold after sitting beside him for hours.

One thing was for certain. Despite her wishes, he could not simply let her go.

He would find her.

And convince her to marry him.

The Lord Mayor's special committee on the Condition of England Question was to meet at two of the clock at Mansion House. Urgent reports had been delivered by special messenger overnight to each committee member, detailing intelligence received by the Home Office that Spenceans, unhappy with the deteriorating economic state of England, were planning to gather *en masse* and overthrow the British government by taking the Tower of London and the Bank of England.

The committee consisted of high-ranking members of Parliament. It was an appointment Sebastian did not take lightly, for he knew he was not assigned to the committee based on merit but because of fortunate birth. It was imperative to the honor of his family, honor that he serve to the best of his ability and distinguish himself, however he might.

He had just disembarked from his carriage and was approaching the impressive front façade of Mansion House when he noticed a young lady with golden ringlets gesturing to him from across the street. Her face was familiar to him, though he could not recall where they had ever met. At first he was certain she had mistaken him for another.

She waved her handkerchief. "Your Grace," she called out in a tone so soft that she barely heard her over the rumble of passing carriages.

He crossed the street to her. "May I be of some assistance, miss?" She was tall, but very thin, and so girlish in shape that he wondered at her age. Barely out, if that, he imagined, yet she was standing here unescorted.

She looked up him, her eyes filled with disappointment. "You . . . you do not remember me?"

"I am afraid I do not." Sebastian fumbled through his memory, but he did not recall ever seeing her.

She raised her lace handkerchief dramatically and sobbed into it. "Dear heavens. What ever shall I do now?"

Sebastian gently placed his hand on her shoulder. "You are distressed. Please, tell me how I may be of assistance."

At that moment another carriage drew up before Mansion House and two members of the House of Lords stepped out onto the pavers. They turned and paused to look at him, there with his hand upon the girl's shoulder.

"Your Grace, you must remember, you must!" She looked up through tear-filled eyes. "I was in the library during the gala at Blackwood Hall. You . . . we . . . oh, dear Lord, I am with child!"

A jolt coursed through every vein in his body. "Dear miss, I am quite certain we have never been introduced."

"We have. At your gala, and again at the Lord Mayor's dinner."

Sebastian squinted. Yes, he did remember making her acquaintance at the dinner—but she was not his lover in the library. Siusan was.

"Are you so dishonorable that you would deny me, leaving me to explain this to my father alone?" Her voice was growing louder, and passersby were beginning to watch them.

"Your father?" Sebastian was readying to ask her if he could help her find him, so deep was her distress, when she spoke a name that turned him cold.

"Yes, Lord Aster." She gazed up to Mansion House. "He is inside, awaiting the meeting of the special committee. I heard you were to attend, so I thought I would speak with you here privately rather than at a ball or a rout."

Sebastian studied the miss. No, she couldn't be the woman in the library. She was thin and lacking the curves of a woman. And yet, how did she know about what happened in the library?

"Miss . . . Aster," he stammered, "I cannot discuss this with you presently." His head was beginning to spin. "May we meet on Friday in Hyde Park? By the fountain near the Park Lane gates at noon."

Miss Aster nodded. "Very well. Friday at noon." She started to walk away from him, but turned suddenly. "You *will* be there . . . or I fear, Your Grace, you may very well live to regret your decision."

Chapter 16

Ambition is a poor excuse for not having sense enough to be lazy.

Edgar Bergen

White's Club
St. James Street, London

With a few spare guineas in his pocket, courtesy of his dear sister Su's published lessons, Grant took inspiration from his brother Sterling, the eldest of the Sinclair siblings, and set out to turn pence into pounds at the card tables.

While the other members of the club had witnessed his skill at any number of games, it never failed to amaze Grant how many of the gentlemen gamesters would lose everything in their pockets, then continue to join him at the tables again and again. When would they realize that the cards one was dealt had very little to do with the outcome of the game and that deftness at reading emotions on the faces of the other players was the true key to winning?

Grant sipped a whisky at a small table near the bow window and assessed the potential players in the club. His favorite players possessed over-confidence, a taste for strong spirits, and, most importantly, fat purses. This fortuitous blending of qualities in men unfortunately seemed in short supply that night. So when his gaze lit upon an animated young man wearing an ill-fitting frock coat, Grant decided to approach the lad for sheer amusement.

"I am telling you, the wager is a sure thing, and is being listed in the betting book as we speak, sir." The innocent-looking lad was telling this to a heavy, balding lord who was so topped with brandy he could barely hold his eyes open, despite his obvious interest in the proposition.

"Did I hear mention of a sure bet?" Grant sidled up to the young man. "My favorite sort." He set his hand on the young man's shoulder. "Tell me more."

The young man looked him in the eyes, clearly distrustful of him. Grant softened his expression and manufactured a smile that stretched from his mouth to his eyes. The young man was instantly relieved.

"All right then." The lad looked about the smoky room and gestured Grant and the older man closer. "By week's end, a purchased-his-title nobleman will marry the youngest daughter of a senior member of the House of Lords."

Grant leaned back and frowned. Hardly intriguing.

"You may be swayed to change your mind when you hear that the bride is with child and"— he looked around the club to be sure no else was listening—"the dishonorable groom-to-be is none other than the Duke of Exeter, the Lord Mayor's new favorite."

Grant's eyes went wide. "The hell you say!" After Siusan said that the duke had claimed that he loved her outside the theater, he doubted very much the duke was simply going to beg off from Siusan and marry some chit just out. "I do not believe a word of it."

"Then take that position on the bet." The young man was grinning. "Six club members are waiting over there to do so the minute the wager is entered in the book."

"Is that so? Weel, I might join their number, but instead of standing in a bloody queue, I vow I should like a whisky whilst I wait my turn."

And some more information from you, lad, if you please.

He looked at the older man sitting at the table. He was asleep. "I do not care to drink alone. Join me, sir?" Grant gestured to his table beside the window.

"I do not mind if I do." The lad tugged his collar high about his head, leaving his ferret-like nose and weak chin nearly concealed beneath his neck-cloth. He followed Grant to the table, and there they sat for over an hour, until the young man had taken his fill of spirits and was now sleeping with his head on the small table for all the world to see.

And Grant had all of the information about the sure bet—information he felt compelled to deliver to Siusan at once.

Grant found Siusan sitting in the front parlor with her sewing basket beside her on the tea table. But she wasn't stitching. Instead, she was using her silver scissors to clip out her columns from the stack of newspapers beside her on the carpet.

She was singing merrily, even after she noticed that Grant had entered the room.

"What are you so bleeding happy about? Bought a new frock . . . or a fan perhaps?"

"Neither. I received a letter from our father this afternoon."

"Well, I see you have not slit your wrists, so I must assume you have instead dosed yourself with laudanum to dull the pain of his words."

"No need for such dramatics this time. For you will be amazed when you hear what the letter says."

"Who is next to be cast out the house?" He cocked his head. "Ah, I see the smile on your lips. Priscilla, eh?"

Siusan laughed. "What a thing to say. Nay, no one is being cast out to the pavers."

"Then what is it? I can only tease you for so long before I grow frustrated with your delay."

"Well, it seems that Da's man of affairs—known better to us all as the Grim Reaper—" She lifted a single eyebrow and Grant nodded his head all too knowingly. "Has been sending our father my columns and the newspaper report of my heroic rescue of the Duke of Exeter. It would appear he is aware of my alias, Miss Siusan Bonnet."

Grant's eyes became suddenly serious. "No repercussions from that?"

"Thankfully, none at all. In fact, Da claims that I have changed and, through my work and drive, I may have redeemed myself." She set her scissors atop the pile of newspapers and grinned.

Grant eased back into the tufted chair near the fire. "He said you *may* have changed, is that right?"

"Aye, which is why he is coming for Christmas to observe my transformation himself." Siusan stacked her clippings and set them inside her sewing basket. She peered up at Grant, all levity shorn away. "I am so close, Grant. So close to winning back Da's favor and respect." Then her lower lip quivered. "But it would take so little for him to learn why I ventured into teaching lessons and what else happened the night I saved the Duke of Exeter. Oh, Grant, I feel as though I am standing before a great precipice, and the smallest breeze might cast me down into its depths."

Grant scratched his head. "I admit, Siusan, you do play awfully close to the edge, but I have heard something today that may change your position."

Siusan set her scissors on the table and leaned forward. "Do tell me your news is good."

"Perhaps." His eyes did not quite agree with his words. "I was offered a bet at White's this afternoon. A nobleman will marry the pregnant young daughter of a senior member of the House of Lords before week's end."

Siusan shrugged. "The wager does not interest me, nor should it you."

"Ah, but see, Su, it should interest you because the groom is said to be the Duke of Exeter."

Siusan came to her feet. "What? This cannot be."

"Something was afoot. I knew it, and so I was a most kind host to the young man offering the bet and filled his belly with the strongest whisky White's possessed. Within an hour I learned the full story. Su, the bet is crafted as a losing proposition for the duke. If he denies responsibility, the lass will tell her father that the duke forced himself on her. If he marries her, he will be admitting that he bedded a prominent lord's young, innocent daughter—thereby losing favor and respect in the House of Lords."

"He could not have done this."

"Aye, you are correct about that, for the alleged intimacy supposedly occurred in the library at the duke's gala. And, the interesting bit is, the duke cannot deny that Miss Aster was his lover because he never saw her face."

Siusan's knees wobbled beneath her and she sank down on the settee. "I am the only one who can exonerate him."

"Aye, but telling the duke you were his faceless lover will do nothing to free him from this web. You would have to make a public announcement of some sort."

"Then that is what I shall do."

"Careful now. I think you are thinking irrationally owing to the stunning nature of what I have just told you. Think about this. The moment you admit that you were the woman with the duke in the library, you forfeit your own honor—and Da's damnable respect."

"And my family." Siusan felt suddenly dizzy as the blood seemed to drain from her head down to her feet.

The morning of Friday, November 15
Spa Fields, Islington, London

The air was frigid and spitting snow as the first public meeting of Spenceans took place. Sebastian stood alone, shivering, before a large contingent of constables and faced down the protestors, his mission, to prevent a riot.

By noon, more than twenty thousand people had come from as far away as Yorkshire, Nottinghamshire, Leicestershire, and Derbyshire, and as near as Cheapside, all to protest outrageous food prices, loss of textile jobs because of mechanization, and the government's and Regent's blatant waste of public funds.

A raucous cacophony of shouts and taunts filled Sebastian's ears. There were too many of them. If violence erupted, he and the constables didn't stand a chance of survival.

Sebastian had to act immediately, before it was too late. He climbed atop a wooden crate. "Hear me!" A quiet pulled through the crowd like an ebbing tide. "Rioting and seeking to overthrow the government will not solve our problems—it will only make them worse. We need to work together as one people to devise a plan."

The crowd murmured and began to stir. A few at first drew closer to listen, while others hung back, as if fearful of becoming caught between the constables and mob should emotions become stoked to a roaring blaze.

Sebastian raised his hands and pointed at the

crowd. "I call upon *you* to send forth your wisest leaders to meet with the Lord Mayor and his committee dedicated to solving this problem for the good of England! Be part of the solution!"

"Why should we believe you? How many of us have been made promises by the government, only to learn that they were lies?" Sebastian peered out at the crowd. He knew that voice.

"Who said that?" Sebastian rose up on his boot toes, but the crowd was too large to discern where the voice had even come from. "Step forward and we will address your comment. I will tell you why things will be different this time—because you will be helping to craft the plan to pull England from this crisis!"

The constables spread out behind the Duke of Exeter, unsure what the response to his offer would be.

Four men stepped forward and crossed the land between them and the constables. Sebastian leaped down from the crate and offered his hand to each of them.

The Spenceans' leaders called out to their followers to go home this night and let them speak with the government to learn if what this man claimed was true—that a peaceful solution could be found. A solution to the shortages must be found.

Gradually, the crowd dispersed from the fields.

True to his word, the Duke of Exeter returned to Mansion House with the four Spenceans, who were ushered into chambers with the Lord Mayor at once.

The next morning, *The Times* proclaimed the Duke of Exeter a statesman of the first rank for his skill in averting a riot at Spa Fields and working with the Lord Mayor to achieve a solution supported by all.

He hadn't slept in nearly two days, but it had all been worth it. Sebastian leaned back in his carriage and closed his eyes. Disaster had been averted this Friday.

Friday?

Bloody hell! His eyes snapped open, and he sat straight up on the bench. Disaster hadn't been averted—because he had agreed to meet with Miss Aster in Hyde Park yesterday at noon!

Her threat had been clear enough. She'd make him regret it if he failed to arrive at the appointed time. She would confess what happened in the library to her father, the powerful Lord Aster.

And Sebastian and his family name would be ruined. His grandmother would be devastated. She had placed so much trust in him. To what end?

Sebastian decided his only option at that early

hour was to send Miss Aster his card that afternoon, explaining his absence. He would bank on the notion that she would have seen the newspaper—realized his absence was unavoidable, a matter of vital importance to England, else he would have met with her.

Sebastian slumped back against the squab, defeated. It did not truly matter if he had met Miss Aster in Hyde Park anyway. He was no closer to coming up with a solution to his own problem than Parliament was to solving the crisis of shortages.

He scrubbed his face with his palms.

And there was still the task of finding Siusan and telling her about Lord Aster's daughter. What could he possibly say to her? He'd told her outside the theater that he loved her. Damn it all.

How did one tell the woman he loved that he might be required to marry another, for the sake of honor?

Honor he did not possess.

Chapter 17

Know the true value of time: snatch, seize, and enjoy every moment of it. No idleness, no laziness, no procrastination; never put off till tomorrow what you can do today.

Lord Chesterfield

Priscilla looked as pale as the soft-boiled egg Mrs. Wimpole had just set before her for breakfast. Siusan sat down across from her sister at the dining table. She could tell from her expression something was amiss.

"How did you sleep, Siusan?" Priscilla was trying to appear bright, but her brow was drawn, and she was clearly biting the inside of her cheek as she awaited a reply.

"Not well, given that I must decide between my family and honor." She leaned over the table closer to her sister. "Though my worries ought not stop you from telling me what is gnawing at you this morning."

Flattening her palm atop the newspaper, Priscilla slid it across the table to Siusan. "Your column was replaced this morning . . . by something else."

"Replaced my lesson? By what?" Siusan wrinkled her nose in annoyance and snatched the newspaper up.

"With an article, special to the *Times* . . . about you."

Siusan wrenched her head up and peered at her sister, expecting her opinion on the article. She always had an opinion. "Well, what say you, Priscilla? Will I burst into tears the moment I read it? Will I be required to leave town? Drop to my knees and confess my sins to all of London? Will I dance on this table in joy? What?"

Priscilla merely shrugged her shoulders. "I honestly do not know what to make of this article though I can understand its relevance and interest to readers of your ladies lessons column." She flicked her fingers at the newspaper. "Go ahead. Read it."

Reprinted from the *Bath Times*

Readers of this publication's widely read excerpts from The Handbook of Elegance *will be eager to learn that the identity of the author has been revealed. It was previously believed to be Miss Siusan Bonnet, an etiquette instructor teaching in Bath at Mrs. Huddleston's School of Virtues. After a lengthy investigation, the true author has been identified to be Lady Siusan Sinclair of Mayfair. The daughter of the Duke of Sinclair, the Scottish author is a highborn lady true, a fact that avid readers of her lesson excerpts have likely long suspected.*

What readers will not have known, for her ladyship has taken great measures to conceal this from all but her immediate family, is that Lady Siusan Sinclair was recently the victim of a near-fatal carriage accident during last month's devastating blizzard. Somehow, she still managed to extract herself from the wreckage and drag the driver, the Duke of Exeter, to shelter. Though freezing to death herself, our brave heroine rode the carriage's horse through knee-deep snow and the dark of night to save the duke, who had been badly injured during the accident.

> *Shortly thereafter, Lady Siusan Sinclair re-*
> *turned to London to convalesce in the company*
> *of her family residing in fashionable Grosvenor*
> *Square.*
>
> *A full recovery is expected and excerpts*
> *from* The Handbook of Elegance *will resume*
> *next week.*
>
> *Orders for Lady Siusan's manual for ladies,*
> *due to be published by G. G. and J. Robinson*
> *on the first of December, have already ex-*
> *ceeded expectations, and a second printing of*
> *the manual has already been scheduled to meet*
> *the early demand.*

Siusan set the newspaper on the table and thrummed her fingers atop it. "Quite interesting, indeed." There was no doubt in her mind that the article was written by Mr. Hercule Lestrange, the curious *on-dit* columnist who had come to interview her at the school. But why, when his usual *on-dit* columns spared no blood, was he so kind and complimentary of her, painting her as a respectable lady and genuine heroine?

"But the article is not all. Because it was first published in the *Bath Times* last month, the publisher forwarded along a packet of letters from its readers. The packet arrived this very morning.

Priscilla rose and picked up a silver salver stacked with letters from the hunt board. "Astonishing, really. They are all for you."

Siusan tore open the first letter and scanned it. "It is from the headmistress of a school in Aberdeen, wishing that, if I ever return to teaching, she would be greatly honored if I accepted a position at The Northern School for Young Ladies." She opened another. "This one is from a publisher in Bristol requesting that the press be considered for the second book in my continuing series of lessons for ladies." She turned to Priscilla. "*Another* manual, what an interesting idea. Perhaps I will focus the next manual entirely on creating a fashionable home for pennies."

Priscilla handed her a letter she held back from the pile. "And there is one other—different from the others."

Siusan was so awed by the letters she was reading she barely heard her sister. "What was that, Priscilla?"

"There is another you should read next." Priscilla held the letter out. When, after several moments, Siusan did not respond, Priscilla snatched away the letter her sister was reading and replaced with another letter.

The instant she saw the heavy-handed script,

she trembled. It was from her father, and somehow she knew this letter would not be as complimentary as the last. Had he discovered why she'd
fled London for Bath? Too many horrid possibili-
ties for his letter swirled in her mind. "I-I cannot
read it." She shoved it back into her sister's hand.
"Please, Priscilla, will you read it and tell me what
it says?"

"Very well." Priscilla broke the wafer and shook
the letter from its folds. "If you are sure."

"I am." Siusan was growing ever more agitated.
"Please, do not delay. Read it!"

The letter was short, Siusan could tell that much
through the ink darkening the foolscap, though
Priscilla spent an inordinate amount of time
studying it.

"Aloud, please. Lud, say *something*." Siusan
imagined all manner of hurtful words scrawled
on the paper. *You have disappointed me more so than
any of my children.* Ivy had received that. *Ye will be
cast from the house with nary a penny to yer name,
Sterling.*

It was interesting, though, how a focused threat
from their father seemed to motivate rapid and
dramatic changes in both her sister and her
brother. Positive changes, for after surviving their
ordeals, both had been welcomed back to Edin-

burgh and into their father's good graces once more.

She only hoped someday, he would forgive her for disgracing the family.

And so, Siusan held her breath and waited for his dire words of warning.

Priscilla looked genuinely confused. "It is as I said before. He has never been more proud of one of his children for showing responsibility than you, Su." Priscilla tossed the letter across the table to her. "See, here. Nothing to fear. Only praise . . . and, that he will be in London on the first of December, to be with you when your book is published."

"But . . . that is less than two weeks!" Siusan leaped up from the table and began to pace. "He cannot come now. I haven't decided what I am going to do."

The hourglass had been turned. Now she had less than a fortnight's time to make a decision that would change her life . . . or Sebastian's forever.

It was very late when Sebastian finally returned to Blackwood Hall after two days of meetings with the committee and the Home Office. Reports about the England Question were conflicting, and yet one bit of intelligence remained sound from every source. There would be another riot, soon.

A lone candle burned in the parlor when Sebastian entered and walked toward it to pour himself a glass of brandy to calm his worried thoughts.

"At last, you have returned." He turned to see his grandmother sitting in the chair behind him. "Where were you for so long? Visiting *her*?"

Sebastian stilled. Did she know about his issue with Miss Aster? "I beg your pardon, Grandmother. I do not know to whom you are referring." Sebastian squinted in the dimness to better see her.

His grandmother's voice was strained, almost as though she'd been crying. "Lady Siusan Sinclair." There was a harshness to her tone as she practically spat Siusan's name.

While he felt somewhat relieved that she was not referring to Miss Aster, Sebastian did not care for, nor understand the venom in her tone.

"Do you know who she is, dear boy? Who that hoyden truly is?"

Sebastian stared through the dimness at his grandmother. She was acting very strange and uncharacteristically cruel.

"No? Well, I shall tell you, my dear. Do not believe that drivel in the newspaper. She is not a respectable woman, and you cannot be connected with her in any way."

"How can you say that about her? You know I would have died had she not risked her life to save mine!" Sebastian crossed the room and stood before his grandmother, his fists clenching reflexively. Her lids were heavy and an empty glass sat beside her.

"She is a Sinclair, one of the Seven Deadly Sins you may have heard wicked tales about since you have been in London. Seven brothers and sisters so uncontrollable, so wild and wanton that their own father cast them from his home until each of them redeemed himself or herself and restored honor to the Sinclair name. Your Siusan has not done so."

"I do not give a fig about the tales told amongst the gossipers of the *ton*. And I thought you above such baseness as well, Grandmother." She flinched at that. "I know Siusan a damned sight better than you or anyone else in Society. And I tell you, Grandmother, she is a good, courageous, and kind woman—"

He paused then, suddenly sure of the future he saw for himself. Sure of the woman he most desired to share that future with him. Siusan.

"If Lady Siusan Sinclair will accept me, I fully intend to marry her!"

His grandmother's lids snapped wide. How

ironic that only a few days ago she was urging him to marry someone exactly like Siusan, and now she was fretful that he would do just that.

He stalked back to his glass, filled it, and drank it down in one draught.

His grandmother was sputtering at the thought. She snatched up her glass and brought it to her mouth, grimacing when she realized it was empty. "Your father went astray and dishonored this family in more ways than you know. It is up to you to restore that honor."

"I cannot change the past, Grandmother. I realize that now. All I can do is live *my* life the best way I know how. Will my actions make others forget my father's mistakes, I cannot say. All I can do is try to be a better person. And with Siusan, I am that man."

"You are a great fool if you believe you can restore our honor with *that woman* at your side. Hear me, boy. You must put as much space between you and that sinful creature before it is too late! She is poison to you! Believe me when I tell you that she will ruin you, destroy your standing in the House of Lords."

Sebastian turned slowly and peered through the low light toward her. "It is already too late, Grandmother. My heart is hers. I love her."

Chapter 18

That destructive siren, sloth, is ever to be avoided.

Horace

The Sinclair residence
Grosvenor Square

Penned inside the tall stone walls, the bitter wind raced around the perimeter of the back garden like a corralled horse. Dried leaves swirled in circles around Siusan's ankles, catching and pulling on the lacings of her boots and on her stockings.

"What are you doing out here on such a bitter day as this, Su? There is a fire in the parlor hearth. Why do you not come inside and sit with me there for a spell?" Grant sat down next her on the marble bench and shivered. "Ye'll freeze your backside off sitting on this. It's like ice."

Siusan shrugged and gazed out at the sturdy boxwoods, their leaves still lush and green while the rest of the garden was withered and brown. "I have a very difficult decision to make, Grant, and I canna allow the laughter and simple pleasures of being with my family to sway my final decision in any way."

"Och, Su, we're as tightly bound together as the stitches of silk you fashioned to bind Sterling's wounds together after a bout." A momentary grin touched his mouth, and even in this dire moment, Siusan chuckled inwardly at the memory. "Even sitting on a block of icy stone canna force more than twenty years of life together from your mind."

"Nay, I suppose not." Siusan sighed, but after a moment in thought, turned to Grant. "How am I to make this decision?"

"What is the decision, as *you* view it?" He squeezed her gloved hand in his warm bare hand. "Remove what anyone else might have told you, or might think, that could affect your own decision."

Siusan sat very still. "I canna, for while my decision will affect my life, it will also change the lives of others, people I care deeply for, as well."

"Tell me what *you* are trying to decide." He leaned forward on the bench in order to better see her face.

She withdrew her hand from his and pressed her fingers together as if in prayer, then held them to her lips.

Siusan rocked a little, forward and backward, almost the way her mother had rocked her when she was small child. It was a little thing, but it calmed her at times when life became complicated.

Pondering Grant's sage advice for a few moments more, she finally lifted her fingers away from her mouth and turned to look at Grant. "This could be the most difficult decision I have ever made—because you can't help me with it. No one can." She lowered her gaze, then met Grant's gaze. "I must choose between allowing Da and the rest of Society to see me as a respectable woman. Not as one of the Seven Deadly Sins."

"This does not sound like such a hard decision. It is what you have always wanted. What we all have wanted since we came to London."

"It is what I want. For the first time in all my life, Da claims to be proud of me. People I do not even know seek my counsel. Members of the *ton* who practically gave us the cut direct, nearly baring their teeth when we entered a ballroom, are sending cards, begging my attendance at events." She turned her gaze up and met his, and gave her shoulders a dismissive shrug. "This is the life I've always dreamed about, but I fear that to claim it would be wrong of me."

"Why would it be wrong? Siusan, you have changed. You are no longer the woman you were before you left for Bath. Far from it. You've grown. The mask that hid your true identity has fallen away. Whether you meant to or not, you have shown the world the Siusan your brothers and sisters have always known—a kind, caring, talented, and respectable woman."

Lowering her head, so he could not see her tearing eyes, she nodded. "You are right, I canna hide anymore. I need to face life . . . but also the pain that accompanies it." She raised her head and faced him, let him see the tracks of the tears rolling down her cheeks. "I canna allow the Duke of Exeter to shoulder dishonor that he rightfully should not bear. I canna let him be forced to marry a lying chit and accept the disdain of the House of Lords and all of Society because I choose to remain quiet and hide my own indiscretion."

"Siusan." Grant pulled her against him and hugged her.

"Please, let me finish." Her voice was quavering now, but in her heart she felt the truth of her words. "If indeed I have changed, if I possess true morals, then I must admit that I lay with the Duke of Exeter in the library, and I must do so publicly."

Grant's gaze was serious and questioning. "If you do this, you will certainly lose Da's respect, and because he will view your act of intimacy with the Duke of Exeter as dishonoring the family name, he may well send you off to carve out a new life, *alone*."

"I know." A tear hastened down her cheek and dripped from her jaw.

"Society may shun you, and so may the duke himself. He may claim to love you, but you must prepare yourself for the possibility that even he may turn from you so that he may preserve his own family honor."

"I realize this too." She gulped back a sob. "But if I do not accept my responsibility, then I have not changed at all. You are right when you say I have shown my true face to the world. Now I must accept the consequences of a life built on truth, and embrace the woman I have become."

Grant hugged her to him again. "Do your brother a wee favor, Su."

She leaned back and blinked up at him.

"Consider your decision a little longer. Do not act until you are completely certain of it. Be *sure*, Su, because whatever you decide will change your life, but in very, very different ways."

Rising, he took her hand and pulled her from the bench. "Now, what say you? Shall we go inside and thaw our bums by the fire?"

Siusan smiled. "You do realize that if you wore woolen breeches instead of silk on days like this, you would not need to worry so about freezing your bum."

Grant laughed. "Perhaps, but then I would not look so damned fine either, would I?"

When they entered the parlor, they saw that they were not alone. Reflexively, Siusan cowered behind Grant the moment she saw their father sitting in the tufted chair next to the fire, stroking his long white beard.

"Father." Grant bowed. When he bent, Siusan was exposed behind him.

Siusan moved beside Grant and curtsied gracefully. As she rose, she saw several dried brown leaves clinging to her walking frock. Her father's thick eyebrow lifted as he noticed them too. "I beg your pardon, Da, we had not expected you to grace our home for another sennight. Please forgive our appearance."

The Duke of Sinclair extended his hand to her. "Come here, my dear child. Ye are dressed sensibly given the unusually frigid day—unlike yer brother, who I observe still wastes coin on fribbles and fancy dress." Though she expected him to lift his attention from her to frown at her brother, he did not remove his gaze from her. "Please be seated, Siusan."

Grant moved beside her like a guard.

"Grant, I should like to speak with yer sister privately. Leave us." His brow lowered in his seriousness.

Grant lifted his chin. "I should like to remain, if you do not mind. This room possesses the only warm hearth in the house, except the kitchen, of course."

"Then by all means, hasten to the kitchen, and while ye are there, ask Mrs. Wimpole if she might brew some tea for this weary traveler."

Grant turned his eyes toward Siusan, with a look that communicated that he would not leave her, no matter their father's wishes, if she needed him to stay by her side.

As she sat down on the settee near the window,

she sent him a quick nod, releasing him. No need for Grant to endure their father's disdain unnecessarily.

Her father watched Grant exit the parlor and did not speak until his son's boots could be heard descending the stairs into the kitchen. "Ye have surprised me, Siusan."

Though his recent letter had expressed his pride in her, days had passed since he penned it and, by now, everything might have changed. She had no notion what his man of affairs in London might have reported.

She focused on his face, watching for any sign, but, alas, his tone gave nothing away, and she could not tell if his *surprise* was one of pleasure or disappointment.

"Did I surprise you?" She stilled her features. Two could play at this.

"Ye must know of what I speak." Then he confounded her with a smile. The expression was so alien to his features that she leaned forward over her knees, unable to refrain from staring at his tilted lips in utter amazement.

Siusan knew, however, to remain quiet. It would be most unwise to offer up any details of the past week's goings-on when she was not certain how much he actually knew.

Raising her eyebrows, she simply waited for him to speak again.

"From what I hear, ye are a great heroine, my dear."

She felt her cheeks coloring and hoped he would see her blush as an expression of modesty rather than embarrassment when the memory of Sebastian's naked body warming against hers suddenly flashed in her mind. That intimate press of skin, far more so than riding through the snow, was truly what saved Sebastian's life . . . and her own.

"And more than that, ye have taken it upon yerself to work to earn money to support yer family. Ye did not choose to gamble, or fight, or trick others into handing ye their purses. Ye *taught*, ye wrote columns, and even penned a book."

There was that smile again, but something did not feel the least bit authentic about it. Or maybe it was she who did not feel genuine—after all, she had not worked out of some great sense of providing for her brothers and sisters. Nay, she went to Bath, and took a position as a schoolmistress, for the sake of hiding from a man she had been intimate with, knowing he mistook her for another. And not caring.

"How I wish yer brothers and Priscilla would

have the fortitude to follow yer lead. But they are worthless and will be until . . . if ever . . . they learn what honor means, to oneself and to the family. But ye, Siusan, ye have learned this lesson and made yer father most proud."

She felt nauseous. Here she sat, being lavished with praise for her transformation into an honorable woman. But she hadn't changed at all. If she had, she would be racing through London to confess to the Duke of Exeter that she had been his lover in the library.

She alone had it in her power to restore his honor and save him from a loveless marriage!

Rising from the settee, she crossed to the secretary and withdrew from the desk a piece of foolscap. She dipped a pen in the ink and hurriedly penned a note.

"Siusan, what are ye doing?" Her father pounded his cane on the floor. "Sit down at once."

Ignoring him, she drizzled the page with pounce, then shook it off and folded the paper, sealing it with a wax stamp.

Eyeing Poplin, the house's lone manservant passing before the doorway, Siusan started for him before she had any opportunity to fashion an excuse for walking away from her father.

"Siusan!" He called out to her. "Return at once."

"I cannot, Father. I have an urgent errand to attend to—one about which I am already terribly delinquent." She whisked her cloak and bonnet from the hooks near the door.

Perplexed, Poplin looked at her, then at her father in the parlor. From the pounding of the cane, he was coming after her. She had to leave immediately.

"Please, see this is delivered at once." She pressed the folded letter into Poplin's hand. "Deliver it yourself. Give it to no one else but the addressee. Do you understand?"

The old man was trembling slightly, but he took the letter from her and whisked it behind his back as he opened the front door for her. Siusan rushed out into the square, then turned on the Brook Street to summon a hackney to transport her to Blackwood Hall.

Where she would confess her sin to Sebastian . . . and to anyone else he required.

Chapter 19

A great deal of laziness of the mind is called liberty of opinion.

Unknown

Blackwood Hall

It was twilight when Siusan arrived at her destination and peered out the carriage window at Blackwood Hall rising from the hillside. There was nary a cloud in the dusky sky, and the stars were already blinking as bright as the many candles in the windows above.

It was rash coming here without even sending a card. Sebastian might be in Town for all she knew, coming for her. More likely, though, he was too consumed with the young woman . . . who claimed she was with him in the library at the gala . . . and who was with child.

How had this Miss Aster chit known what had occurred in the library? Siusan, herself, had been there, and she hadn't even known that it was the Duke of Exeter she'd been intimate with in the darkness. Clearly, the duke hadn't known that she was his lover. So, how had some barely out miss cleverly assembled all of the puzzle pieces of that night—wedging herself in to replace Siusan—to complete a scene Sebastian would take for truth?

There was only one explanation Siusan could muster. Miss Aster has a connection with Basil Redbane, the man who had fashioned the bet at White's. Then, finding her own self round with child, the girl blames it on Sebastian, knowing somehow that he did not know the identity of the woman he had bedded in library.

Well, he'd know it now.

And soon, the whole of London would know.

When the carriage halted, the driver stepped down, opened the door, and handed her out. She pressed coins into his hand and had started for the hall's huge double doors when she reconsidered. "Please wait, if you would. I should not be long." The driver agreed and climbed back onto his perch. What hackney driver worth his whip wouldn't prefer a paying gentry miss to a long, fareless drive back to London?

The front doors opened before she had ascended the first two steps, and to her astonishment, Gemma bounded out to greet her.

"Oh, Lady Siusan! You have come. I told my Guardian you would, but he seemed certain you would not." Gemma grasped Siusan's hand and pulled her up the steps and into the great entry hall, where she took Siusan's cloak and bonnet and handed them to a hovering footman, who promptly disappeared into the shadows.

Siusan was staggered by the sudden onrush of emotions. Until that moment, she hadn't realized just how much she really missed Gemma and all of the other girls. She bent and hugged her former student to her, her eyes welling with happiness. "Och, look at me so flustered. I have missed you so." She straightened as it suddenly occurred to her that the girl should have been in school. "Why are you here? Why are you not at Mrs. Huddleston's School of Virtues?"

Miss Gentree lowered her eyes. "I begged Her

Grace to remove me from the school once you had gone. Everything changed so miserably. Mrs. Huddleston began teaching your classes. And it"—her voice began to quaver—"was terrible. We were never permitted to leave the school, nor were the other teachers. We were locked in our rooms at night and not freed until morning." She threw her arms around Siusan's waist. "But I am so pleased you have come, and my uncle will be as well."

Siusan took the girl's shoulders in her hands and eased her back until she could see her face. "Your . . . *uncle*?"

"Gemma meant her *guardian*." When Miss Gentree gasped, Siusan whirled around to see Sebastian's grandmother standing a few feet from them.

Siusan honored the duchess with a deep curtsy. "Duchess."

Miss Gentree stepped back from Siusan and, again, lowered her gaze. "Yes, I . . . I meant Lord Wentworth, my *guardian*. He is so kind to me I sometimes think of him as family." She lowered her head.

"No, Gemma," came Sebastian's voice from the end of the grand hall. He hurried forward, hold-

ing Siusan tightly in his gaze as if she might flee if
he blinked. "Gemma is my niece—she is my late
brother's daughter."

"She is your *ward*," the duchess hissed.

"Yes, she is, but she is also my niece. Your great-
granddaughter."

Miss Gentree seemed moved by Sebastian's
claim, but it was the duchess's piercing gaze that
prompted her to speak. "My father was not married to my mother. So, I am not truly family."

"Yes, Gemma, you are," Sebastian insisted,
reaching out for her. "We share blood. You are
family, and from this moment forward you will
be presented as my niece." Tears started down the
girl's cheeks, and Sebastian hugged her to him
as he stared down at his grandmother until she
turned and stalked away.

"Lady Siusan has come." Miss Gentree reached
out and took Siusan's hand.

Sebastian seemed somewhat startled. "You
mean, Miss Bonnet."

"She has always called me Lady Siusan . . . in
class." Siusan smiled at the girl.

"But you *are* Lady Siusan! I read the article in
the newspaper. I was looking for your lesson, but
instead, a column all about you was in its place.

You are a true lady. You are Lady Siusan Sinclair."

"Aye, I am." Siusan smiled a little embarrassedly, then turned her gaze up to Sebastian. "But, if you do not mind, Gemma, I urgently need to speak with your uncle alone."

A pleased smile tilted the girl's lips, and without a single word of protest, she walked down the hall and started up the huge sweeping staircase.

"*Siusan.*" Sebastian reached out for her. "There is something I must confess to you—"

"And I you. Please, may we retire to the library?" She gestured to the passage cutting off to the left from the grand hall.

"The library?" Sebastian rubbed his forehead. "So you already know."

"More than you are aware, and that is what I must speak with you about—in the library." Without waiting for him, she started forward.

"Allow me to show you the way—"

"I know where I am going." Her stocking began to slip as she walked, but she did stop to adjust it. As they grew closer to the library, she felt her cheeks flush pink.

Together, they crossed the grand hall, then turned down the dim passage for the library. A light pressed through the seam of the closed door.

Siusan looked up quizzically at Sebastian, wondering if someone was already inside . . . perhaps Miss Aster.

"I was sitting in here a few moments ago." Sebastian opened the door and gestured for her to enter. "It seems I have retired here frequently since I came to London."

"You are trying to remember." Siusan set her hand on the sofa and followed it around to the other side. She sat down, just as she had the night of the gala; then she drew her skirts up to her thighs. One stocking puddled about her ankle, while other was tied high with blue ribbon.

Sebastian stared at her.

"I had barked my knee and was sitting just here in the darkness, rubbing the sting from it, when you entered."

"Siusan, what is this folly?" Sebastian walked forward until he was standing next to her looking down.

"I thought you didn't see me at first, but then I saw the angle of your head and followed where your gaze might have traveled. The moonlight had fallen across my thighs, and you were looking down at them. You thought I was someone else."

"Siusan, why are you doing this?" He shoved his fingers through his hair.

"That someone was named Clarissa."

"How did you know her name?" Sebastian's eyes widened. "I never told anyone her name. Yes, it is shameful, but I was to meet Clarissa, a courtesan, in the anteparlor, or here during the gala. I could not remember which. Later, I learned she had never come to Blackwood Hall at all."

He came and sat on the edge of the sofa, peering at her, appearing perplexed.

"But *I* was here. You started kissing me, like this." Siusan leaned back against the sofa cushion and pulled him to her. He'd said once before that because it had been dark in library, his memories were mostly physical sensations. So, she would help him remember them. She pressed her lips to his, softly at first, then harder and more passionately.

He pulled back in protest. "Siusan—"

To force him to remember, to really believe her, she would have to do more. "Your hands were here." She grasped his wrists and set one hand on her inner thigh, dragging his fingers over her skin. She moved his other hand to her chest, brushing his fingers over the upper swell of her breast, before cupping his hand completely over it. "And here. And you were touching me like this—"

"Siusan!" He pulled back from her, staring at her like it was the first time he'd ever seen her. And maybe it was. The first time he'd really seen her—for the woman she really was. He pulled her gown down to cover her legs, then turned away in silence.

"Nay, Sebastian. I want you to look at me. I want you to see me, in the light, and know who I am." Her heart was breaking, but she needed to do this. Needed to free him from the lies. She sat up and grabbed his face with both hands and turned his face toward hers. "I am the woman you were with in the library that night. I. Lady Siusan Sinclair."

He stared without blinking for so long that his eyes began to water. Then he turned and took something out of a box sitting on a high bookshelf. He knelt before her. In his hand was her missing stocking ribbon.

She lifted her skirts over her knee and drew up her stocking. "You did not take advantage of some innocent miss in the darkness as you've been told. No matter how many glasses of brandy you may have had, Sebastian, you were with a woman who knew exactly what she was doing."

Sebastian tied the ribbon around her leg, securing her silk stocking. Then he pulled away and
shot to his feet. He began to pace, again shoving
his hands roughly through his hair in agitation.
He stopped before her and peered down. His
face was reddening, and his fists were clenching.
"Why, Siusan? Why did you let me make love to
you when you knew I thought you were another?"

"At first, I had thought only to escape the library. But then you kissed me, and I had been so
lonely that night. It was the anniversary of my fiancé's death." She wanted to look away in shame,
but she could not allow herself to do that. She had
to be strong, to make him understand that he had
done her no wrong. "When you kissed me, I let
myself imagine it was he kissing me, touching me
so intimately, the way he used to do."

"You imagined I was your fiancé?" His left eyebrow twitched.

"Only at first. But then you touched me, aroused
me, brought out a passion in me that he never
could. I could not imagine him any longer, but
nor could I stop myself from needing to feel you
inside me. I wanted you, and though I knew that
what I was doing was wrong, you, Sebastian, felt
so right."

He stared at her as she took his hand and eased

his fingers from a fist, then brought his fingertips to her mouth and gently kissed them.

"Why didn't you tell me after—"

"Afterward, I was ashamed of having given in to my passions. But, more than that, I was afraid you would learn who I was. I had put my family's honor at risk. I could not let Society learn of my indiscretion. I hoped you would forget me and what we shared here."

"I didn't know whom I bedded and feared I had ruined an unmarried woman. I had to find you . . . to make amends for my deed."

Siusan nodded. "When I later learned that you were tracking me, I knew I had to leave London for a time."

"That is when you went to Bath."

"Aye. A friend made arrangements for me to go to ground in Bath, working as a teacher to pay for my room and board. Until then, I had never worked a day in my life. I had only one skill, being a lady."

Sebastian continued to stare at her. His face frozen in suspended disbelief.

"When you came to see your . . . niece, I did not know who you were. I had, so far as I knew, never seen you before. You were introduced as the Marquess of Wentworth, not the Duke of Exeter."

He sighed. "I used my secondary title for Gemma's sake . . . and admittedly my own. I worried that if it became known that Gemma's unmarried guardian was a duke, both she and I would receive unwelcome attention from the students and their well-meaning mamas. It was foolish of me." He exhaled a long breath. "Believe me when I tell you that my use of the title was never directly intended to conceal my true identity from you."

"Neither of us knew we had shared an intimate moment with the other. And yet . . . I fell in love with you." She shook inside, waiting for his reaction, but still he did not speak. "How was I to know that the man who had so awakened my body would also awaken my heart?"

To her surprise, Sebastian slowly withdrew his hand from hers and turned and leaned on the sill to peer out of the window into the darkness.

It felt as though her heart were being crushed inside her chest. "Sebastian, you owe me nothing. Nothing. But neither do you owe Miss Aster anything. You are not the father of her child, if one exists in her belly at all. A Mr. Basil Redbane saw someone, me, leave the library right before you emerged. I do not know the details, but my brother learned that, through a proxy, Redbane had entered a wager in White's betting book. The wager was that you would marry the daughter of a high-ranking member of the House of Lords within a week. While most would take this bet, thinking it impossible, Redbane's young accomplice explained to my brother that the bet was solid, because you could not remember the woman you bedded during the gala. Miss Aster is posing as that woman—the woman you now know . . . was I."

Sebastian's shoulders tensed, but he did not turn from the window.

Siusan moved behind him, and she could see that he watched her candlelit reflection in the glass. "Sebastian, there has been no dishonor . . . except on my part. And I will confess my wrongdoing to anyone you wish—beginning with Lord Aster. I have already sent my letter of confession to him."

He flinched when she mentioned the letter, but still, he did not turn or utter a single word.

"I love you, Sebastian."

She had offered up her own honor to preserve his, the very same way she had risked her own life to save his. Sebastian looked down at his hands resting on the sill. His eyes welled, and he could not allow her to see them. He just needed a little time to collect himself.

A moment more, then he could tell her he loved her.

Then he heard the door open, and in the reflection of the room he saw Siusan leaving. He whirled around.

She wasn't going to leave him again after sacrificing herself. Not this time.

He raced though the doorway, where he found her leaning her forehead against the wall in the passage, hands pressed over her mouth, her shoulders shaking.

He approached her slowly, then eased his hands over her shoulders and kissed the side of her neck. "I love you, Siusan."

She turned her wet, reddened eyes up to him. "I know, Sebastian. But we both realize that what we feel does not matter." She tried to step away, but he held her firm. "I sent my confession to Lord Aster. My name is soiled beyond redemption, but your honor has been restored. We can no longer have any relationship. You know as well as I, Sebastian, you must sever all connections with me. We can never, ever, be together again."

She did not have to say it—to preserve his

family honor. He knew what she meant, and the painful truth of her statement.

His strength drained from him. Sebastian lowered his hands and, though this felt so wrong, and it took every bit of restraint he possessed, he allowed Siusan to walk down the passage and out of his life.

For two hours Sebastian sat alone with a single crystal of brandy, not bringing it to his mouth even once.

Since he'd become the Duke of Exeter, whisky had become his close companion. It tamped down his nerves before appearing as Duke of Exeter the night of the gala. It launched him on his mission to locate the miss he believed he'd taken advantage of in the library.

It quieted his worries and gave him courage to attempt ice-slickened roads during a roaring storm. And, before Siusan arrived that evening, it had kept him company while he rehearsed his confession to Siusan—that he must marry another to preserve his honor.

He turned the glass around, letting its amber contents sparkle in the light of a candle. Why had it taken him so long to realize that brandy had never helped him at all—it only birthed greater woes.

His courage had to come from within himself. It was time to shoulder the responsibilities of the Duke of Exeter—and prove what true honor really was.

And he would begin with Lord Aster.

By the time Sebastian's carriage reached Berkeley Square, it was hardly an appropriate time to call upon anyone, let alone the senior member of the House of Lords.

He approached the door, about to set the knocker to its rest, when it swung open and, to his astonishment, he was standing face-to-face with Basil Redbane. He narrowed his eyes.

"Your Grace, damn me! You about startled the life from my breast." Redbane slapped one hand to his heart, while with the other he waved someone behind his back from the door.

Sebastian stepped closer and peered over Redbane's shoulder. Miss Aster stood to the left of the door, her hand cupped over her mouth. "Good evening, Miss Aster." He gave her a quick nod. "I have come to speak with your father . . . though I must assume he and your mother are not at home." He glared at Redbane, whose cheeks, even in the dimness of the lamplight, were glowing like embers.

"Oh, Basil. What are we to do?" Miss Aster wailed. "He is certain to tell my father that you—"

Redbane shot his face around to her and growled. "Shut up, you stupid chit. Let me handle His Grace."

"Do not fret, Miss Aster, since your father is not available, I shall speak with Mr. Redbane about recent developments." Sebastian looked over Redbane's shoulder. "Shall we speak inside . . . or in my carriage."

"Oh, in your carriage, please, Duke. My parents should return from the musicale very soon." Miss Aster set her hand on Redbane's arm. "Please, Basil." Though her eyes were filled with worry, she batted her lashes coquettishly. "Please."

Redbane sighed and followed Sebastian down to the grand Exeter town carriage.

The moment the carriage lurched forward, Sebastian raised his fist.

Redbane raised his hands. "Now, now, Your Grace, let us not be rash."

"Why not? What would you do to someone who tried to force you to accept responsibility for his own by-blow?"

"Figured that bit out, eh?" Redbane's hands remained in the air, protecting his face.

"And then, sought to profit from it by placing a

bet through a proxy at White's." Sebastian sucked his lips into his mouth and raised his fist higher.

"Well, I credit you, little brother. I did not think you'd puzzle it through. Truly, I did not."

Sebastian's face muscles fell slack, and he slowly lowered his fist.

"Oh, so you hadn't figured the last piece, eh?" A smirk slid over Redbane's lips. "We are brothers . . . born on two very different sides of the blanket in the very same month. I was born on December 3, and you on December 19. Only, our father was not married to my mother, but instead to yours. You became a nobleman, while I became a tradesman, destined to live in the shadow of your splendor."

This was all coming too fast. It could not be that he and this man shared the same blood. "Are you saying—"

"That when Quinn died so suddenly—and oh, yes, he knew all about me—except for that one slip of Fate, I would have become the Duke of Exeter." His top lip curled back like a snarling dog's. "How do you think it felt all those years being ignored by our father, watching him teach you to ride? Standing in the shadows, learning a trade while you were being packed off to fine schools. Watching you squander money when I had to sweat blood for every penny. And even when I managed to make something of myself, you stepped in and accepted a lofty position backed by no more merit than an accident of birth."

"You have done very, very well for yourself, Redbane, and you cannot fault me for the circumstances of my birth just as you cannot fault yourself." Sebastian studied Redbane. As he looked at the man, he saw his father's eyes and heavy jowls. This was no lie. This man was his brother.

"That's rich, coming from you." Redbane sneered.

"If your hatred of me lies so deep, why would you wish me to raise your child with Miss Aster? That makes no sense. Were you to marry her, your political career would surely benefit. Instead, you wish me to accept your responsibility."

Redbane laughed. "Because, dear brother, though I was deprived of everything your noble birth ensured for you, my son would be the next Duke of Exeter."

"And he would never know you and all you did. Would never know who you are." Sebastian looked hard at Redbane. "Listen, man, marry Miss Aster. Raise your son to be the man you would have been. You have the means. Choose honor, because it is the right thing to do, Redbane, and you will never, ever, be like our father."

Redbane's mouth had fallen open, and he was blinking hard.

Sebastian glanced up through the window and saw that the carriage had ringed the square twice, and they were now approaching Aster House. He hammered his fist on the carriage wall, and the driver pulled the team to a halt and climbed down from his perch. The door opened, and the steps were let down. Silently, Redbane descended the steps to the road, then climbed the stairs to the walk.

"Be the honorable gentleman you aspired to be." Sebastian called out to him. "The past is over, there is nothing we can do to change that. But you can shape your future, and that of your child, or you can become our father and live only for yourself. The choice is yours."

Chapter 20

Life is not long, and too much of it must not pass in idle deliberation how it shall be spent.

Dr. Samuel Johnson

Sebastian squinted through the window as his carriage rolled to a stop before the Sinclair town house. The light of a single candle in one of the third-floor windows drew his eyes up to a woman peering down at him. During the past hour, clouds had drifted across the earlier clear sky, and whirling white flurries now spun through the air, obscuring his vision. *Siusan?*

Flinging open the carriage door, he charged up the snow-dusted stairs to the door. It was late, but he had waited too long already to set everything to rights with the woman he loved.

He had just reached for the brass knocker when the front door opened a hand's width, and Lady Priscilla Sinclair squeezed her face into the small opening. She appeared to be wearing naught but a nightdress wrapped with a mantle.

"You have to leave at once," she hissed. "Our father is in residence, and he will not take a liking to a gentleman, duke or not, calling for my sister at such an hour."

Sebastian shoved his boot into the gap to prevent her from closing the door. "I am not leaving until I see her."

From the concerned expression on her face, she clearly took his words for truth. She turned her head and glanced behind her, then cracked the door open a bit wider and slipped through, pulling it nearly closed. "She's not here, so *please* leave."

He could see that she was telling the truth as well. "Where is she? Has she returned to Bath?"

Tears budded in Lady Priscilla's eyes. "Our father does not yet know she has left London, but she has."

Sebastian abruptly grasped her shoulders, startling her. He lifted his hands away, holding them momentarily in the air. "I apologize, Lady Priscilla, but I must know where she has gone."

She rubbed the tears from her eyes. "My sister has left for Aberdeen—to protect you. She means to accept a teaching position there." Lady Priscilla started to scoot back through the door.

He reached for her arm. "Scotland? When did she leave? Did she hire a carriage—" In his agitation, his tone grew louder and his grip on her tighter.

"Please be quiet. *Please*. My father cannot learn of this until tomorrow, when she will be safe from his reach." She tried to tug her arm away.

Sebastian held her arm firmly. "Lady Priscilla, I cannot allow her to leave. Not when I have yet to ask her to marry me."

Priscilla's dark slashes of eyebrows shot toward her hairline. "But she was sure there was no future for the two of you. Your honor—"

"What honor would I have left if I dishonored your sister in a misguided attempt to right my father's years of wrongs? I am my own man, I have my own sense of honor—and tonight that means I must find Siusan." He opened his fingers one by one and allowed her to lower her arm as she considered his words.

"Grant ordered a traveling coach from Gower Mews and summoned it to the corner for her the moment our father was asleep. From what I saw, it is large but slow."

"My thanks, Priscilla." Sebastian turned and started down the stairs. "Wish me luck."

"If you hurry, you might still catch up with her— but I do wish you luck convincing her to return to London. Su is stubborn when she has set her mind, but I know too that she loves you deeply— enough to summon the courage to do what she fears most in life—leave her family." She gave him a small wave, then moved back inside the house.

He turned again to leave but was stopped once more when a man called out to him. "Your Grace." A small, balding man, who he remembered as Poplin. "Your Grace, might I impose on you to please apologize to Lady Siusan for me and inform her that the addressee was not at home and therefore, per her explicit instructions, the letter was not delivered." The little man lifted his wiry eyebrows meaningfully.

Sebastian hesitantly took the letter and briefly looked down and saw Lord Aster, Berkeley Square, inked on the front. He looked up for further information, but Poplin had already disappeared inside.

Her confession was never delivered.

* * *

Tiny flakes of snow caught in Sebastian's lashes as he peered through the open window of the carriage for any sight of Siusan's coach. In the carriage's lamplight he could see the tracks of another vehicle that had gone before, but those wheel ruts were quickly filling with snow.

Glimpses of their carriage accident pricked at his mind, and a growing fear began to nag. Not fear for himself, but for her.

Suddenly his driver called down to him. "There's a coach straight ahead, Your Grace."

"Run it down." Sebastian leaned his shoulder out the carriage window and peered through the darts of snow ahead. Two lamplights illuminated a large carriage.

"He's got a team of six, and I've got but two, though I shall give it all I've got." Sebastian heard the crack of the driver's whip in the air, and the carriage surged forward.

As the carriage gained on the coach, it became clear the road was not wide enough for the two vehicles to move side by side. "It's not stopping. Are you able to pass and force the coach to stop?" Sebastian yelled up to the driver.

"Road is too narrow, but I can stop them."

A moment later, the report of a gunshot rent the air. The coachman pulled his team to a halt.

Sebastian leaped from the carriage and rushed to the coach door, pulling it open. "Siusan?" He peered inside. *Damn me!* He lurched back in surprise when an old woman looked back at him. "I beg your pardon, dear lady. I thought you were someone else."

Just then, Siusan leaned forward from the front bench of the coach. "When has that ever stopped you before?"

She gave him a small smile and gestured to the old woman. "Mrs. Patterson is headed for Edinburgh. There was only one traveling coach available this night, and she graciously agreed to share."

He tipped his hat at Mrs. Patterson, then reached for Siusan's hand and drew her out of the coach. "Siusan, please you cannot leave London."

She pulled her hand back. "I must. Do you not understand, I must, to preserve your family's honor?"

"No, Siusan. If you leave, you will take my honor with you." He shook his hands, palms up. "Please, at least listen to what I must say to you. I love you. I love you and cannot live another day without you."

Siusan's eyes rounded, and she cupped her hand at her brow to shield her eyes from the driving snow as she stared back at him. She did not move or speak for a long while as she considered his words, though when she did, she called out to the driver. "Would you please remove my portmanteau from the coach? It seems I am no longer headed for Aberdeen . . . at least not on this snowy night."

Mrs. Patterson tittered, then slid back on her seat and allowed the door to be closed. "Good eve, Lady Siusan."

Sebastian was bursting with relief. He passed Siusan's bag to his own driver. "Back to London, Bertrum." Then, he opened the door and handed Siusan up inside his carriage.

Climbing in after her, Sebastian spread a blanket over them both.

Siusan's expression was serious. Instantly, she hushed him with a finger across his lips. "Before you begin, I must tell you that I wrote a letter to Lord Aster advising him that you are not and could not be the father of his daughter's child because she was not the woman whom you bedded during the gala. I was. I also confessed that I took advantage of your inebriation to conceal my own identity, and that you should be held entirely blameless in this matter."

Sebastian kissed her finger. "Are you through?"

"*Nay,* do you not understand? In order to maintain your honor now, you must sever your connections with me. Forever."

He held up the letter Poplin, the butler, had given him. "Is this the confession you sent to Lord Aster?"

Siusan's eyes went round. "Aye, but where did you get it?"

"I went to Lord Aster's house earlier this night, but instead encountered Basil Redbane—"

"The man who placed the anonymous proxy bet at White's!"

"Yes, but he was not alone. He was with Miss Aster. We spoke briefly, during which time he admitted that he was the father of Miss Aster's child—and though I am not certain of it, I believe he will marry her."

"But . . . the letter."

Sebastian handed it to Siusan. "It was never delivered. It seems Lord Aster was not at home to receive it, and so, your butler, per your instructions, never delivered it."

Siusan turned it over in her hands. The seal had

never been broken. She raised her eyes slowly until her gaze met his.

"Siusan, I love you, and no matter the circumstances, I always will. You have shown me what true honor and courage are. This is the greatest lesson you've ever taught because you imparted it by example." Sebastian rose and did his best to kneel before her in the wobbly carriage. He took her hand in his. "Siusan, will you do me the great honor of becoming my wife?"

Siusan's eyes welled, and her lips quivered as she prepared to answer. "Aye, Sebastian, I will." Her voice was a mere whisper to his ears.

His balance was uncertain, but his intent was sure. From his pocket, he withdrew a large sapphire set in a ring of gold and eased it onto her finger. "This ring belonged to my mother, who taught me what love was, and now I wish for you to have it, the woman who made me remember."

"I love you, Sebastian."

"I love you too . . . Miss Bonnet."

Siusan stared into his eyes.

"Well, I do. I love Miss Bonnet, because through her, I met the love of my life—you. I love you, Lady Siusan Sinclair."

Siusan shook her head but grinned as she cupped her hand behind his neck and pulled him into a deep kiss. His arms came around her and slowly he guided her back down against the bench's cushion.

Nearly two hours later, Sebastian's carriage rolled up before Siusan's house. "I shall return in the morning to request an audience with your father and ask for your hand in marriage." Sebastian leaned down and kissed her.

"And if he refuses?" Siusan pressed her lips and held him close, as though it were the last time.

"I know his acceptance is important to you. So I shall ask again, and again if needed. He will accept my offer, Siusan. I will not stop until he has. I can be quite persistent." He stepped out of the carriage and helped Siusan down, then escorted her to the door.

Siusan touched the latch and was pleased that it had not been locked. "Good night, my love. I will see you in the morning." She pecked his cheek as he passed her her bag, then she slipped inside.

She hurried into the parlor to watch his carriage leave the square, but when she entered her father was sitting beside the fire. "Father."

"So that was the Duke of Exeter, was it?" His face was expressionless.

"Aye, Da, it was." Though the parlor was warm,

Siusan shivered but shed her cloak and shook off the cold. "And you should know that on the morrow, he will ask you for my hand in marriage."

"His family name is tarnished with dishonor. Why should I approve such a union?"

"Because he is an honorable man, a good man, a kind man. He should not be held to blame for his father's past misdeeds. A son should not have to atone for the sins of his father. Have you not taught us that we must atone for our own sins— restore honor to ourselves to restore it to the Sinclair name?"

The Duke of Sinclair raised a white eyebrow at that comment. "Aye, I did."

"This is what I am trying to do. I have made a great many mistakes, but had I not made them, I would not have learned the value of honor. I would not have learned to love and be loved. I would not have learned that I am happiest when I am working. And that I will never lose my brothers and sisters, even if we are apart, because as a family, we are one."

"Aye, Siusan, ye are right. This is why family is so important and why we must all strive to overcome our weaknesses, to become strong, so when one of us needs support, we are able to give it." He set his cane to the carpet and rose, then crossed the parlor to Siusan. "Ye've grown, cast off that which held ye in a place of pain. And now, ye're a strong woman, and I am proud that ye are my daughter." He reached out and hugged her to him.

Tears of great happiness rolled down her face, and she began to laugh. Never had she been so happy, but one thing could make her joy complete. "And the Duke of Exeter?"

Her father took her shoulders in his hands and straightened his arms to look at her. "He will have my blessing."

The aged Duchess of Exeter was standing before the grand staircase when Sebastian returned to Blackwood Hall. "It is morning. Where have you been all night? You stormed out of here so angrily that I worried for your safety. Thought you might do something rash and—"

"Die in some freakish accident like the other Dukes of Exeter?" Sebastian shook off the notion and started for the parlor.

"Do not mock me, Sebastian." She narrowed her eyes at him as she followed him into the parlor. "The Curse of the Duke of Exeter exists."

Sebastian flung himself onto the sofa and covered his face with his palms. He was too exhausted for this, but he'd let talk toy with his mind and alter his actions for long enough. "The Curse of the Duke of Exeter does *not* exist."

"How can you deny the evidence?"

"I do agree that the men in this family have a foolish, adventurous streak about them—and that, Grandmother, is what killed them. Not some ridiculous curse."

"A ball of lightning struck your grandfather!"

"Well, if a man chooses to walk across a flat field in a thunderstorm, he may be struck."

His grandmother gasped. "Your own father died in a flood of beer!"

"Because when the beer vats burst, he went swimming in it while drinking all he could. I ask you, what sane man would do that?"

"Your brother's death was—"

Sebastian rubbed his eyes. "My fault. It was a hot day, and I'd just purchased my high-perch phaeton. I bragged about its speed and challenged him to race it around the park. When he didn't return . . ." He sucked in a deep breath. "He'd tried to remove his neckcloth, and it somehow had gotten entangled in the wheel, snapping off his—" Sebastian swallowed deeply. "There is no curse. Never has been. We look for adventure, though sometimes we are reckless and pay the ultimate price."

His grandmother's eyes were tearing. "You share their blood. How will you avoid a fate to rival theirs?"

"Because I know why they died. It wasn't Fate. It was recklessness. I won't make the same mistake." Sebastian pushed up from the sofa and started for his bedchamber. "If you will excuse me, Grandmother, I must bathe and dress."

"Why? Where are you planning to go? You just returned home."

"To Mayfair, to call upon the Duke of Sinclair and offer for his daughter, Siusan."

His grandmother reached out and caught his sleeve as he passed her. "Wait, Sebastian."

He looked down at her. "I cannot be dissuaded. Lady Siusan Sinclair has offered up her own life for mine twice already. I have never met such an honorable, kind, and loving woman. I love her, Grandmother, and I will marry her."

She drew him close and hugged him. When she pushed away she was smiling. "Then I shall love her too. We are family after all." She clapped her hands together as a notion struck her. Allow me to throw a glittering gala in honor of your engagement!"

Good Lord. A gala.

Sebastian shuddered inwardly at the thought. "Actually, Grandmother, I have read in one of Siusan's columns that small dinner parties are becoming all the crack."

"Really?" She peered into the air as if assessing his statement. "Perhaps you are right. Yes, I think I quite like the idea of fashionable dinner party. I shall begin planning the menu at once."

Sebastian chuckled as his grandmother scurried out the parlor door ahead of him.

One month later
Bath Abbey

Siusan's happiness was nearly complete. In a moment, she would marry Sebastian Beaufort, the fourth Duke of Exeter.

Her father offered his arm, she took it, and together they moved slowly through the great abbey.

As she approached the altar, where Sebastian waited, the morning sun was shining through the soaring windows of Bath Abbey, making the gold embroidery glisten atop her white satin-and-lace gown.

On her shoulders was her mother's velvet cloak, lined with whitest ermine.

Another lesson. It is possible to be warm and entirely fashionable.

Nearest the altar stood her family. On the right were her brothers, Grant, Killian, Lachlan, and even Sterling, with his wife, Isobel. On his left, her sisters, Priscilla and Ivy with her husband, Dominic Sheridan, the Marquess of Counterton. Her heart swelled at the sight of them all together, the way it used to be.

She beamed as she walked past Miss Hopkins and Miss Grassley, who gestured madly at the man beside her, her fiancé, to the amusement of the gaggle of Siusan's former students, who were trying very hard to remain ladylike.

The Duchess of Exeter stood nearest Sebastian, with Miss Gentree at her side.

As she and her father reached the altar, she took Sebastian's strong hands, and within minutes, he swore before God to love and honor her all the days of his life.

She peered down at her hand, her eyes swimming with tears of joy, as Sebastian slipped a circlet of gold onto her finger.

And then the ceremony was over. The tears

she'd held in her eyes during the ceremony cascaded down her cheeks. Still, she didn't care.

This was the happiest day of her life. And from this moment on, she and Sebastian, the man she loved with all her heart, were married.

That evening

After the wedding breakfast and festivities had concluded, a grand ball was held in the Upper Assembly Rooms in honor of the marriage of the Duke of Exeter and Lady Siusan, the new Duchess of Exeter.

All of Bath Society was present at the glittering event, at least, or so it would be reported in the *Bath Time*'s *on-dit* column, according to Mr. Hercule Lestrange, who amazingly seemed to move through the crowd without drawing notice.

When Siusan and Sebastian quit the dance floor, she noticed that her sister was watching with the queerest expression on her face. "What is it, Priscilla?"

"I was just thinking." Whatever it was she was thinking about must have taxed her mind, for her brow was drawn.

"What were you thinking?" Movement caught her eye, and she looked to see Grant standing behind Priscilla shaking his head fiercely, but with a most amused smile upon his lips.

"If you had just observed my claim on the duke at his gala ball, none of this would have ever happened." She lifted a single eyebrow as if to punctuate her point.

Siusan promptly leaned over and kissed Sebastian's lips, then settled her hand atop her belly, smiling. "I know."

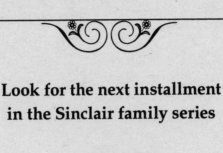

**Look for the next installment
in the Sinclair family series**

**Coming 2012
From**

Avon Books

ord Grant Sinclair never could abide the ignorant. And though the company of the four thick-brows he'd joined at the card table an hour before had fattened his pockets considerably, their inane conversation prickled his patience.

What addlepates they were. Why, their mugs practically screamed out the exact cards they held in their stubby thieving fingers, while they turned the blame for their own idiocy on being light on luck.

What a ridiculous notion.

Being blessed with good fortune had nothing to do with winning at cards. Nay, it had everything to do with watching for tells, those tiny, almost imperceptible flinches, grimaces, or smiles, that communicate even the most wily of liars' honest reaction moments before their minds have the good sense to mask true emotion. Tells were Grant's bread and butter.

His brothers, and aye, his sisters, too, had developed perception of others to a fine art. That was not to say that this skill always benefited them, for indeed, many times, knowing what another is thinking only boosts one's supreme self-assuredness to a level that leads him to attempt too great risks, thinking he has a clear advantage. That forged a path to recklessness . . . and sometimes to a blackened eye.

Or worse.

Much like tonight.

Grant realized his mistake the moment he won the fifth straight hand, chuckling inwardly as he dragged more than fifty gleaming guineas across the card table. A heap of sweet gold glittered before him, and yet he held his countenance impassive. A misstep, it seemed, for his lack of reaction, which would have warranted from anyone else a hoot at the very least, drew the attention of the other players.

"Why, ye're a bleedin' cheat." The player's words slurred, courtesy of the bottle of fine brandy Grant had paid the waiter to serve to their table time and time again over the past hour.

He couldn't help himself but redirected the attention from his skill at cards to the brandy. "Hardly. But I am a Scot, as well as a Sinclair, and holding our spirits is something at which we excel."

"Well, I don't think that's it at all, you sotting shark." This man was a fair bit larger than the first, and Grant felt it was only wise to refrain from baiting him. "Here's what I reckon. Ye've colored the cards or numbered them somehow." He and the other males—for in that particular gaming hell, Grant was sure he was the only gentleman present—flipped over their cards and held them up before their crimson-threaded, glazed-over eyes. "How else would you always know exactly what we're all holdin' in our paws?" The hulk came to his feet . . . followed by the other players.

As if on cue, they whisked back their coats, revealing knives, guns, and even a small meat hook.

Bollocks.

Now, Grant was a very large man, by any standards, but the four muscle-bound thugs had the advantage of numbers—and weapons.

Blast. Time to quit the premises. Promptly.

Hooking the tips of his fingers beneath the edge of the table, he flipped it over upon them. Not terribly original, but, hell, he didn't have more than a moment to consider his escape.

The cost would be his bounty, but his life was more precious. His most recent pile of ill-gotten guineas spilled out upon them and clattered across the floor.

The thick-brows scrambled, providing Grant just enough time to whirl around and dash out the door.

The air was icy, and, for a moment, the thought crossed Grant's slightly inebriated mind that the fogged plume of his breath would lead them straight to him, wherever he ran, like a trail of bread crumbs.

He hastened to the top of St. James's Street, hoping at that time of night, a hackney would be waiting at the stand. No such luck. He could already hear the gamesters bellowing at him from down the hill.

Despite the hour, he saw candlelight glowing in the windows of a building up ahead. The room appeared crowded, and if he was stealthy enough, he decided he could slip inside and lose himself in their number. He made for it.

The pounding of his footfalls sounded amplified in the still of the night, twisting his nerves tighter. He hurried to the door and, to his relief, found it unlocked, and he was able to enter freely.

A gathering of several people stood at the front of a large, rectangular room. A bench in the front and a number of simple wooden chairs stood cheek by jowl in rows of six with a narrow aisle down the middle. Plainly dressed women filled the chairs on one side of the aisle, while men and older boys were on the other.

Not a word was spoken, though every soul turned around to peer at Grant as he entered. He nodded in a friendly manner, but he could see from their disapproving eyes that he had intruded upon some sort of meeting. And, while he knew he should leave at once, he simply could not. Not with Mr. Meat Hook prowling about outside. And so, he smiled sheepishly and quietly closed the door behind him.

At the front of the room stood a young, very beautiful woman wearing a sullen expression that contrasted so completely with her snowy white frock. She was all but surrounded by a stern-faced gentleman, a well-dressed man, and a woman, who, between audible sobs, dabbed a handkerchief to her eyes.

The young woman's green eyes lifted and sought out Grant's own. He smiled at her and immediately a flash of borrowed relief swept her finely sculpted features.

"Is that he?" The tall, elderly man barked, pointing rudely at Grant.

She lowered her eyes as she nodded. "I told you he would come. He would not leave me to face this alone."

What in God's name is she going on about?

"You, there, friend. Come forward. We have been waiting for you." The tall man beckoned Grant forward.

"Are you referring to me, sir?"

"I am. Come forth." It was not a request.

On the other side of the wooden door, Grant could hear the muffled voices of the cardplayers as they called out to each other. It was certain they would discover him if he did not find some way to conceal himself in plain sight. And so, he did what any man being pursued by a snarling pack of armed thugs would do—he walked down the aisle toward the young woman.

As Grant neared, the miss's wide green eyes pleaded desperately with him. It was clear she needed his help, but in doing what? Her face paled as her chest rose and fell in a rapid succession of shallow breaths.

Damn me. He'd seen this collection of reactions before—just before his sister Ivy lost consciousness the day she was presented to the queen.

Grant hastened to her, and when she reached out her shaking hands to him, he instinctively took them into his own.

Och, aye, she was in a serious tangle, of that he

was certain. But Grant was deep in the stew as well, and so, for the moment, he would accept her plea and become her accomplice in some sort of grand charade.

Squeezing her hands, he gave her a quick nod to impart his agreement with her plan, whatever it might be. After all, better to play along than to be cast back into the street and into the hands of four men desiring to hack him into guinea-sized bits and feed him to the Thames.

What happened next was damned odd.

Nothing. Not a bloody thing happened. They were led to two chairs set side by side and bade to sit. There they remained for several agonizing minutes in complete silence as Grant's pursuers stalked past the windows time and time again.

The congregation did not stir. At one point, Grant leaned toward the young woman to whisper to her. He had to admit, he was feeling more than a little done in from the whisky he'd imbibed during the card game, and, perhaps, he missed the stern-faced man's directions and whether he was supposed to say something.

The moment he parted his lips, the green-eyed beauty flashed a warning glance. He closed his mouth at once.

Finally, she took his hand and drew him to his feet. She turned to him. "In the presence of God and these Friends, I take thee to be my husband, promising with Divine assistance to be unto thee a loving and faithful wife as long as we both shall live." Then, she squeezed his hand.

Damn me to hell. Grant's eyes widened. This was a bleeding wedding! *His.* His keen bachelor's instincts told him to run. He started to pull away, but she tightened her hold.

"Please," she mouthed. Her eyes began to flood with tears.

Nay, this was going too far. Grant started to turn, meaning to quit the premises at once, but at that very moment the door opened and one of his pursuers stalked in. Everyone turned to face the newcomer.

Grant turned back around and angled toward the young woman. If he could just remain where he was for a few moments, the wastrel might not see him and leave.

"Please." The miss peered up at him. "Help me," she whispered.

Grant stared down at her. How could she possibly ask him to do this? She didn't even know him.

Then it occurred to him that that was likely

exactly why she wanted his help. They didn't know each other. His name could not be upon any wedding license, for until a few minutes ago, they'd never even seen each other. The marriage ceremony was not valid in the least. He exhaled. "Very well."

"Repeat after me, while the Friends are still distracted by the man in the back of the meeting house. I assume he is looking for you?"

Grant nodded. Had a thug not been prowling the perimeter of the room, this whole adventure would be vastly amusing.

"Then, sir, we have an agreement." A sigh of relief escaped her full, pink lips.

"Aye, we do." *Why the hell not?* After all, what a chuckle his brothers and sister would have when he told them over breakfast that last eve he married a chit he'd never even met. "Begin."

She peered up into his eyes and spoke.

Trying not to slur, Grant repeated her words softly, but in a heartfelt manner so as to make the ceremony more believable to all present. "In the presence of God and these Friends, I take thee to be my wife, promising with Divine assistance to be unto thee a loving and faithful husband as long as we both shall live."

The door slammed closed, and Grant could not help but whirl around. *Thanks be. He is gone.* His breathing came easier now. Another moment, and it would likely be safe enough to leave the building.

The young woman dragged him to a table in the front corner of the room. She took up a quill and dipped it into the ink. "One last thing. Please, sign your name here, and we are finished."

The entire congregation had left their chairs and were moving toward them, and so, not wanting this farce to continue any longer, he scribbled something. The two older men who had been standing with the young woman took up the quill pen and signed the document as well.

He gave a parting glance at the visibly relieved young woman, as the congregation enveloped her, then he dashed from the room and back into the empty street.

The next morning
The Sinclair residence
Mayfair

"Excuse me, Lord Grant."

Grant lifted one eyelid but he was not about to move from his pillow. "What time is it, Poplin?"

The Sinclair family's elderly manservant stood before Grant's bed. "Noon, my lord."

"Too early. Need sleep," he groaned, pulling the coverlet over his head.

"I must inform you that you have a visitor, my lord."

"Poplin, my head pains me." Indeed, Grant's head throbbed with every word. "I am in no condition to receive a visitor."

"Forgive me, my lord, but your sister was quite certain you would wish to receive this caller."

"Who is it?" Grant rolled onto his back and lifted the edge of the coverlet from his face.

"The caller did not provide a name, though I believe Lady Priscilla is correct in her assumption that you would wish to receive this caller."

Grant opened his eyes. The old man was clearly discomposed. He could not even meet Grant's gaze. "Why are you and my sister so convinced I would wish to entertain a visitor now?"

"Because, my lord," Poplin cleared his throat, "she claims to be your wife."

Grant hadn't even bothered to dress. He donned a striped dressing gown, tied it at his waist, and stormed from his bedchamber. Hurrying down the stairs, he rushed into the parlor.

And there she was. The green-eyed beauty he'd . . . well . . . Christ, did he marry her last eve? Only they weren't married. Nay. It was a charade, nothing more!

"There you are, Grant," crooned Priscilla, the youngest of the seven Sinclair siblings. "I realize you must have been in a great hurry to greet your beloved wife, but you might have considered wearing breeches at the very least for my sake." She grinned over the lip of her teacup.

The young woman rose. "My lord."

Grant narrowed his eyes and walked toward her, but stilled his step when his brother Lachlan entered the parlor. "Well, who have we here, Priscilla? Care to introduce me to your lovely friend?"

The woman turned to look at Lachlan, then trained her eyes on Grant once more. "I fear I am no longer a Friend, my lord."

Lachlan chuckled and turned his attention to Grant. He playfully punched his brother in the shoulder. "Och, now, what have you done to deserve that, Grant?"

"He married her. Isn't that right, Grant?" Priscilla's lips lifted with the promise of more mischief.

Lachlan burst out laughing, but when no one joined in his merriment, he stopped abruptly. "She is jesting, Grant, isn't she?"

"I don't even know her name." Grant studied her without reservation.

"I am Miss Felicity Lightfoot."

"Or, rather you *were* until last night. Now, you are Lady Felicity Sinclair." It was evident that Priscilla could barely contain her laughter. "I know, the marriage happened so suddenly that your elevation and new name will take time to become accustomed to."

Lachlan grasped Grant's shoulder and shook him. "What in blazes is going on here?"

"I honestly could not tell you, but I intend to find out." Grant pushed away his brother's arm and headed for Priscilla. He whisked her dish of tea from her hands and pulled her to her feet and marched her toward the passage.

"Lachlan, will you escort our sister to the dining room?"

"Absolutely, if you promise to explain—"

The moment Lachlan and Priscilla had passed through the parlor door, Grant closed and locked it behind them without a word of explanation.

"Miss Lightfoot, please be seated. By the sound of things, we have much to discuss." He gestured to her chair, and she quickly sat down. "Let us begin our interview with a simple question—*why*?"

Her lower lip trembled. "I had nowhere else to

go . . . and you were so very kind in marrying me."

Grant raised his eyebrows at that. "We are *not* married."

"Oh, but we are." She sounded so sure of herself.

"Do you take me for a fool, Miss Lightfoot. There was no license. Ergo, we are not legally married."

Suddenly, there was a persistent knocking at the parlor door. "Grant!"

He turned toward the door. "Lachlan, please leave."

"Nay, Grant. There is something you must know," he yelled from the other side of the door. "Something very important."

"Excuse me, please, Miss Lightfoot. My brother has something in his head that cannot wait, it seems." He rose, shaking his head as he stalked to the door. He turned the key and opened the door a hand's width. Lachlan and Priscilla were standing just on the other side, each with a crystal glass in hand. They had obviously been listening at the door and using the glasses to amplify the sound. "What is it that could not wait"—he lowered his voice to a low whisper—"until I have finished my discussion with this . . . madwoman."

Lachlan was shaking his head fiercely. "She isn't mad, Grant, she is a Quaker."

"What are you rambling on about?"

"The government does not require Quakers to possess a wedding license in order to wed legally." Lachlan's eyes were wild.

"But . . . banns were never read," Grant protested.

"Nor do they need to be."

Grant's mouth flapped open and closed as he struggled to apply some logic to this. "Oh, blast it, get in here. I may need your help."

He swung the door wide, and Lachlan followed him inside. Priscilla did not wait to be asked but practically skipped into the parlor uninvited.

Miss Lightfoot crossed her arms over her chest.

"Grant, dear, I believe she heard every word," Priscilla quipped. "Did you, Miss Lightfoot?"

"Indeed I did." She unfolded her arms and set her gloved hands atop her knees. "There was no officiant, no minister, or priest to join us."

Grant clapped his hands together. "There you have it, Lachlan. You see, I am not married."

Lachlan shook his head solemnly. "Quakers marry each other in the presence of God and the meeting of Friends."

Shoving his fingers through his hair, Grant dropped back onto the settee. Slowly, he looked up at Miss Lightfoot. "So, this is true . . . we are married—*legally* married?"

"Yes." She rose from her chair and walked into the passage. Grant and Lachlan exchanged confused glances. When she returned, she carried a leather valise, and from it she withdrew a scroll of parchment. She handed it to Grant. "Our marriage certificate."

Grant opened the scroll to review an ornately illuminated document.

Priscilla moved beside him and peered over his shoulder at the parchment. "Look, there is your name, Grant Sinclair—oh, hardly legible at all, but there—and yours"—she looked up at their visitor—"Felicity Lightfoot."

Beneath their names were others. The meeting of Friends. Their witnesses to the marriage. And there were dozens of them.

Grant began to feel nauseous. "If you knew this was legal, why in God's green earth would you do this?"

Miss Lightfoot lowered her head. "A young man I met in a shop stole a kiss from me last week. His amorous display was witnessed by two of the meeting's elders. My guardian was informed, and I was to be read out of the meeting last night. My guardian's wife was greatly distressed and convinced the clearance committee to allow me to marry this young man before being read out, so I would not be ruined." She turned her bright eyes up to Grant. "I didn't even know the man's name, and so I could not give it. They thought I was merely protecting him from retribution by my guardian. I knew there would be no marriage—how could there be?—and yet I couldn't tell her. She was so frightened for me."

Grant sighed. "And so when I unexpectedly walked into the meeting, and everyone assumed I was the young man you were to marry—"

"I didn't know what else to do. I went along with it."

"You just went along with it?" Grant dropped the certificate to the table before him.

"Well, so did you. I don't know why, though I expect it had something to do with that man who interrupted the meeting. I kept expecting you to walk out. *That* I could explain to my guardian and his wife. But you never did. You went through with everything. You even signed the certificate."

"I was sotted!"

"You made your mark."

"Because you told me I would be finished once I did!"

"Well, *my darling,* now we are married—and the fault of our union lies with the both of us." She lifted an eyebrow.

Everyone remained silent for several moments, no one daring to speak.

Then Poplin entered the crypt-silent parlor. "Shall I refresh the tea, Lady Priscilla?"

Priscilla's expression instantly shifted from stunned to absolute delight. "Not just yet, Poplin, but would you please take Lady Sinclair's valise to Ivy's former bedchamber?"

Grant's mouth fell agape.

Priscilla grasped Miss Lightfoot's hand and drew her from the chair. "Come with me, Felicity. I may call you that, mayn't I? We are sisters now. Oh, how wonderful is this? I have so missed having a sister in the house. You cannot imagine what it is like to live with a houseful of men! But now I shall not have to, for I have a new sister, and my brother has a wife!"

Grant wilted. *Damn it all.* So he did.

Unforgettable, enthralling love stories,
sparkling with passion and adventure
from Romance's bestselling authors

At Avon Books, we know your passion for romance—once you finish one of our novels, you find yourself wanting more.

May we tempt you with . . .

- **Excerpts** from our upcoming releases.

- Entertaining **extras**, including authors' personal photo albums and book lists.

- Behind-the-scenes **scoop** on your favorite characters and series.

- **Sweepstakes** for the chance to win free books, romantic getaways, and other fun prizes.

- Writing **tips** from our authors and editors.

- **Blog** with our authors and find out why they love to write romance.

- **Exclusive content** that's not contained within the pages of our novels.

Join us at
www.avonbooks.com

AVON

An Imprint of HarperCollins*Publishers*
www.avonromance.com